SING IN THE MORNING, CRY AT NIGHT

BY BARBARA J. TAYLOR

Also available from Kaylie Jones Books
Unmentionables by Laurie Loewenstein
Foamers by Justin Kassab
Starve the Vulture by Jason Carney (forthcoming)
The Love Book by Nina Solomon (forthcoming)

Published by Akashic Books

ISBN-13: 978-1-61775-227-8
Library of Congress Control Number: 2013956835

First printing

Kaylie Jones Books
www.kayliejonesbooks.com

Akashic Books
Twitter: @AkashicBooks
Facebook: AkashicBooks
E-mail: info@akashicbooks.com
Website: www.akashicbooks.com

Dedicated to my father, Carl

In memory of all my Pearls

This is my story,
This is my song . . .
—Fanny J. Crosby

PART ONE

Where Leggett Creek, in beauty springs,
In fair Chinchilla's shade
Where the Red Robin sweetly sings:—
Her holy dust is laid.

—George W. Bowen

TO REVIVE WITHERED FLOWERS

> *Fill a bowl with water so hot that you can scarcely bear your hand in it; throw a little salt in the water and put the flowers in immediately. The effect is wonderful.*
>
> —*Mrs. Joe's Housekeeping Guide,* 1909

Widows and spinsters. We're the backbone of the church. Visit the shut-ins, polish the collection plates, wash and iron the baptismal robes. Wrap them in blue paper to keep them from yellowing.

Every Saturday morning we clean the sanctuary. Takes a good deal of water. And elbow grease. Start in the front and work our way back. No reason. Just habit.

Mix a spoonful of kerosene into your bucket. Adds a shine to the woodwork. Glass too, if you dry it with newspapers.

Cleaning's more difficult after a funeral. The family takes the flowers graveside, but you can still smell them. Stronger when it's a child. Don't know why, but we've all said it. We'll say it again soon enough. That's how life is.

Buried the Morgan girl this past summer. Tragic. Only nine years old. The candle of Grace's eye, as we Welsh say. And Owen's, most likely, since Daisy was the first of their two children.

Reverend Halloway preached himself proud. Not easy under such circumstances. Seen better than him fall to pieces while performing a service for a youngster.

Owen too. A rock, if we ever saw one. Patience of a saint. Holding his wife on the right and that other daughter of his on the left. Job himself could not have done better.

Of course, strength like that can't last forever.

Now, Grace, she's another story. Just have to look at her to know. She'll take the easy way out. Go batty, like her mother. Not that we can blame her. Who's to say we'd manage any better? Hope we would, though.

And then there's Violet. Lost her only sister—accident or not. Can't hold a body accountable at eight years old. Probably didn't do it out of meanness.

Makes us wonder is all.

CHAPTER ONE

GRACE LAY IN BED, listening to Violet mill about the kitchen, but for what? Breakfast, that was it. Something to eat before heading off on the first day of school. "I'm her mother," Grace murmured. "Her mother," she repeated, pushing herself up, swinging one leg onto the floor and then the other. She heard a milk bottle clank against the lip of a metal cup and pictured the eight-year-old sitting at the table. "I'm *her* mother," she said again, this time tasting the anguish as it rose from her stomach. She leaned forward, wretched into the pot beside the bed, crawled back under the covers, and shut her eyes. "Lord, forgive me," she prayed, waiting for the back door to close behind Violet.

An hour later, Grace dragged herself into the kitchen for a cup of tea. Neither the blackberry root nor the quince seed had done much for her dyspepsia. She'd try the spearmint leaves this morning. After putting the kettle on to boil, she stared at the wall calendar—an advertisement for the George Sherman Coal Company.

Cleanest Anthracite in Scranton, PA.

Every miner in the neighborhood had one tacked up in his house. "Sherman's idea of Christmas cheer," Owen had said last December, tossing it on the table along with what was left of his wages, after paying his tab at the company store. Grace had been the one to hang it. She'd waited until noon on New Year's Day, to avoid the bad luck that comes with putting a calendar up too soon.

As if luck were that easy.

As if found pennies or four-leaf clovers could have saved her child.

September 4, 1913. Had it been two months already? Fresh tears started down Grace's face. My Daisy, she thought. It's really true.

When Grace turned, she found Grief sitting in his usual chair at the table. His wasted appearance and blanched complexion always startled her. He had first come to her twenty years earlier, a few days after her father's suicide, just enough time for one so young to grasp the finality of death. Grief would sit on the corner of her bed, attired in a slim gray suit, loose about the shoulders, but clean and ironed. "What's to become of us?" he'd whisper, opening and closing the glass buttons on his shoes with the sterling silver hook he carried in his pocket. For several months, his gangly frame cast a long shadow over her bedroom. "My poor Gracie."

He showed up a second time after her sister Lizzie passed away, and later that year when her mother followed. He'd grown into his clothes by then and had a hint of a beard. And he began coming around again once the miscarriages started. He'd undo his coat and loosen his tie, lingering a bit longer each time. Daisy's birth eventually shooed him outside, and Violet's seemed to have chased him off for good. But he reappeared soon enough, after Rose, Grace's blue baby, died at the hospital. That night he rolled up his shirtsleeves, unpacked his belongings, and made himself at home. She knew then that he'd always return, so she prayed to have long stretches between visits. Her prayers went unanswered, and now, nine months later, he sat across from her, his hair matted, collar soiled, shirt unbuttoned below a rope of neck.

She shuffled to the sink and started in on Violet's breakfast dishes. *Busy yourself*—Owen's advice when she'd tried to talk to him about her pain. Easy for a man who spent twelve hours a day in a mine. Backbreaking work, yes, but still, it was time away from home. How could he know the torment of changing a bed in the room where Daisy's dresses hung on a bar, waiting for Violet to grow into them? Or the agony of discovering Daisy's favorite hair ribbon wedged between the cushions of the couch?

"He'll never understand." The soothing ripples of Grief's voice lapped against Grace's ears.

She brushed the crumbs off Violet's plate and ran a wet dishtowel across it. "He's a good man."

"Who's gone back to the drink."

Without turning toward him, she wagged her finger at the reflection in Owen's shaving mirror propped on the windowsill. "You have no proof of that."

"But *you* do. I saw you catch the whiskey on his breath last night."

"You saw no such thing." She abandoned the dishes and slumped into the chair across from him.

He slid his hand toward her, but she did not offer hers in kind. "So be it," he said, as he fished the buttonhook out of his pocket. "But what about Violet?"

"What about her?"

"I'll say it if you won't." He scraped at the sludge under his fingernails. "Violet's the one who killed Daisy. It's her fault. We both know it."

"Those words have never passed my lips!" Grace pounded her fist, knocking an empty teacup off the table. Porcelain shards peppered the floor. "Now look what you've done." She swept the pieces onto a rag rug, lifted both sides, and shook it into the wash tin. "You're not wanted here. Never were."

"Just the same. You hold the words inside." He pulled out his shirttail, wiped the hook clean, and put it back in his pocket.

"Where they belong." She set the rug in place and went to the stove to brew her tea. Grace thought about the words, those words, beads of buckshot—solid, heavy, cold. Each leaden syllable primed to explode. All along, she'd been swallowing them whole, choking them down with roots and seeds and leaves.

"Come now. Ease your pain." Grief pressed up against her back and pecked at her ear. Blood rose to his pallid cheeks. "Blame Violet. Give voice to your heart's truth."

Grace trembled at both his touch and his suggestion. I'll not say the words, she thought. Better to push them deeper into her belly. What if the accusation shot past her lips while she scrubbed floors or sipped tea? *You killed Daisy!* What if she opened her mouth to pray, and fired the words instead? *Our Father, who art in heaven.* What happened to Eve when Cain slew Abel? Did she still love her child?

Grace pulled away from Grief and sat down at the table. "What do you know of me?"

"I know your fears. Your pain." He tucked in his sullied shirttail and combed his parched fingers through his oiled hair. "We're two halves of the same whole. Twins, born on the same day, tied together for eternity." He stepped closer.

"Not another word about Violet, do you hear?" Exhausted, she dropped her head and wept.

"Poor Gracie. What's to become of us?" Grief lifted her chin and blotted her tears with the back of his hand. "Stay with me," he whispered. "I won't leave you."

A late-summer breeze pushed through the screen door, momentarily rousing Grace to a larger world, one with Owen, and yes, even Violet, and love. Her feet stirred, but her body remained rooted to the chair.

"Let's do something about that pain," Grief cooed. Grace nodded but held onto the words. "So much pain," he continued. "So many tears." He wiped her cheek again.

Grace leaned forward and pressed her lips against the hollow of his open hand.

CHAPTER TWO

WHILE THE THIRD GRADERS PRACTICED their cursive, Miss Reese called Violet into the hallway. On her slow march up the aisle, Violet looked to her classmates for some hint of her wrongdoing, but they kept their eyes trained on their papers.

"I'm sorry for your loss," Miss Reese said when Violet stepped into the hall.

She nodded. She wasn't in trouble. There was some relief in that. The teacher was simply offering her sympathies. Violet should've been used to it by now. She should have been able to say *thank you* the way she'd been instructed so many times throughout the viewing and the funeral, but once again, the words stuck in her throat. She still didn't know what words to use for Daisy being gone, but *thank you* hardly fit.

The teacher continued: "Your sister was a student of mine last year."

Violet and Daisy had spoken about Miss Reese on several occasions. "She smells of rose petals," Daisy had said, and standing this close, Violet realized it was true. Neither sister had ever had or even known such a young teacher. And so pretty. Violet had had Miss Philips the year before, a stern woman, all teeth and bosom, who wielded a switch with a marksman's accuracy.

Miss Reese knelt down, and her long skirt billowed, sending a puff of air in Violet's direction. "I said, your sister was a student of mine last year."

Violet wondered at the repetition and nodded again, this time more vigorously.

The teacher pulled a handkerchief from the sleeve of her shirtwaist and held it out.

Violet had neither sneezed nor spilled anything, the only two reasons for a hanky in school, so she said, "No thank you."

Miss Reese stood abruptly, shook out the folds of her skirt, and sent Violet back to her seat, alongside Olive Manley.

Later that morning, after the children had been released for recess, Violet sat on the steps listening to her teacher describe the morning's encounter to Miss Philips. "Not a tear in her eye after only two months."

"An odd duck," Miss Philips said, her eyes trained on a spirited game of kick the can. As if to clarify her remark, she explained, "Only one in the yard that day other than Daisy herself. We'll probably never know the truth."

Violet glanced up and noticed several of her classmates listening to the women with rapt attention.

After recess, Olive slid into the empty desk next to Lydia Parker.

"And what's wrong with the seat I gave you?" Miss Reese asked.

Olive's eyes nudged at Violet.

"Perhaps you'd prefer to spend the rest of your day in the corner."

"No ma'am." Olive crossed over and dropped into her seat next to Violet, without looking at, speaking to, or brushing up against her.

* * *

When Miss Reese rang the bell for lunch, Olive popped up before the clapper finished sounding. The other students quickly followed suit. Violet remained seated, wiping down her pen tip and arranging her books, until she felt certain the room had emptied. She padded out to the schoolyard, convinced that self-imposed isolation somehow suggested she had a choice in the matter.

As she started down the hill for home, Evan Evans, known in the neighborhood as Evan Two-Times, bounded into her path from behind an oak tree.

"Slowpoke."

Violet kept her head forward and her eyes straight ahead as she tried to move around the boy.

Evan mirrored her steps so she could not pass. "How come you're alone? Everyone's way ahead." He winked in the direction of some overgrown elderberry bushes, and giggles rose up from behind them.

"Not you," she said, still refusing to glance at him or his pals in the covert. "Unfortunately." Everyone knew Evan to be a bully like his mother Myrtle. Violet had no intention of showing weakness.

"I'd be happy to see you home."

"No thank you." Violet glanced toward the street, but a milk wagon prevented her from crossing.

"Wouldn't want to worry your ma . . . considering." The bushes shook with nervous laughter.

"Will you please move?"

"Can I ask you a question?"

"You're going to make me late."

"Did you really kill your sister?"

Violet slammed Evan Two-Times against the tree with such force that the back of his head knocked against the trunk. "Ask me again. I dare you."

He rubbed his scalp and winced. "Ma's right," he said, pushing Violet into the elderberry bushes, causing the crouching boys to scatter like hens. "You are crazy." Evan took off down the hill after his friends.

Violet tried to wriggle free of the bushes but couldn't get a grip on anything to push off of. Just as she started to cry, two hands reached in and pulled her to her feet.

"Thanks," she managed, too ashamed to look up.

"He had it coming, but good."

"Stanley?" Violet said, recognizing his pinched voice. Of all the saviors in the world, hers had to be Stanley Adamski. Stinky Stanley. Stupid Stanley. Not that she had ever called him those names, but she'd never spoken against those who had, either. For one thing, Stanley did have an odor, which surprised Violet. According to her mother, Polish women had spotless kitchens, so it stood to reason that their children would be clean as well. For another, even though Stanley was a year older than Violet, he hadn't yet made it out of second grade. He failed due in large part to his poor attendance, but that didn't stop the bigger boys from calling him a dumb Polack. And from Stanley's view, all the boys were bigger. He stood four feet tall on his tiptoes, at least six inches shorter than anyone else his age. Even Violet had an advantage over him.

"Thanks again," she muttered, brushing leaves off her pinafore. "Mother's expecting me," she added over her shoulder as she started running down the hill. Once safely on her front porch, she turned to see Stanley waving at the top of the block. She pretended not to notice and darted inside.

Violet pussyfooted into the kitchen so as not to disturb her mother. She found an old biscuit and smothered it with molasses. If she closed her eyes and let the syrup linger on her tongue, she could almost taste Christmas with its ginger cookies and candied sweets.

"Is that you, child?" her mother called from the bedroom.

Violet eyed the biscuit, the last one in the house. "Can I get you something?" she yelled back.

"A cup of tea."

Violet stoked the fire and placed a half-full kettle on the stove. Brewing tea would make her late getting back to school by a good ten minutes. She hoped Miss Reese wouldn't make a fuss.

After steeping the leaves, Violet spooned cream off the top of the milk and into the tea. White foam bubbled on top. "That's money in your pocket," she said, scooping some into her mouth. It was one of her mother's favorite sayings.

"If you won't be needing anything else . . ." Violet said, as she set the cup and saucer on the table next to her mother's bed.

"Watch!" Grace snapped, snatching a framed photograph, the one taken of Daisy and her friends on the day disaster struck. In the picture, Daisy stood on the far end of the second row, her long hair pulled up in a bow, her white baptism dress illuminated by the sun. While the other six girls stared straight into the camera, Daisy glanced beyond it, her mind seemingly running ahead, her body leaning out, poised to follow. Grace pored over the smile, the laughing eyes. You couldn't know, my pet, what the day would bring. Of course not, she thought with some relief. She studied the other girls—Flo, Ruth, Marion in the first row, Janie and Susie in the second. No signs, no indications of what was to come. And then, as impossible as it seemed after two months, Grace noticed Violet for the first time. Somehow she'd managed to squeeze into the photograph. Her closed right hand covered most of her mouth; her left clung to the skirt of Daisy's dress. Violet had been worried about spoiling the picture. She knew she didn't belong.

"I best be on my way," Violet said uncertainly. In that instant, the sour smell of vomit reached her nose and choked her. "Been sick again this morning, I see." Violet held her breath, walked over to the chamber pot, and lifted the container with both hands. Emptying it would delay her another five minutes.

When she finally got out the door, Violet found Stanley waiting for her at the bottom of the steps, holding two fishing poles.

"Ever play hooky?"

CHAPTER THREE

BY THE TIME THEY GOT TO LEGGETT'S CREEK, one of the better fishing spots in the Providence neighborhood of Scranton, and cast their lines, Violet had discovered that Stanley was anything but stupid. He could do numbers in his head, even his times tables up to eight. He could name at least forty of the forty-eight states, including Arizona and New Mexico, which had only been added the year before in 1912. And he could call birds better than the birds themselves.

"Shush," Stanley said. "Hear that?"

"Hear what?"

"That blue jay," Stanley whispered as he pointed across the creek toward a thick line of hemlocks.

"I can't see anything." Violet stood up and stretched on her toes to see what Stanley saw.

"Listen."

Violet sat down, closed her eyes, and focused on the bird's triple-noted whistle, a high-pitched *twee-dle-dee, twee-dle-dee,* like the old nursery rhyme. The song repeated several times, and then a nearby blue jay, too near for Violet's comfort, returned the call. Violet leaped up with arms flailing in an attempt to shoo the bird. She'd heard from her neighbor Tommy Davies that blue jays would peck a soul to death. No need to take chances.

Stanley sat at the edge of the creek, doubled over in

laughter. "That was me, you silly goose." He blew into his cupped hands, and the bird sang again. He straightened right up when he saw Violet's red face. "Aw, come on. I'll teach you if you like."

Violet stood, arms folded, mouth turned down, until Stanley had apologized half a dozen times. She thought six an adequate number of "I'm sorrys," especially since she really did want to learn how to call birds.

"We'll start with the sparrow. He's an easy one. Think of your mother when you've let her down."

Violet's eyes flashed with tears.

"Or a teacher when you've made her real mad," he added quickly. "That's a better one." He raced on: "You know, when she makes that *tsk, tsk* sound with her tongue on the roof of her mouth." He fired off a series of eight or twelve trilled *tsks*, too quick to be counted.

Much to Violet's surprise, a sparrow immediately returned the song. "How'd you learn to call so good?"

"Mama. She had what Pa calls *a gift.*"

Had. Violet paused to digest so small a word.

"Rheumatic fever," Stanley added, in answer to her unasked question. "It'll be a year next month."

So that explained it, Violet thought. No mother to make him go to school. She glanced at Stanley's dirty face and clothes. No mother to make him wash behind his ears or change his britches. She pulled in her line, rethreaded the half-dead worm on the hook, and cast back into the water.

"You're not doing it right," Stanley said, flinging his line out twice as far as hers. "It's in the wrist."

"Who made you boss?"

"I'm older," he said. "Been fishing longer." The tip of his pole bent toward the creek. "See?" He smiled broadly as a mud-colored sucker with a hook in its cheek broke the surface of the water. "Biggest one yet."

"Sing in the morning," Violet warned, "cry at night."

"How's that?" Stanley asked, just as the line snapped. They both watched wide-eyed as the sucker disappeared downstream.

"Don't count your fishes until they're caught." She stifled a giggle before handing him her pole to share.

"You're going to catch hell when you get home," Stanley said as they admired two suckers and a chub strung by the mouth and gills on a piece of rope.

Violet knew truth when she heard it, and marveled at Stanley's ability to express it so effectively. Not only had she skipped a whole afternoon of school, but she'd skipped a whole afternoon on the first day of third grade.

On their way home, they tried to think of an excuse, not that Stanley had any particular need for one, but he wanted to help Violet, especially since fishing was his idea in the first place.

"You best take them all home," Violet said, eyeing the chub she'd caught not an hour before. "If I walk in the house with a fish," she paused to consider her words, "I'll catch hell."

Grace plodded into the kitchen, clamped the meat grinder onto one end of the table, and started in on a supper of *ffagod*, Owen's favorite Welsh dish. She minced the pig's liver and onions before folding them into a bowl of suet and breadcrumbs, seasoned with a light hand. It had been weeks since Grace felt well enough to tend to a meal, and she hoped Owen would notice her effort. After flouring her hands, she started rolling the mixture into egg-sized portions. Not having added any coal to the stove since morning, Grace looked over at the bucket alongside it. Three-quarters full, more than enough to keep the oven going.

She pulled her eyes straight back, ignoring the lightly bruised wall where a few of the blueberries had landed that day. Ignoring the purple pinpricks that would inevitably bleed through this latest coat of paint. Not today. Not now.

Not again.

July 4, 1913. Just two months ago.

Grace had been so happy, full of hope for the first time since she'd buried Rose nine months earlier. Daisy would be baptized that morning. Since baptism could only be performed after a profession of faith, the elders saw fit to limit the practice to those nine years and older. With the girls only eleven months apart, they probably would have accepted Violet's profession of faith as well, but Grace thought it best for each girl to have her own special day.

Grace had even put on the new straw bonnet that her sister Hattie had ordered from Montgomery Ward's summer catalog. She'd never worn so fancy a thing before. A band of moss-green silk circled the bell-shaped crown. A single quill shot out from three crimped rosettes, nestled in the seam of the brim. Topped with such beauty, Grace dared to walk a little taller that morning, not in a prideful way, not that she could see, just a little taller.

But Myrtle Evans had to have her say even before the service started. "A bit fussy for the Lord's house. Some might even say improper."

"Jesus must have liked fine things," Grace replied with a smile. "The Bible tells us they cast lots for His garments."

After church, Grace stomped through her kitchen, yanking flour off the shelf, slamming lard onto the table. Although Myrtle's remark had irritated her, the fact that she took satisfaction in her own response bothered her even more. "Lord, I know full well that pride goeth before a fall," Grace said aloud, working the lard into the flour with a sprinkle of cold water. "I'm heartily sorry for my sinful ways. Amen."

She'd decided to make a huckleberry pie for Daisy. Why not indulge her? After all, it was her baptism day, and later they'd be going to the Providence Christian Church's annual picnic, one of the rare days the mines shut down in Scranton.

She looked up to see Daisy stroll into the kitchen. She twirled once, the air opening the pleats on her store-bought dress, a one-time indulgence.

"When did you become old enough to be taken into the church?" Grace's eyes locked on her daughter. "So grown up. My pet. Be marrying you off before we know." She pushed a colander of huckleberries in Daisy's direction.

"Never," Daisy laughed. "Though I expect I'll be promoted to the Junior Choir, seeing I'm a member now." She picked through the berries, tossing the green and the spoiled into a bowl.

"More than likely." Grace dropped the ball of dough into the bowl to rest and turned to adjust the damper on the stove.

Daisy began singing. "*I come to the garden alone . . .*"

"My favorite," Grace said. "Get Violet to play the piano. I love to hear both my girls."

Daisy stood up, took two steps toward the parlor, and called, "Vi-o-let!"

"If I'd wanted someone to stand in my kitchen and yell, I'd have done so myself."

Daisy moved into the parlor and turned down the hall of their one-story house toward the bedrooms, Grace and Owen's on the left, the girls' on the right.

Grace picked up an empty milk bottle and began to roll out the crust. Two things she knew how to handle, piecrust and babies. *And babies*. She shook off the thought before it had a chance to take hold. "Lord, I'm grateful for the ones you let me keep. Amen."

Two pairs of feet marched back into the kitchen, but Daisy pushed through the doorway first. "Tell Violet to listen to me."

"I'll do no such thing." Grace stirred the berries into a bath of butter and cinnamon sugar and poured the mixture into the pie shell.

"Daisy is telling me what to do again." Uneven bangs framed Violet's angry brown eyes, the cropped hair a reminder of a lice incident earlier in the summer.

"I'll not have bickering today of all days." Grace bore three finger holes in the middle of a second crust, lifted it on top of the pie, and pinched the two shells shut with thumbs and forefingers. "And you," Grace nodded toward Daisy as her elbow landed in her sister's side. "What kind of example are you setting?"

Daisy dropped her arm and stared at the floor. Grace lifted the pie and stepped toward the oven. She looked back briefly to see if the girls were behaving and caught sight of Violet shoving her hip into her sister's side. Daisy teetered, and for a split-second, Grace thought Daisy might grab hold of the table and save herself. They both locked eyes as Daisy missed her chance, knocking into Grace and tumbling to the floor with her mother and the pie.

"Owen!" Grace yelled loud enough to be heard out on their front porch, and the front porches of the neighbors on both sides. "Take hold of your girls before I get my hands on them."

Grace lined the *ffagod* on a plate wondering how she could have been so angry over a pie. If only I'd been more patient that day. If only I hadn't taken Myrtle's comments to heart. If only I'd worn my cloth hat to church. Sobbing, she wiped her hands on her apron and went back to her bedroom.

After fishing all afternoon with Stanley, Violet arrived home late to find uncooked *ffagod* on the table and her mother in bed. She wanted to feel relieved about the lies she wouldn't have to tell, the day she wouldn't have to explain, but fear kept tugging on her sleeve. She wondered about her father and the late hour, then set her attention to finishing supper.

CHAPTER FOUR

OWEN PUSHED TWO EMPTY GLASSES toward the barkeep. "Shot and a beer."

"Ain't nothing sold on credit."

Owen reached into his pocket for a few more coins, found a greenback instead, and handed it over. He knew better than to stop at Burke's Gin Mill on his way home from work, but he couldn't help himself. A few men standing around a bar, each with one foot resting on the rail and the other planted on the sawdust-covered floor, made for a peaceful moment.

The door squeaked open behind him, and he turned to see Joey Lewis and his brother Bobby, both timbermen down at the Sherman Mine, regulars at the beer garden. He waved, turned toward the bar, and threw back his whiskey.

"Well, I'll be damned. Thought you was a teetotaler," Joey said, slapping Owen on the back. "What are you drinking?"

Owen held up his hand. "This here's my last." He drained the beer, pocketed his change, and turned to leave. "Need to look in on Grace. And see about Violet's first day."

Joey and Bobby nodded solemnly. They were neglecting wives and children of their own. "One more," Joey said, pulling out a handful of nickels.

Owen hesitated. The men were decent enough company, but he didn't go to Burke's for company.

"For the motherland," Bobby added, and he started in on the first verse of "*Hen Wlad Fy Nhadau*," "Land of Our Fathers."

Mae hen wlad fy nhadau yn annwyl i mi,
Gwlad beirdd a chantorion, enwogion o fri . . .

Joey and Owen couldn't help but join in.

Ei gwrol ryfelwyr, gwladgarwyr tra mâd,
Tros ryddid gollasant eu gwaed.

Four whiskeys later, they started their national anthem again, this time in English.

The land of my fathers, the land of my choice,
The land in which poets and minstrels rejoice;
The land whose stern warriors were true to the core,
While bleeding for freedom of yore.

The three men raised their glasses, "*Iechyd da*, for our beloved Wales," putting Owen in mind of the last time he'd seen home.

Sixteen years earlier, his mam had packed the family Bible in his suitcase. "Always remember," she had said, "sin will keep you from the Bible, but the Bible will keep you from sin." Owen kissed her and headed for the train station with a leaflet in his pocket promising, *High wages for skilled miners*. He took one last look at his hometown of Aberdare, with its winding dirt roads and rolling green hills, and set off for New York by way of Liverpool. During the crossing, he met Graham Davies from the town of Flint in the northeast corner of Wales, and the two became fast friends. Once in New York, Owen and Graham continued by rail to Scranton, Pennsylvania, where according to the advertisements, *Anthracite Is King*. They were confident they'd find jobs in the coal mines.

The first year, they worked out of the Marvine Mine in the Hunky Patch, a Scranton neighborhood of mostly Poles, Lithuanians, and Hungarians. In late 1899, that operation shut down for a few months while the drillers went about finding new veins. Owen and Graham moved on to the Sherman Mine in the Providence section of the city, on the recommendation of Hattie Goodfellow, the widow who owned the boarding house. "Not one to take guff," she said of the mine owner, "but he's fair. No need to keep your eye on the scale," she added, referring to the rumor that the Marvine superintendent underreported the weight of the miners' coal cars, cheating them out of pay.

While prosperity seemed slow in finding them, Owen and Graham earned enough money to pay for their room and meals with a little left over to buy the beer that washed away the last of the coal dust at the end of the twelve-hour workday. Hattie overlooked the trips to the gin mill as long as her boarders didn't try to carry drink onto the premises. Not known to take guff herself, the men obliged.

Of course, Owen's drinking days had ended when he married Grace. "There's no place for the demon alcohol in a Christian home," she'd told him. As long as she promised to stay by his side, he would have agreed to any sacrifice.

"Another round," Joey said as he flagged the barkeep.

"I've had my last pint, boys. I'm headed for home." Owen staggered out the door well after one in the morning, wishing he had a full moon to light his way. Grace would be angry, and he couldn't blame her. Nothing worse than a drunkard in her eyes. Thinking time might sober him up, he crossed Market Street and stared up at the redbrick church, anchoring the northwest corner of Providence Square. It featured twelve stained-glass windows and a white steeple that aspired toward heaven. Providence Christian Church, he thought, sitting down on the steps for a breather. The very place that had led him to Grace.

About two years after they'd arrived in Scranton, Owen and Graham took a stroll up to the square on the last Saturday in August. According to Hattie, it was Old Home Week, a time when residents past and present gathered to celebrate the founders of their neighborhood with parades; music; red, white, and blue buntings; and fireworks. American flags adorned porches and storefronts, and shop owners advertised their wares at special prices. Women sat at tables in front of their churches, selling a variety of foods; *halupkies* from the Poles, corned beef from the Irish, pickled herring and onions from the Jews—a taste of the old country, whichever one that might be.

As they approached the fair, Owen spied *pice ar y maen*, Welsh cakes, arranged three to a plate, and he smelled home for the first time since leaving Aberdare. For a moment, he remembered Mam working the lard and measuring the currants at the kitchen table. He said a silent prayer for her and meandered over to the Providence Christian Church's table. Graham followed.

Owen froze at the sight of the two girls seated in front of him.

"May I help you?" asked the one on the left.

Owen simply stared at her, wishing he'd had a drink or two to loosen his tongue.

"Would you like to buy some Welsh cakes?" asked the one on the right. "A penny a piece, or three for two cents." She smiled broadly, her teeth perfectly straight, her cheeks inexpertly rouged. Graham returned the smile. Owen remained transfixed on the first girl, with long brunette curls and the bluest eyes he'd ever seen.

Graham ignored his friend, searched his pocket, found a nickel, and passed it to the redheaded girl on the right. She pushed forward two plates and said, "Kindly return them when you've finished eating." She placed the nickel in a cigar box and retrieved a penny.

Graham held up his hand. "A donation for the church." The pair shared another smile before he managed to shove Owen away from the table.

"What's got into you?" Graham asked, handing Owen a plate.

"I'll take the chubby one." Owen's first words.

"You don't say." Graham patted his friend's shoulder and laughed.

Owen paused to collect his thoughts. "I'd like to court the one on the left. If she's not spoken for. Her with the pretty blue eyes."

"So long as you leave one for me."

Owen and Graham began attending the Providence Christian Church of Scranton the very next day, two services every Sunday and one on Wednesday nights. The chubby one, the girl on the left, made no offer of her name. Owen reminded himself that a proper lady waited to be asked. Each time he saw her, he tried to muster the courage, but failed.

The one on the right, Louise, wasted no time introducing herself to Graham. She told him about her life as the child of a maid in the Jones household. How Mrs. Jones refused to allow her daughters to "consort" with Louise, even the youngest, who was her age. The two played together anyway, but in secret, the beginning of a lifelong friendship. She also made mention of a scandal resulting in Mr. Jones's demise. With the family disgraced, the youngest Miss Jones was forced to take a job as a maid herself, "her with the pretty blues eyes."

Graham passed all of this along to Owen, who only became more nervous when he realized Miss Jones had been raised with certain advantages. Even if she's not living that life now, he thought whenever she sat in the same pew at Christian Endeavors, a Sunday school class for the young adults of the church, what could I offer so fine a woman?

Owen's paralysis persisted, even after three months of church attendance. When she'd glide past him to collect the Bibles, he couldn't breathe. If she stood to make an announcement about a covered-dish dinner or a visiting missionary, he'd avert his eyes so that his affection would not spill out.

And then came Thanksgiving.

Hattie had invited Owen and all the men without family to share in a meal. Owen donated the bird, one he'd shot a couple of days before in Chinchilla, the next town over. When Hattie called everyone to the table, she suggested Owen sit at the head, since it was his turkey they were serving.

"A beautiful bird," one man said admiringly.

"Chester never looked so good," Owen said with a wink. Chester was Hattie's prize rooster and the bane of every man who boarded there. In addition to his sunrise duties, Chester crowed whenever someone tried to sneak in after Hattie's ten o'clock curfew. He also nipped the ankles of anyone he disliked, and he disliked everyone except Hattie herself.

"Chester may be the ugliest bird God gave breath to," Hattie said, "but he's the best watchdog I ever had." She sat down on Owen's right, near the kitchen door so she could clear the table and refill dishes. "And I know that's not

Chester on my platter because he'd have bitten your nose off by now." Everyone laughed.

Just then, Miss Jones with the pretty blue eyes rushed into the dining room full of apologies, her cheeks flushed, her brow dappled with sweat. On one side, strands of dark hair pulled free from her bun and fell across her face.

Owen looked at Hattie. He'd seen the two women talking together at church on occasion, but it hadn't occurred to him that they were more than acquaintances. They never sat together that he could recall.

"The colonel's dinner took longer than expected. I hope you didn't wait for me." Miss Jones paused for a moment, glanced at Owen stuck to his seat, and pulled out her own chair. "We had forty-eight people. Can you imagine?" she asked him, turning to the right. "I'm Grace. Grace Jones," she said. "Hattie's sister." Owen didn't stir. "I believe we both attend Providence Christian."

Owen wanted to speak, to tell her how lovely she looked with her hair pulled back and a silk flower behind her ear. He yearned to tell her how sweet she smelled, an intoxicating blend of lilacs and vanilla, but he couldn't find the words.

"I work as a live-in maid for Colonel Watres, like my sister, before she married." Grace unfolded a linen napkin and arranged it on her lap. "Over on Quincy Avenue. And I also teach piano to his children."

Hattie interrupted: "Owen, will you lead us in the blessing?"

His throat clamped shut so tightly that words, even if he'd been able to find them, could not escape. He took a sip of water, closed his eyes, and with great effort, managed to loosen a single syllable: "Grace."

After an embarrassing silence, Graham jumped in. "That's prayer enough. Amen and let's eat." He grabbed a bowl of cooked rhubarb and spooned some onto his plate.

Red-faced, Owen pushed himself away from the table and hurried into the kitchen. He took a few swigs from a flask in his pocket as he paced back and forth. Occasionally he stopped and mumbled "Simpleton" or "Half-wit," then started up pacing again. Just as he began his fourth pass across the kitchen, Grace pushed through the swinging door with an empty bowl in her hand.

"I'm not much for rhubarb myself," she explained, "but the others sure seem to like it." She laughed easily and strolled past Owen toward the stove.

He watched her back, the curve of it, the dampness of the blouse clinging to it. She turned toward him, and in one decisive movement, he grabbed her arm and pulled her into him for a kiss—hungry, urgent, necessary. He tucked the errant strands of hair behind her ear, pressed his lips against it, and closed his eyes. When he opened them, he found Grace on tiptoe, stretched toward him, her eyes wide. Betrayed by her own eagerness, she blushed and tumbled backward, her boot heels slapping against the linoleum floor. She scowled at Owen, who smiled broadly, suddenly emboldened by her chagrin and the contents of his flask. He pulled her in and kissed her again, allowing his lips to linger this time.

Grace and Owen married at the Providence Christian Church six months later, on May 11, 1900, the same day he signed the Temperance Pledge under his father's signature in his family's Bible. If he'd had his way, they would have wed sooner, but Grace wanted to wait for the lilacs to bloom.

Owen smiled at the memory, stood up unsteadily from the church steps, and continued home. Though nowhere near sober, he knew enough to step around the side and enter through the kitchen. The front door took coaxing, and he didn't want to run the risk of waking the whole house at two o'clock in the morning.

"Look at you," Grace said from her seat at the table. She turned up the wick on the oil lamp and eyed him head to toe. Broad-shouldered. Muscular. Hair as black as coal. Still handsome, but his hollow-cheeked countenance startled her till she noticed his reddened nose poking through the coal dust. "A fine example for our children."

They both gasped at the slip and wondered at the weight of it.

Grace found her voice again: "I don't want drink in my house, Owen Morgan. I'll not have it."

Indignation pushed past Owen's guilt and settled in, making itself at home in his mouth. "Your house, is it? *Your* house?" he yelled. "I suppose it's your pay that puts food on the table and a roof over your head?" Owen grabbed the back of a chair to steady himself.

"Do you want to wake Violet?" Grace turned down the lamp as if to quiet him.

"Your house," he continued. "And I'm what? A guest now?"

"A common drunkard, more like it."

"You best hold your tongue, woman. I'll not stand for it."

"As if you could stand," she countered.

He slammed the chair across the room, upending it. Grace jumped back in fear.

"I'm so sorry." Owen reached for Grace's arm, but she recoiled. "I didn't mean to . . ." He righted the chair and sat down at the table across from her. "What kind of man am I?" He started to cry. "Look what you made me do."

Anger swelled inside Grace, running off any hope for sympathy. She could feel the rigidity in her stance, in her soul. She knew she was looking down on her husband, judging him, but she could not help herself. "Get out of the house this minute." She punctuated her statement with a fist to the table. "My father never took a drop of liquor in his life. I'll not have a drunkard for a husband." She stood up, hurried to the door, and held it open.

Owen pushed himself up and stood facing her. "Your father was a scoundrel. You and your highfalutin ways." He took hold of the door. "Your father was nothing but a no-good coward."

Grace slapped Owen across the face. He returned her blow without hesitation, and staggered out the door.

TO KEEP AWAKE IN CHURCH

To keep awake in church when inclined to be drowsy, lift one foot a little way from the floor and hold it there. It is impossible to go to sleep when your foot is poised in the air. This remedy, though simple, is very effectual and never fails to keep a person awake.

—*Mrs. Joe's Housekeeping Guide*, 1909

Let the Catholics sprinkle their babies. At Providence Christian we baptize by immersion, the way the good Lord intended. We used to "dunk" in the Lackawanna River. Had to cut away the ice in the middle of winter. Now we have an indoor baptistery. Souls can just as easily be saved near a modern coal furnace.

We try to help out wherever we can. Last fall, after Pearl Williams's husband took up with that trollop from Bull's Head, dark-skinned, I-talian most likely, we organized a pound party. Asked folks to donate one pound of food apiece to get the Williamses through winter. Members of Providence Christian did not disappoint. Pearl got herself enough flour, sugar, and canned goods to last a year. And we're happy for her, even if she didn't think to share her bounty with those of us who toiled on her behalf.

Missionaries, evangelists. We feed, house, and raise money for them all. There's talk Billy Sunday might come to Scranton to preach next spring. Now that would be a thrill. Played outfield for the Chicago White Stockings before he found Jesus.

Had his picture in the paper just last week. A fine-looking man, even old Miss Proudlock says so.

Wish we could do something for that poor Morgan girl, though. Traipsing all over town with that little Polish boy. Just makes matters worse. Most likely lonesome for her sister. Then again, growing up in Daisy's shadow couldn't have been easy. Never knew a more perfect child. Those eyes. That voice. And smart as a whip. It's a wonder Violet wasn't more jealous, if you ask us. She did have one advantage over Daisy, though. Never knew a child with more promise at the piano. Of course, that's all over now. Has to be.

Tending to the needs of our flock—that's our mission. Probably the same for Catholics, Episcopalians, even Jews. We're proud to do the Almighty's work. It's the Christian thing to do.

CHAPTER FIVE

HATTIE HAPPENED TO BE OUT SWEEPING the front steps when she spotted Grace trooping toward the boarding house. Even before her sister reached the yard, Hattie could tell she was distraught. Grace had the habit of chewing her lower lip when she was troubled. Hattie put down her broom, grabbed two shawls, and led Grace upstairs and out to the second-floor porch for a little privacy.

After some coaxing, for Grace had always needed coaxing, even as a child, she told Hattie that Owen hadn't come home in almost a week. Hattie's hand flew to her heart, but before she could say a word, Grace explained, "He's rented a room over Burke's. A gin mill, of all places."

Hattie wasn't entirely surprised. He'd taken Daisy's death about as hard as any father could.

Once Grace opened up, she recounted the whole night, including Owen's drunken antics and the argument it had caused. Grace was upset about his leaving, of course, but Hattie couldn't help thinking his comments about their father bothered her sister even more.

Owen had been right, Hattie thought, as she tried to comfort Grace. Mean-spirited, but right. Not that this excused his behavior, but their father had been a "no-good coward." Old wounds opened and anger festered anew, surprising Hattie with their intensity.

Growing up, Hattie and her family had lived in a grand home, with the largest wraparound porch on North Main Avenue. Green-shingled second and third stories sat atop a ground floor of fieldstone. Six gables poked out of the roof, much to the disappointment of Hattie, who thought they should have seven like the house in Nathaniel Hawthorne's novel.

Hattie and Grace's father, Ivor Jones, a third vice president for the Delaware and Hudson Railroad, had amassed his wealth by investing in the mining industry and businesses associated with anthracite. As his fortune increased, so did his enemies, who accused him of making his money on the broken backs of the poor. Not that those in his circle were concerned about the poor, more likely they were simply jealous of his knack for using them to his advantage. At the same time, Ivor Jones sat on the board of the Hillside Home, an almshouse and insane asylum on the outskirts of Scranton. Unlike most board members, he spent time with the wards, and many a preacher praised Ivor's dedication to these hapless souls.

In the fall of 1888, Bronwyn Jones, Ivor's wife, had given birth to a son named for his father. Ivor Jr. made four children in all, including Hattie, thirteen; Lizzie, ten; and Gracie, seven. Although Ivor Sr. had always shown affection toward his children, at least in public, he seemed particularly taken with the boy.

"God has seen fit to grant me a son," Hattie would often hear him say at church. "It's about time," he'd add, "don't you think?" and chuckle.

But soon, their idyllic life began to crumble. Evidently her father had been offering more than just sympathy to the female residents of the Hillside Home and his enemies exposed him as soon as they'd gotten wind of the scandal. The D&H directors dismissed Ivor from the railroad, and investors pulled their money from his interests, bankrupting the family in a matter of months. By the spring of '89, her father had hanged himself from a rafter in the attic. Unable to cope with the loss of her husband and her sudden poverty, Bronwyn had a nervous breakdown herself and became an involuntary occupant of Hillside. Hattie and her sisters were sent to the Home for the Friendless. There, they could expect to spend their days with other abandoned and orphaned children until they reached adulthood. The baby had been given to the Athertons, a childless couple in the Green Ridge section of town. From what Hattie would learn long after, the woman was barren, and they welcomed Ivor as their own, changing his name to Peter, like his adoptive father. A few years later, after the death of her husband in a mine explosion, Mrs. Atherton and the baby moved to Baltimore to live with her sister. Neighbors lost track of them after that.

The Home for the Friendless, a monolith of stone walls and turrets, stood on the hill near Jefferson Avenue like a guard dog poised to strike. Mothers and fathers pointed the structure out to ill-behaved children as a warning. *If you don't straighten up, it'll be the Home for you.*

Those inside the walls knew differently. The place was better than some and no worse than others. "At least they feed you here," one girl said to Hattie at breakfast. "And not a one of them will take a switch to you." And it was true. The women who ran the institution offered serviceable beds, three meals a day, schooling, music lessons, and religious instruction. Yet it was not their own, and Hattie vowed to one day earn enough money to make a home for her sisters and mother.

Four years later, on her seventeenth birthday, Hattie found employment as a maid with the Watres family. She received room and board, and a small salary. By year's end, with the money she'd saved, she secured three rooms over the bakery on West Market Street. Though it lacked the decorative moldings and vaulted ceilings of her youth, the place was very much a home.

First, she assumed custody of her sisters. Brother Kinter from the Providence Christian Church vouched for Hattie's character, and the women in charge gladly handed Lizzie and Gracie over to make room for other unfortunates. Next, she took her mother out of the Hillside Home, initially on short visits, then overnight on weekends, and finally to stay for good. That first year as sole provider proved difficult. If it weren't for the generosity of church members, particularly Michael Goodfellow, owner of a local boarding house, she knew they would not have survived. As it was, they lost Lizzie to influenza the following winter, a blow from which Hattie never truly recovered.

That spring when Michael proposed, he offered to give Hattie the world if she'd only marry him. As it turned out, she didn't need the world, just a room for her mother and sister to share. Her mother Bronwyn could often be heard saying, "This is no place for a lady," when she sat out on the boarding house's modest front porch; but in spite of her insults, Michael always treated his mother-in-law with kindness and seemed overwrought when she succumbed to consumption that same year.

Now that was a man, Hattie thought. Unlike Owen, Michael stayed put until '98, when the good Lord carried him home. Diphtheria, God rest his soul.

Hattie glanced across the porch at her sister, wondering how best to handle Owen's absence. Her heart told her to move Grace and Violet into the boarding house right away so she could take care of them. It would certainly make her feel better to have them close by. But was that what was best for Grace? She was a woman, not a child, with a family of her own. And what about Owen? If he was ever going to find his way back home, Grace had to be there.

"I'll have to sell the piano," Grace finally said as she stood and wandered to the edge of the porch.

Hattie stiffened in her rocker. "Why on earth would you do something like that?"

When Owen had left her boarding house to marry, he and his friend Graham had carried the red-lacquered Tom Thumb piano ten blocks uphill to the new home. Though a third smaller than most uprights, and in spite of its wheels and handles, the instrument proved to be about as difficult to move as a mule in a coal mine. Owen had never told how he'd acquired the piano—Hattie's best guess, a winning hand of cards; Grace thought barter a more likely explanation—which he presented to his wife as a wedding present.

"It's what I can spare for now," Grace explained, "and it'll keep a roof over our heads for another few months."

"You'll do no such thing," Hattie said, a little louder than she intended. "As much as I hate to take up for Owen right now, you and I both know that if he has breath in his body, he'll provide for you and Violet."

"And we both know what drink does to a man." Grace took off her shawl and handed it to her sister. "I have my family to consider."

"You can come here," Hattie offered. "There's plenty of room, and I'd like the company."

"Company is the last thing you need. And besides, I don't want to leave my home." Grace paused for a moment and blinked back tears. "How will she know where to find me?"

"She'll come with you, naturally."

"Daisy . . . I mean Daisy."

My sister's worse off than I realized, Hattie thought, as she decided to take matters into her own hands.

CHAPTER SIX

THE NEXT DAY, OWEN WAITED outside the colliery for Graham's twelve-year-old son Tommy to finish with the mules. Four years had passed since Tommy had started in the mine, and in that time, he had moved up from breaker boy, where he sorted coal from slate bare-handed, to mule boy, where he worked the animals and took care of them in their underground stable. Owen paced in front of the mine's entrance. He knew Tommy would be out soon, and there was an errand he wanted him to run.

Owen had just opened his growler, ready to take a swig of beer, when Hattie turned the corner and marched toward him. He dropped his head in shame.

"She intends to sell the piano." Hattie didn't see the need for a proper hello.

"Why on God's earth would she do a thing like that?" Owen asked, still looking down.

"For the money, what else? I hear it's two rents you're paying now."

"And what kind of man would I be if I didn't do for my wife and daughter?"

"The kind of man who leaves his family at the first sign of trouble." She nodded toward his hand. "The kind who carries a pint for his dinner."

Tommy Davies walked up at that moment and tipped

his cap, "Ma'am." He turned toward Owen and asked, "What is it you need, sir?"

"Go straight home, and see that Grace gets this." Owen handed the boy what little was left of his pay after he'd taken care of the rents and the tab at the company store.

"Yes sir." Tommy nodded and hurried away.

"Be sure to tell her," Owen yelled after him, "she'll not have to sell the piano."

Tommy waved back and ran up the hill.

Hattie wanted to tell Owen that she saw good in him yet, but loyalty to her sister prevailed. "It's the least you could do," was all she managed.

"The very least," Owen agreed.

Hattie went on her way without so much as a goodbye.

The Tom Thumb piano, Owen thought, as he headed toward Burke's. That she would sell it had never entered his mind.

It had been Good Friday, one month before their wedding. Owen remembered because Grace had asked permission of the landlord to plant morning glory seeds along the front porch of the coal company house on Spring Street, where they'd live once they were married. According to Grace, most of the other flowers could wait until May, but morning glory seeds had to be planted on Good Friday in recognition of the Lord's sacrifice, and in order for the seeds to sprout in a timely manner.

She was still working for the colonel but intended to give up her position once she started keeping house with Owen.

One night, about a week after their engagement, Owen had asked Grace if she'd miss her work.

"Only the lessons. If I'm ever fortunate enough to come by a piano, I'll teach the neighbors' children."

Unsettled by the thought of Grace missing anything, Owen decided to find a piano in time for their wedding. It was the evening before Good Friday that Graham told Owen about a little Tom Thumb down at the horse track along the Lackawanna River. A trainer by the name of Carl had won it from a barkeep up the line in a game of chance. According to Graham, the barkeep had it on good authority that Carl's dice were loaded. After asking around some, Graham found others eager to make the same accusation.

"He's a mean little son of a bitch," one of the men said. "Deny his own mother if there was money to be made."

Along the way, Graham also discovered that the trainer ran cockfights out of the feed barn at the track the second Friday of every month—high stakes, serious gamblers only.

On the morning of Good Friday, Owen had gone down to the track to see about the piano. Carl kept it in his room off the stables. He used it as a shaving stand, propping his mirror on the music desk, setting his aluminum shaving mug and brush on the covered keys. An unopened cake of barber's soap lay next to them, and a horsehide razor strop straddled the top of the instrument. He made due with an overturned apple crate for a seat.

"Come on in and set down," Carl said, sitting on the edge of the bed as he offered the crate to Owen. "What can I do you for?"

"Come about your piano," Owen said, "to see what you might take for it."

"So you wants to get a piano. Don't play myself." Carl held up his hands and wiggled his fingers, five on the right hand, four on the left. "I'd end up missing a few keys." He laughed.

"It's for my bride-to-be."

"Ah, love." Carl reached for the strop and started sharpening a razor. "How much?"

"Thought we might barter."

"Then you're wasting my time," Carl said as he put down his razor, stood up, and gestured toward the door.

"Heard you run cockfights here."

Carl dropped his hand and sat down again.

"Might be I have a bird that could win a man some money," Owen continued.

"You raise fighting cocks?"

"Got me a beaut."

"That so?"

"Yep." Chester—a bird too ugly to let live. "He's yours for the piano. Won a total of fifty dollars with him in three counties." Owen hoped the Lord might turn a blind eye when it came to swindling a swindler.

"Then you won't have no problem paying for that instrument outright." Carl got up again, and this time Owen stood as well. After a sizable pause, Carl said, "I'll tell you what. You bring that bird of yours tonight, and if he wins you enough money, I'll let you buy the piano."

The men shook hands, and Owen started up the road, wondering what he'd tell Hattie about her rooster.

That afternoon, Owen lied to Grace for the first time. "Graham got himself into a peck of trouble." He looked at the ground, afraid she'd see deception in his eyes. "I need to help him out tonight."

No matter how many times Grace asked, "What kind of trouble?" Owen refused to elaborate.

"You won't even miss me. Morning glories sure'll look pretty come summer."

Grace turned on her heel, into the servants' entrance at the colonel's house, and let the door slam behind her.

In the end, Owen decided not to tell Hattie about her rooster. He'd already told one too many lies and couldn't stomach another. If Chester survived the night, and Owen thought he might just be mean enough to, Owen would return him to the yard in time for his sunrise duties. And if Chester didn't make it, Owen would have enough time to think about what to tell Hattie on his way home.

Graham scooped up the bird while Owen tied string around his beak and feet. Chester managed to inflict wounds on both men before they could secure him.

When they got to the track, they found Carl standing outside the feed barn, checking the crowd—a little light this particular night, even for a holy day. "Who's this?" he asked, pointing toward Graham with a thumb.

"Raises fighting cocks with me," Owen said. Chester reared up, as if to expose the lie.

"Shoulda mentioned him before," Carl said, but he pointed both men toward the door. "You're third up."

Inside, about fifty men sat on makeshift bleachers surrounding a pit fifteen feet around. Owen noticed some of the men down on the barn floor, poking at the birds, pulling at their wings, getting them riled up.

Carl strutted in and announced the rules: "All wagers before the bell. Cocks fight till they're dead or crippled. I'll call it."

The crowd started to settle in.

"First up, a fighter out of Chinchilla. Hold that bird high."

A barrel-chested man waved a rooster in the air. Its feet scrambled frantically above the man's head.

"And a cock out of Bull's Head, another one of Harry's."

Harry held the bird in one hand and waved to the crowd with the other.

"Place your bets."

Various sums of money changed hands while two boys, no more than sixteen, grabbed up the birds and strapped razors to their spurs. Each boy held his charge aloft.

"Are we ready?" Carl asked, poised to strike a nearby bell. The boys nodded. "Begin!"

At the sound of the bell, the cocks were thrown into the pit. Shouts from the crowd overpowered the high-pitched squeals and squawks below. A flurry of wings, feathers, and bloody talons rose and fell, pecking, slicing, and tearing at anything either one could get ahold of. They rose and fell again, and then only one stood up, just barely. His right side had taken the brunt of the blows. An eyeball dangled from its socket by a single cord of muscle. A wing hung down at an unnatural angle like a cracked tree limb after a storm. His foot was shy two claws.

Carl walked over to the pit and declared the barrel-chested man the winner. He scooped up his damaged bird, untied the razors, and held him aloft in victory. Harry snatched up the loser, removed the blades, and threw him in a crate at the back of the barn. Money changed hands, new bets were placed, and the next two cocks were held up for fighting.

Owen sat stunned. He'd never seen such a spectacle, and though he hated Chester, he couldn't find it in his heart to throw him in the pit.

"I can't do it," he told Graham, getting to his feet.

"Go on," Graham said. "I'll catch up later."

Grateful he didn't have to explain himself further, Owen carried the rooster out the door and home to Hattie's.

The next morning at breakfast, Hattie asked, "Which one of you nitwits tied Chester's beak shut?"

Owen silently cursed himself for the oversight.

"That's a terrible thing to do to one of God's creatures, and I'll not have it again." All of the men nodded and kept on eating.

On their way to the mine that morning, Graham said, "I got myself in a bit of a fix last night."

"What's that?"

"Bet most of my wages on the fifth fight, a cock outta the Patch."

"How much?" Owen asked, figuring in his head what money he could spare.

"A sure thing, I says to myself when I saw him. Now *he* was a fighter."

"Nothing sure in this world."

"True enough."

"How much?" Owen asked again.

"Don't need no money, if it's all the same to you." A smile broke across Graham's face. "Just need help moving Grace's new piano."

Owen hurried into Burke's, paid for a whiskey, and threw it back. Wiping his mouth on his sleeve, he mumbled something about a piano. The barkeep poured a fresh shot and pushed it in Owen's direction. "On the house."

Owen glanced up, surprised.

"You look like the sorriest man in town."

He nodded, picked up his whiskey, and headed over to a table in the corner.

CHAPTER SEVEN

BY LATE SEPTEMBER, Violet had only attended school a handful of days. She'd go as far as the oak tree on School Street and wait to hear the two-syllabled *chew-chew* of the cardinal. She'd reply with a series of sharp *chip, chip* whistles, the only call she was able to imitate accurately. Stanley would step out from behind the elderberry bushes where he'd been hiding until the boys passed on their way down the hill.

"Fish are biting," he'd announce, handing her one of two poles. Off they'd go until the end of the school day.

Violet had even stopped going home for lunch, something her mother never seemed to question. She also never asked Violet about the suckers and chubs she'd started bringing into the house every now and again. If anything, she seemed relieved not to have to think about supper.

On the few occasions when Violet did show up for school, Miss Reese smiled at her politely and went about her lesson. Only once did the teacher pull her aside and address the matter of her absences.

"We've missed you in school," Miss Reese said, and she sounded sincere.

Violet took a deep breath, wondering why she hadn't prepared for this moment. Should she lie? If so, what lie would she tell?

"Tending to your mother," Miss Reese paused as if searching for words, "considering the circumstances, is admirable."

Miss Reese seemed to think she understood the situation, so Violet thought it best not to contradict her.

"It speaks to your character. A pleasant surprise for all."

For all? Violet wondered at the remark, but remained silent.

"I'm sorry about school, but I'm proud of you nonetheless." The teacher managed a smile, one where the corners of her mouth lifted without alerting the eyes of their intention.

Violet burst into tears and this time gladly accepted the handkerchief Miss Reese held before her.

"What happened to fishing?" Violet asked one morning late in September as Stanley popped out of the bushes without his poles.

"I'm tired of fishing," he explained. "And I'm tired of fish."

"So now what?"

Stanley smiled and started up the hill.

Twenty minutes later, enough time for him to teach Violet the saw of wren, they arrived at a grove of trees just beyond Leggett's Creek.

"Apples? Why didn't you say so?" Violet twisted an apple off a lower branch, shined it on her sleeve, and took a hearty bite.

"And I'm the one they call stupid," Stanley said as he scrambled up into a tree. "I'll drop them down. You try and catch them. No one will want to buy them if they're bruised."

Violet took three more quick bites and threw the core deep into the tall grass. She bent her legs, cupped her hands, and yelled, "Ready!"

* * *

After half an hour, the pair had picked more fruit than they could possibly carry. Stanley loaded his pockets, while Violet gathered her skirt as a sack, taking great care not to show her bloomers along the way.

"Let's go." Stanley led Violet to a side road, in the opposite direction of home. "No sense taking chances."

Two hours later, after they'd sold, dropped, or eaten all their apples, the pair headed back toward Providence Square with a nickel between them.

"Murray's?" Stanley suggested. "They have a whole counter in the back with nothing but candy."

"What if we're seen?"

"Who's going to catch us? School hasn't let out yet. Everyone else is either working or starting supper."

Violet stopped to consider his points.

"Peanut brittle sure would taste good right about now." Stanley smacked his lips together.

"And gumdrops," she added as they started down the hill toward the square.

The screen door yawned open, brushing against a cowbell suspended overhead.

Violet followed Stanley past bolts of fabric, men's hats, and a fine china display.

"Be careful!" a woman shouted from somewhere in the store, Mrs. Murray, the owner's wife, by the sound of it.

"Yes, ma'am," Stanley returned as he continued toward the back. He paused to admire a bounty of chocolate, while Violet went in search of her favorite treat.

"No fooling around." Mrs. Murray, a rake of a woman, stepped behind the candy case and grabbed an apron off a nail. She wrapped the strings behind her thin frame and around front again. With fabric still left over, she tied a substantial bow over her hollow stomach. She obviously never sampled her own wares. "What can I get you?"

Stanley piped up first: "Peanut brittle." He placed the money on the counter.

"And gumdrops," Violet added. After all, that nickel was just as much hers. "Red ones, please."

"You'll take what color I give you," the woman said as she shoveled a scoop of gumdrops into a paper sack. "No more brittle till tomorrow. Sold the last of it this morning." She swiped the nickel off the counter, tossed it into the register, and moved toward the front of the store.

Violet handed the bag to Stanley. "You can have the red ones if you like."

Looking first to see their color, he popped two green candies into his mouth. "What a pickle puss," he said when Mrs. Murray was out of earshot, and he started toward the door.

Violet spied the widow Lankowski near the entrance. A giant, standing six feet tall, she had at least a head's advantage over most of her Welsh neighbors. She was also the only Catholic on Spring Street. All Violet had to do was look out her parlor window to see the proof, a foot-tall statue of Mary planted in the woman's front yard. And if that weren't enough, she was childless, making her even more suspect in the eyes of the children who seemed to prefer passing on the Morgan side of the street.

Violet grabbed Stanley by the collar and pulled him down behind a cracker barrel to the right of the china. She pointed and mouthed, "The widow." Without a word between them, they agreed to wait the woman out.

"We Catholics are just as eager to meet Billy Sunday," the widow Lankowski was explaining to Mrs. Murray. She straightened her fingers as far as her swollen knuckles would allow and raised her right hand. "God as my witness."

Mrs. Murray nodded while she cut several yards of black muslin from a bolt on the table. "Glad to hear it," she said, turning to wrap the fabric in a sheet of brown paper.

"We're all God's children, are we not?" the widow said.

"Ain't that the truth." Mrs. Murray cut a length of string, tied it around the package, and handed it to her customer. "That'll be one dollar even."

"And a bottle of Lydia Pinkum's."

Mrs. Murray motioned the widow to follow her to the right side of the store. "For what ails you," she said, pointing to an assortment of bottles stacked on the shelves behind her, all promising to cure any number of female ailments.

"I'm fit as a fiddle," the widow said. "An ounce of prevention is all."

Mrs. Murray ran her finger across a ledge in search of the tonic. "There's more in back. Just be a minute."

The widow glanced around the store before turning to the counter, where she pulled out a small red book and pencil, and recorded her purchases.

Stanley saw his chance and yanked Violet left around the barrel. "Move," he whispered, keeping hold of her hand. Both pairs of feet scurried toward the door, but their eyes remained fixed on the widow's giant frame. As they reached the front of the store, Stanley finally breathed and smiled, "I thought we were in for it."

The screen door yawned, the cowbell rang, and the children collided with Myrtle Evans just as she crossed the threshold.

"What in the world?" Myrtle placed a hand on the head of each child and pushed them backward into the store. "Mrs. Murray?" she shouted. "Come here this minute."

"She's in the storeroom," the widow Lankowski called out, moving toward the entrance. She eyed the prey trying to wriggle free of Myrtle's talon grip. "And what do you have to say for yourselves?"

"Probably trying to rob her blind," Myrtle offered as she dug her nails in a little deeper. "Mrs. Murray?" she called again.

"Where are your manners?" the widow asked, looking at Violet and Stanley. "Apologize to Myrtle Evans."

Violet willed her lips to move. "Sorry," she managed a beat before Stanley. Their apologies overlapped like songs sung in rounds.

"Now if you'd waited for me at the counter like I told you, none of this would have happened."

The children's eyes sprang up and their mouths popped open as they pivoted toward the widow.

"They're with you?" Myrtle asked, relaxing but not abandoning her hold.

"I asked the children if they wouldn't mind helping me this afternoon. Gout's acting up."

"That so," Myrtle said. "For someone who's afflicted, you move real good."

The widow allowed her left leg to slacken under her long skirt, as she leaned against a table of bed linens. "I'm embarrassed to say, I didn't think to ask their folks first. I'd be much obliged if we could keep this matter between us." When Myrtle didn't answer, the widow added, "We both know Grace doesn't need bothering now." She glanced in Stanley's direction. "And who knows what his father would do. Beat the daylights out of him, I suppose."

Stanley reared up, but Violet grabbed his wrist and squeezed.

Myrtle Evans said nothing, her lips pulled tight like a drawstring purse.

"By the way, I've been meaning to ask you if that was your Evan I saw pushing over poor Mr. Bonser's outhouse on Thursday night. Sure looked like him, but I couldn't say for certain. Eyes are about as bad as my gout." She stood up straight and waited.

"Apology accepted." Myrtle dropped her hands to her sides. "Consider the matter forgotten. You'll not hear a word about it from me."

"That's awfully kind of you, Myrtle. The children and I are sure grateful."

Mrs. Murray came back out, carrying a bottle of Lydia Pinkum's. "One dollar and sixty-three cents, all together."

The widow Lankowski paid Mrs. Murray, entered the price of the tonic in her red book, and handed the bottle to Violet and the muslin to Stanley. She said, "Good day," as she ushered the two out through the screen door.

Dumbfounded, the children accompanied the widow in silence over and up to Spring Street. When they arrived at her back porch, she took both packages and held up a finger as a signal to wait. The pair exchanged glances, but stayed put. Stanley stared through the open door, as Violet nervously glanced around the yard. Her eyes settled on a statue of Jesus, similar in size to the one of Mary out front. Orange marigolds circled the stone savior, while gold and purple pansies flanked His outstretched arms.

A minute later, the widow returned to the door with an oatmeal cookie in each hand. "A little thank you for your time. I'm making molasses taffy Saturday night. Come around after church on Sunday."

Both children nodded, still unable to speak.

The widow peered at Violet. "Remember me to your mother." She turned her attention to Stanley. "If you'd like to accompany me to Mass this week, I'd be much obliged. Haven't seen your father since long before your *matka* passed, God rest her soul, but that's no reason for you to stay away. Eight o'clock. No later."

"Yes ma'am," Stanley managed as he backed down the steps.

Violet finally found her voice when they crossed over to her house. "I didn't know you were a Catholic."

"Neither did I."

CHAPTER EIGHT

OWEN SAT IN FRONT OF BURKE'S, where he rented a furnished room by the week, balancing his beer-filled growler on one knee. He could see the pink edges of daybreak above the black culm banks as he watched for Tommy Davies. In the month since he'd left home, he'd started meeting the boy at the square, so they could walk to work together.

Owen had started carrying beer in his lunch pail, but only so he'd have something to drink at the end of his shift, when the pain became unbearable. He knew the mine held countless dangers and alcohol only added to them. No telling how a man might meet his end. Burned, suffocated, drowned, buried under tons of coal. Roof squeezes happened often enough. Sometimes a man miscalculated the number of pillars needed to support the ceiling in a gangway or chamber. Other times, a roof fell in spite of the properly spaced columns of coal. The odds of a squeeze always increased when their bosses ordered them to "rob the pillars" after a mine had been worked to its limit. Countless times, Owen had been sent to some back chamber to take as much coal from the pillars as possible. Like all the other miners, he knew the practice was illegal and could cause a collapse, but he also knew that speaking up would get him fired.

The stories of fallen miners always made several passes through town, offering information to satisfy each listener.

The women usually focused on the tragic loss. He was someone's husband, son, or brother. The miners pored over the grisly details. Was he intact? Did he have all his limbs? Was the face recognizable? That's why they wore those round metal tags each time they stepped foot in a mine. Often, a man could only be identified by the number pressed into the center of the oversized coin.

Everyone who heard the stories listened for a mention of last words. Such remarks seemed to bring comfort to the listener. They suggested the miner had not died alone.

"Morning," Tommy said as he crossed the street.

Owen nodded his greeting as he stood. "How's everything next door? Grace still letting you fill the coal pails for her?"

"Yes sir." Tommy studied his feet as he spoke. "Most days."

Owen could hear discomfort in the boy's voice. His mother, Louise, had surely sided with Grace, as well she should. She'd probably instructed her son not to answer any questions Owen might ask about his wife and daughter. *Let him come home and find out for himself*, he could hear her saying. Nonetheless, Tommy was his only connection to Grace at the moment, so he continued: "And you're tending to the ashes?"

"As best I can. Don't see her around much, though," he added in anticipation of Owen's next question, the same questions every day.

"And Violet?"

"Don't see much of her, either. Probably inside with Mrs. Morgan," he reasoned.

"I trust you'll tell me if something needs doing around the place."

"Yes sir."

Owen decided not to press the boy further. The two

turned the corner in silence and plodded toward the colliery.

Although men had been working this part of the Sherman for better than fifteen years, folks still referred to it as the "new mine." Long before George Sherman was born, his father Oskar had opened a slope mine on the land. Men blasted and picked their way through eight chambers in about as many years before exhausting most of the resources. Engineers knew that rich veins of anthracite lay far below the mine's floor, and by then, excavation methods had improved enough to get at them. Oskar Sherman had two choices: convert the existing mine into a vertical one with multiple underground levels, or dig a companion mine adjacent to the old one. Since the slope mine still had about a year's worth of anthracite left in its walls, he instructed his engineers to blast alongside the existing operation. His decision proved to be a lucrative one. Between mining the walls and robbing the pillars, his men had enough work to see them through the colliery's expansion, and they brought in enough money to pay for it.

Tommy stopped at the above-ground stable. "Be needing some salve for one of the mules. His harness keeps chafing."

Owen nodded goodbye and continued on to the mine's entrance.

A dozen men stepped into the cage and, after a signal of two whistles, were lowered into the mine to begin a twelve-hour shift. Owen pegged in with the fire boss where he received his assignment: continue driving the new gangway on the fourth level. After adjusting the flame in his lamp, he fingered for luck the numbers *1-9-4* on his metal tag and waited for the other men to pass by. Like every morning these days, Owen walked the rail alone, and remembered.

He knew he should have stepped inside the moment he heard the squabble in the kitchen, but he'd figured Grace could handle it this one time. After all, she seemed to be in better spirits lately, and a man deserved an hour of leisure now and again. Owen required no other holiday than a pipe, a copy of the *Scranton Truth* newspaper, and his rocker on the porch. Unlike most folks, he reveled in the scorching Fourth of July sun. He liked weather in all its forms. Hot, cold, rain, snow, no matter. Variety. Outdoors. Life. The coal mine was another story. Stagnant air, sunless hours, a constant temperature of fifty degrees. An underground womb stripped of its soul. Owen thought himself fortunate to have had daughters. The mine might support his children, but it would not claim them.

He stood up and called through the front door, "Everything all right in there?" Silence after a ruckus always alarmed him. Owen stepped into the kitchen and found Grace sprawled on the floor in a huckleberry puddle. He eyed each girl to determine the course of events. Daisy stood not two feet away, her white dress speckled in purple. Violet hung near the door.

"Now look what you've done," he directed at Daisy for no other reason than proximity. He squatted down next to Grace, pushed errant wisps of hair in the direction of her bun, and lifted her off the floor. "And don't think you're excused," he said to Violet. "This has your hand all over it. Moping all morning. Nothing more disappointing than a jealous child."

"Hooligans, the pair of you." Grace twisted the back of her long skirt around front to inspect the damage. "Ruined."

"It's her fault." Daisy pointed at her sister. "She started it."

"Not another word, young lady." Owen scooped the berries into the dustbin. "I expected more out of you. Your mother working so hard to make the day nice, and what do you do? Ungrateful, that's what I say."

Tears welled in Daisy's eyes, and Owen immediately regretted his impatience. Words of apology circled his mouth, but reprimand fell into line ahead of them. "Outside, both of you, while you still can."

That was the moment he couldn't bear. The shame of it consumed him. The last time he'd ever see his daughter whole, and he'd turned away from her to tend to Grace. "Let's get you cleaned up," was all he'd said as he guided his wife toward their bedroom.

Up ahead in the mine, Owen heard Davyd Leas, one of the elders from Providence Christian, leading some of the men in prayer as he did every morning before they started their shift in earnest.

"Yea, though I walk through the valley of the shadow of death . . ."

Owen walked past the men and onto the gangway, refusing to acknowledge any God who would take his child.

CHAPTER NINE

THE FIRST WEEK OF OCTOBER, Stanley suggested they go downtown. He liked to spend time over at the Wholesale District on lower Lackawanna Avenue, where men of all sorts, Welsh, Irish, Italian, Pole, Negro, even the Turks, loaded up their wagons with the produce, meats, and dry goods they'd sell in their own neighborhood stores. It always thrilled him to meander through the maze of vendors whose accents were as thick as their cigars.

Halfway to their destination, Stanley paused in front of a large white sign, lettered in black. "*Do your part to lead souls to Christ*," he read aloud. "I wonder what that's about."

"Probably some message from the holy rollers." Violet didn't exactly know what a holy roller was, but she'd often heard her mother use the expression when discussing the "goings on" in other people's churches. "Look!" she yelled, pointing to a sign on the next corner. "There's another one."

The pair ran to the end of the block, and Violet read this time. "*How many persons are going to be steered to the straight and narrow path?*"

"Twenty-nine!" Stanley hollered, and laughed at his own joke. When Violet looked at him annoyed, he added, "It's as good a number as any." Stanley stood back for a moment and examined the barren piece of property, a full city block in size. "They're on all four corners."

Violet nodded, and they headed to the third sign. "*Future home of Scranton's largest tabernacle*," she read out of turn.

"Holy rollers must be building a church," Stanley said. "Hey, what is a holy—"

Violet ran toward the fourth corner before Stanley could finish his question.

"Wait up, so I can read!" Stanley sprinted and the two arrived together in front of the last sign. "*Reverend William A. Sunday*," he paused a moment to catch his breath, "*the world's greatest evangelist, will begin his siege on Scranton, March 1, 1914. Will you join his army*?" Stanley stood, amazed. "Well, isn't that something?"

"What?"

"Billy Sunday."

"Who's he?" Violet asked.

"Only one of the best outfielders to ever play baseball." Stanley shook his head. "Girls! Come on." He tugged on Violet's arm. "Let's get to town while there's still time."

Once they arrived at the Wholesale District, Stanley looked at Violet and said, "I have a better idea." He turned onto Wyoming Avenue.

"Not another one." Violet winced but followed. "Do I need to remind you of what happened the last time you had an idea?"

Stanley stopped in the middle of the block, pointed to a sign, and grinned. "A minstrel show. Sounds promising."

"How do you figure?" Violet knew better than to go inside Poli's Theatre. To begin with, she didn't have the money for a ticket any more than Stanley did. They'd have to sneak in. Just as important, according to the sign on the easel out front, dancing would be "the highlight of the performance." Violet knew full well that Providence Christian Church did not tolerate dancing of any kind, and she was sure that included, the "Shim Sham Shimmy" and the "Buck-and-

Wing," whatever they were, and she told Stanley just that. "How about a game of Nipsey instead?" she suggested. "We can get sticks down by the creek. See who can hit them the farthest."

"I think you're yellow," Stanley said. "Who woulda thunk it?"

"Am not."

"Are too."

"Am not."

"Prove it."

Violet pushed ahead of Stanley, held her breath, and slipped in the side door. After taking a moment for her eyes to adjust, she glanced up and screamed at the oddest-looking colored man she had ever seen. His dark face glistened like wet paint. Skin, the same color as her own, circled his eyes and bright red mouth. He stretched his arm forward and plucked a cowboy hat from a rack to the right of Violet.

"Watch where you're going, kid." He placed the hat on his head and disappeared through a door labeled, *Backstage*.

Violet turned to leave.

Stanley opened another door, this one marked, *Theatre*, and pushed her through. Both of them froze at the sights before them. Electric lights, velvet curtains, and signs pointing to indoor comfort stations, one for *Ladies* and one for *Gentlemen*. Neither of them had ever seen anything so fine in their lives, and they paused to take it in. Stanley pointed to the columns surrounding the stage decorated with garlands of plaster vines and flowers.

A burgundy-jacketed usher started toward them, his brazen buttons catching the reflection of the lights. Stanley yanked Violet by the arm, and into a curtained alcove. They watched as the usher made the turn away from them toward the *Gentlemen's* arrow.

"I want to go home," Violet muttered.

"Not a chance," Stanley said, leading them toward two vacant seats.

As soon as the curtain opened, Violet closed her eyes. She may have been obligated to stay for Stanley's sake, but she didn't have to watch the show. Maybe if she kept her eyes shut, she could escape damnation. She imagined being at home, sitting in the kitchen by herself. She looked around and saw the stove, the table, the sink, and the motto hanging above it. *Rules for Today*. The needlepoint words hit her like the back of her mother's hand.

Do nothing that you would not want to be doing when Jesus comes.
Say nothing that you would not want to be saying when Jesus comes.
Go to no place where you would not want to be found when Jesus comes.

She opened her eyes and looked around. She could think of no worse place to be when Jesus came, and she knew He was coming. Every nerve in her body told her so. She squeezed her eyes shut and saw the words emblazoned in gold thread.

Go to no place where you would not want to be found when Jesus comes.

Thanks in equal parts to her mother and her sister, Violet had had the motto memorized by the age of six. She thought about that day and the horrible pain. It was washday, so it had to have been a Monday. Her mother had just finished filling the copper tin when Daisy accidentally knocked into it, sending boiling water down her sister's backside. It truly was an accident. Violet was convinced of that, but pain was pain. In spite of her mother's home remedies, angry blisters rose up from Violet's skin.

Every night for a week, Violet balanced on a stool bending over the kitchen sink while her mother carefully tended to her burns.

"Read the first two words for me," she'd say.

"*Do nothing . . .*"

"That's right, and the next couple?" Her mother would pass a needle over the flame of a candle.

"*. . . that you . . .*"

"Good," she'd say. "Keep going." She'd slowly inserted the needle into the first blister. Stick, pop, squeeze until the wound was drained of fluid.

"*. . . would not want to be doing . . .*"

Her mother would move onto the next blister and start again.

"*. . . when Jesus comes.*"

"Close your eyes and see if you can say it back for Mother now."

And so it went for seven days, and by the end, she had the motto memorized.

Violet pulled on Stanley till he got up from his seat and followed her out the side door. Given a choice between coward and sinner, she thought coward the more favorable option.

"What's going on?" Stanley asked, stopping to let his eyes adjust to the sunlight. "It was just starting to get good."

"You'll thank me when the Pearly Gates open up to you, Stanley Adamski," she said, as she pulled him toward home.

School had let out by the time Stanley and Violet got back to Providence from downtown. Hungry from all that walking but hesitant to return to their own homes just yet, they found themselves on the widow's porch steps.

"Go ahead and knock," Stanley said.

"Third time this week. Maybe we're making pests of ourselves."

Stanley pushed past Violet. Just as he raised his fist to knock, the back door swung open.

"Well, hurry up." The widow ushered them into the kitchen and headed toward the stove. "Don't want my *pączki* to catch." The children exchanged confused glances. "Doughnuts. I already have some cooling on the sill. Give them a few more minutes, or you'll burn your tongues." She picked up a fork and tipped one up. "Perfect," she said as she flipped all the golden confections frying in the pan. "Stand back," she warned. "The lard's very hot. Violet, you set the table, and Stanley, you pour the milk. Nobody makes *pączki* better than me!"

After the incident with Myrtle Evans at Murray's store, the widow Lankowski had waited for the children to start showing up at her door. She didn't have to wait long. She took to baking sweets and ordered extra bottles of milk to have on hand when they came calling. She thought both were in sore need of a mother's love, though in Violet's case, the widow held out hope that Grace would eventually come around, poor soul. The same could not be said for Stanley. She just had to look him in the eye to know. If his dear *matka* were still alive, maybe things would have been different, but with only Albert in the house, the boy had no chance at all.

God had not seen fit to bless Johanna Lankowski with her own babies. She'd pocketed that hope twenty-five years earlier, on the day two miners dropped her husband Henryk's broken body on her front porch steps. Of course, she had been young enough to marry again but never considered it, even though there had been a few offers. She'd submitted to Henryk's will without complaint, as God required a wife to do, but she vowed not to make the same mistake twice.

Fortunately for the widow, she'd come to America as an eighteen-year-old bride with a gift for languages and lacemaking. Back in Poland, her father, a teacher, had taught her German in honor of her paternal grandmother, and English, so she could read the works of William Shakespeare in his native tongue. Her mother, like most mothers in the mountain village of Koniaków, taught her the art of needle lace, so she could help out when they came up short at the end of the month. She took to the crochet hook like a baby to the breast, quickly mastering the scallop, swirl, and petal patterns handed down from her ancestors. Soon, she began creating her own openwork designs, inspired by nature. In winter, she studied frost blossoms on the windowpanes and reproduced their intricate shapes. In summer, she collected feathers and mimicked their lines. Much to her mother's delight, several of Johanna's cloths adorned the altars in the local Catholic churches, and some of the wealthier women hired her to make baptismal gowns for their children. She could turn cotton string into a work of art as easily as she could turn a page, and although needle lace was her specialty, eventually she could imitate any style of European lace set before her, including point, pillow, and bobbin.

After Henryk's death, she took a job at the Scranton Lace Curtain Company on Meylert Avenue, down past the Sherman Mine. They specialized in what the English called Nottingham lace because the looms that originally produced it came from that town. The seamless fabric created on the factory's machines looked homemade to the untrained eye, but Johanna could tell the difference. No heart. No life. The Lace Company's curtains and tablecloths were too exact, too smooth for human hands.

In spite of her aversion to machinery, the widow quickly moved through the ranks from operator to winder, apprentice to weaver, jobs more often assigned to men than women. As a female, she still did not earn enough to keep herself. Males made a better wage since they had households to support and women could always marry. She took in sewing to earn extra money. At first, she mended a variety of goods, but slowly, she became known in Scranton for her ability to repair damaged lace by hand. Soon, the wealthy wives from all over town started sending their torn curtains and tablecloths to the widow Lankowski. One day Mrs. Dimmick, wife of J. Benjamin Dimmick, the president of the Scranton Lace Curtain Company, sent a servant to the widow's home with an heirloom cloth. It seemed one of the children had gotten his hands on a pair of scissors and cut a gash across the middle.

"You're wasting her in that factory," Mrs. Dimmick told her husband after the widow had stopped by their Green Ridge home to return the repaired tablecloth. "I dare you to find the damaged portion." Mrs. Dimmick handed the cloth to her husband. "I'm sure you have customers who would pay dearly for such attention to detail. Better yet, there are many who still prefer one-of-a-kind creations."

By the end of the week, the widow started working from home for the self-supporting wage Mrs. Dimmick encouraged Mr. Dimmick to offer her.

The widow poured sugar into a paper sack, set it on the table, and grabbed the plate of doughnuts from the windowsill. "Take turns," she said. "Drop a *pączek* into the bag, fold it closed, and shake hard." Stanley grabbed for the doughnuts. "Where are your manners?" the widow asked. "Ladies first." She pushed the plate toward Violet and went back to the stove.

Their bellies full, Violet and Stanley had as much sugar on their faces as they'd had on their pastries. "Don't forget to wash up," the widow said.

They both nodded and took turns at the sink.

"Thank you kindly," Violet said as she dried her hands. "I never tasted anything so wonderful."

Stanley added, "Me too," then smacked his lips and laughed as the pair headed out the door.

The widow sat at the kitchen table long past suppertime thinking about her situation. She had her books, her garden, her lace. All gave her pleasure, though the books caused some of the neighbors to regard her with suspicion.

"Always has her nose in a novel, that one," one remarked in a disapproving tone. "Wish I had time for such folly."

When Violet and Stanley came into her life, the widow realized what she had been missing all these years. "If only we'd had children," she directed toward a sepia photograph staring down at her from a wall. In the picture, Henryk stood behind a seated Johanna, his hands on her shoulders, eyes glaring straight into the camera. He wore the new suit of clothes they'd purchased their first week in America. Like so many immigrants, they'd gone out and bought new American clothes and had their picture taken to show their families in the old country how well they were doing in the land of opportunity. In the end, that had been Henryk's only suit, so of course the widow had him buried in it.

Finally, the widow stood and cleared the *pączki* dishes from the table. It had been a long time since she had allowed herself to imagine how children might have changed her life. Just as sadness started to settle in, she glanced over at her husband's picture once more. Henryk's eyes, cold marbles, stared back at her. "I suppose God knew best," she said aloud, "considering." She pulled a lace-trimmed handkerchief from inside her sleeve and spit the word "*Świnia*," bastard, into its center.

CHAPTER TEN

DUTY AND INDIAN SUMMER, two unlikely conspirators, coaxed Grace into the backyard for the first time since the tragedy. Violet wouldn't be home from school for another two hours, so Grace decided to hang the wash herself. She dropped her basket next to the clothesline, shut her eyes, and tipped her face toward the sky, inviting the sun to warm her bones, to thaw her heart. The rays obliged, and for a moment, Grace convinced herself that a tonic of sun and sky might be enough.

"A little color in your cheeks. It makes all the difference." Grief stood on the other side of the clothesline, examining Grace's features. "At that angle," he formed a frame with his thumbs and forefingers, cocked his head, and closed one eye, "you look like a young girl."

Grace ignored his remarks and held onto the sun, absorbing its heat like the trees, the grass, and the flowers around her. Without opening her eyes, she pictured the spot where she was standing—the back half of her own yard and the beginning of Myrtle Evans's patch of dirt. That's what Owen always called it when he compared their properties. Like everyone else in the neighborhood, both families rented from George Sherman, owner of the Sherman Mine. The company houses looked forlorn, like rows of ragamuffins, some taller than others, but all uniform in their modesty.

Soot from the mine and nearby culm bank fire dressed them in sober shades of gray and brown. Frost from the Pennsylvania winters kicked up the footers and bowed the boards, forcing porches to rest on their wooden haunches like old arthritic dogs. With no more than ten feet between them, huddled houses passed along the secrets contained inside. Mr. Harris, who lived to the right, used the Lord's name in vain whenever he got his hands on whiskey. Louise Davies on the left watched for her husband each night in spite of his death four years earlier. Backyards ran into one another, and neighbors met in the middle to discuss weather or church or those out of earshot.

Yet, from late spring to early fall, Grace managed to color her house in pinks, reds, blues, peaches, and yellows. Sweet peas stretched up the back porch's latticework, hiding the unpainted boards. Trellised roses craned their necks to view the scene below. Delphinium stood watch over the begonias as they fanned out across the soil. Snapdragons waited open-mouthed for lilies of the valley to breech their borders. Come summer, throaty toads from nearby Leggett's Creek crooned from the shade of rocks.

At the slap of a screen door, Grace's eyes popped open. Over on the Evanses' back porch, Myrtle offered an armless rocker to a rather rotund woman. A missionary, if Grace's recollection could be trusted.

"Good afternoon, Grace," Myrtle called over from a second rocker. "So good to see you up and about." She covered her mouth, and whispered something to her guest.

Grace waved a handful of clothespins that she'd retrieved from her apron pocket, peeled a sheet off the top of the basket, and hung it on the line.

"No one likes a busybody," Grief said, pushing aside the sheet that separated him from Grace.

"She's a fine Christian," Grace murmured, smoothing

the sheet back into place. "Not many like her who would open their homes to as many missionaries as she does."

Grief walked the length of the clothesline and stepped around to Grace's side. "She only puts them up long enough for the elders to take notice," he said. "They're someone else's problem, soon enough."

"I'll not have—"

Grief put a finger to Grace's lips, cupped his ear, and tilted his head toward the women on the porch.

"God as my witness," Myrtle's voice penetrated the sheetwall, "she threw that sparkler at her sister."

"I told you!" Grief's voice crackled with excitement as he slapped his knee.

"Don't take my word for it. Ask my sister Mildred." Myrtle started her rocker going. "She'll back me up. We both saw the whole thing from this very porch."

"Myrtle and Mildred. Two peas in a pod." Grief shook his head good-naturedly. "Always have a bone to scratch between them."

Eager to please her captive audience, Myrtle continued: "And then we heard poor Daisy accuse her sister. *Violet!* she yelled just before her dress went up in flames."

When Grief turned around, he seemed to notice Grace's wracked expression for the first time. "You really didn't know?" He studied her for a minute before changing his tack. "I'm not saying it's all her fault. That husband of yours played a part in this little drama." His brow furrowed as he tried to get the words right. "*No telling what might happen when you put trouble in a child's hands.* Isn't that what you told him when he brought those sparklers home?"

"*What harm can come?*" Grace parroted Owen's response, the last words he delivered on the subject. Somehow this detail, of all the details, this snippet of conversation between a husband and wife—for that's what it was and nothing more, or was it?—destroyed her. She leaned forward, her hands trembling, her eyes glazed with tears, picked up a damp shirt from the basket, and pinned it to the line.

Nothing to be done about it now, she thought. You can relive a moment again and again and again. But you can't change it. That's the tragedy of time.

"See? All better." Grief absently stroked the back of Grace's neck. "A little truth," he said. "A bit of a shock at first, but good for the soul in the end."

Grace opened her mouth to speak, though she couldn't imagine what words she would say.

"Hush." Grief smiled broadly, exposing his yellow teeth, and turned back toward the women. "I want to hear the rest of the story."

Grace didn't need to hear the story. She'd lived it that day and every day since. Daisy's screams, raw, feral, fractured, had compelled everyone within earshot to rush outside and bear witness. Grace, clad only in her slip, flew out the door and into the yard.

As Daisy ran toward the house, fire swallowed her dress and seared the flesh beneath.

"Lord Jesus. No!" Grace had screamed, wrapping Daisy's flaming body in a rag rug she hadn't remembered grabbing. She pushed the child to the ground, rolled her over several times, and dropped on top of her, smothering the last of the fire with her own body.

Owen reached the yard on Grace's heels. Burned flesh saturated their senses. Thick, sweet, biting. Heat rose off Daisy's body as he opened the rug. A leathery patchwork of red, black, and mahogany reared up and settled itself where the dress had once been. Owen gingerly lifted the afflicted child, carried her toward the house, and whispered, "Be brave, little lady. Daddy's here."

Owen, Grace, and Daisy entered the kitchen as one.

Violet remained behind, feet rooted to the desecrated soil.

Being the closest neighbors, Louise Davies and Alice Harris showed up immediately. Doc Rodham arrived at the house not ten minutes later. One of the local children had run to get him, though Grace never knew which one. As with any calamity, so many people, including the young ones, claimed to have played a role that day.

Once Owen placed Daisy on the girls' bed, Grace pulled a rocker up and studied what parts of her were still whole. Eyes, lashes, brows, nose, mouth, ears—the head in its entirety, untouched. She struggled to find comfort where she could. A disfigured body could be hidden under clothes; a disfigured face was another matter. It drew any manner of unwanted attention, and that would prove difficult for a girl. Grace's eyes skirted past the worst of it in search of hope. The right hand seemed intact, though the same could not be said of the arm. Still, Daisy was right-handed. Feet, ankles, calves, unimpaired enough for boots. So she won't be a cripple.

Grace held onto the promise of a mouth that could speak, feet that would carry, and a hand to be used in the service of the Lord. "Mother's here," she whispered, confident her daughter could hear her words. Daisy lay still but with eyes open, conscious and alert on the cotton sheet. Another good sign.

Doc Rodham entered the bedroom carrying his medical bag and the piano stool from the parlor. He placed the seat on the floor, cleared a small table, opened his case, and lined up his medicines. "I'm sorry for your troubles," he said, extending his hand to Owen. He draped a stethoscope around his neck and rolled his seat over to his patient. The fire had ravaged the front of her little body, thighs, torso, most of her right arm, and the whole of the left. He discarded the stethoscope, placed two fingers on the pulse at her neck, and looked into her eyes, so blue.

"Hello, young lady," Doc Rodham said to his patient.

"Hello," Daisy answered.

"Thank you, Jesus." Grace added speech to her list of blessings.

"Am I going to die?"

Her directness seemed to momentarily unnerve Doc Rodham, but reassurance of a kind quickly fixed itself on his expression. "Not on my watch." He smiled. "Now, tell me where it hurts."

"My feet," she said. "They're so cold."

"Mrs. Harris!" Doc Rodham yelled loud enough to be heard in the kitchen.

A moment later she poked her head through the door, stole a glance at Daisy, and winced in spite of her best intentions.

"I'll need hot water bottles."

She nodded and ran off down the hall.

Grace found it strange that Alice Harris happened to be waiting for instructions and wondered who else might be milling about her house. The notion unsettled her. Had she even finished cleaning up the spilled pie? And could that have really just happened this morning? Concentrate, she thought, and scolded herself for thinking such things mattered.

"Any other pain?" the doctor asked as he removed the stopper from a bottle marked, *Laudanum*.

Daisy shook her head slightly.

"Thank God," Owen said, "Thank God."

"An ounce of prevention," Doc Rodham said. "Open up." He placed several drops of medicine onto her waiting tongue. "And four drops every two hours," he said to Grace, who nodded.

"What about the hospital?" Owen asked.

Grace whirled around, looked directly at her husband, and said, "We'll not go there again, Owen Morgan. Not after Rose. Not ever." She turned back and looked to Doc Rodham for confirmation.

Doc Rodham shook his head. "No use," he murmured, "she'd not survive the . . ." He glanced at his patient. "Home is the best place for her just now."

Although most of Daisy's clothing had either burned or fallen off, here and there, flecks of fabric cleaved to the skin. Had the doctor not treated his share of miners over the years, whose bodies were burned in explosions, he might have mistaken the remnants for seared flesh, but as he later explained, he could tell the difference between the two. Charred cotton curled up at the ends. Burned skin pursed beneath the surface. Doc Rodham soaked a piece of linen in saline solution, wiped the affected areas, and peeled the fabric off with tweezers.

"Now let's see." He worked at a particularly stubborn section on her torso. "How long have we known each other?"

"Nine years," Daisy said.

"That so?" He picked the loosened material away.

"You delivered me," she said, as if surprised he'd forgotten such an important fact. She eyed her father, but he was turned toward the window.

"You don't say." Doc Rodham spun around to his work table, palmed a syringe, and swung back toward his patient. "You sure have a good memory." He pricked only the largest blisters, the ones stretched to the point of breaking.

Grace grimaced at the sight of the needle, but Daisy seemed not to notice. "Tell me a story."

The doctor gently patted the pierced blisters with cotton batting, soaking up the fluid. "Which one would you like to hear?"

"About the day I was born," she said.

"Now that's a good story," he replied, saturating several linen strips in carron oil. "March 1, 1904. Bet you thought I wouldn't remember." He placed the bandages on top of skin that was only burned, not broken. "You weren't in any hurry to come. Kept your mother waiting all day. When you finally got here, we knew right away that you were special. Most babies squall when they're born, but you came to us singing like an angel." He turned, measured out a portion of boric acid, and mixed it into a jar of Vaseline.

"You're teasing. Babies don't sing."

"My point exactly." He spread the ointment onto the remaining pieces of linen and placed them on the areas where the wounds were open. "Never heard a singing baby before or since." Once all of the burned areas had been treated, Doc Rodham layered cotton over the linen cloths and wrapped bandages over the batting. "That's how I knew you were special."

Alice Harris called from the doorway, and the doctor excused himself. "I don't want to push myself on anyone," she said softly, handing him two hot water bottles. "A sick room's no place for folks that ain't family, excepting you, of course, and the preacher when he comes. Holler if you need." She disappeared down the hallway.

Doc Rodham returned to the stool and finished dressing Daisy's burns. He placed two hot water bottles at her feet, covered her lightly with a sheet, and kissed her forehead. "Now, your mother and father and I are going to step out for a moment." Grace started to object, but he added, "And while we're gone, I want you to sleep. Doctor's orders." Grace remained seated.

"It's best if we discuss the child's condition elsewhere," the doctor muttered to Grace. In Daisy's direction he added, "And give her a chance to rest."

Owen leaned down and gingerly patted the top of his daughter's head. "We'll just be outside if you need us." He turned to Grace and lifted her from the chair. "Five minutes is all."

Grace relented. "Not a second more." She kissed Daisy on the cheek. "Go to sleep, pet. Mother will be back before you wake."

Out in the kitchen, Doc Rodham mentioned something about a blessing, and Grace held onto that word.

"Called *skin death,*" the doctor explained. "With third-class burns, and of course the shock, she's spared from most of the pain. At least for now."

So that was the blessing, Grace realized as she sat for a moment and warmed herself in front of the stove on the hottest day of the summer.

Owen took a breath, closed his eyes, and asked, "Will she make it?"

"Truth is . . ." the doctor lowered his gaze.

Owen reached for Grace's hand and squeezed it.

"I don't see how she'll survive the night. And if she does, she'll likely die of infection in a day or so." The doctor lifted his head and looked straight on. "I'm so sorry, Owen, Mrs. Morgan."

Grace waited for him to continue. As long as he kept talking, there was a chance he might get around to hope, to miracles, to stranger things happening than a child this injured making a full recovery.

Silence. Grace pulled away from Owen and folded both her hands in her lap.

Louise Davies went to Grace and rubbed her arms to stop her from shivering. "Hardest thing to understand," Louise said, "God's will."

"No God that I claim," Owen said, just as Reverend Halloway stepped across the threshold.

* * *

Myrtle's screen door snapped shut, interrupting Grace's thoughts. She reached into the basket and discovered she'd hung all the laundry.

Grief noted the empty rockers on the Evanses' porch. "All good things must come to an end," he said, taking Grace's hand and leading her back to the house.

A PENCIL POCKET

The husband will greatly appreciate a narrow pencil pocket not over one inch wide placed on the inside of coat, cutting through the facing to the right and a little above the inside breast pocket on the left side of coat. It should be just wide enough and deep enough to hold a pencil and a fountain pen. If the husband be a business man who often goes without vest on hot days, he will wonder why he did not have it long ago.

—*Mrs. Joe's Housekeeping Guide,* 1909

Just the other day, Pearl Williams saw Grace Morgan out on her front porch patching one of Owen's flannel shirts. Covered it with her apron, but not before Pearl took note.

"Winter's coming," was all Grace said by way of explanation. "Mending to be done." She gathered her sewing and ran straight into the house without so much as a goodbye. That's how Pearl told it.

Heart-sorry. We all say it when speaking of the Morgans. So sad. Not many light moments in that house, even from the start. Had a hard time of it. Grace especially. Always worse for the woman. Miscarried three times in as many years. Louise Davies birthed two boys in the same stretch with a third one on the way.

We all breathed easier after Daisy. Healthy. Happy. Seemed to lift Grace's spirits.

Violet came too quick is all. Too much for some women. Delicate ones, for sure. Milk dried up early. Baby had to be wet nursed by some of the mothers in the church till she could be weaned. Myrtle Evans heard Doc Rodham say Grace's insides were all tore up. Violet coming so close on the heels of her sister just did Grace in.

No one blamed the child, of course.

Owen did for Grace and the babies best he could. Not a word of complaint. Worshipped the ground that woman walked on. Now he's living over a beer garden, and there's talk the elders might remove his name from the church roll.

Though we don't like to admit it, there are those who say Grace brought this on herself. Poor thing. Wearing fancy hats to church. Teaching her girls to play piano. Correcting their English when they misspoke.

Of course, we don't believe it for a minute. God can't possibly find the time to punish folks for living above their station. Grace's troubles probably have more to do with that slip of hers. Can't think of one good reason why a decent woman would have been out of her dress that day—in the middle of the afternoon. And Lord knows we've tried.

A tragic situation for all. Oh, "How are the mighty fallen," is what we say.

CHAPTER ELEVEN

OWEN SAT IN THE ROOM HE'D RENTED OVER BURKE'S. It contained a bed, a dresser, and two caned chairs. Only one of the seats could be used with any comfort. The legs on the other were shorter in front than in back. He fingered the letter that had been delivered to him that morning. "Now what would the church want with me?" he said aloud. The answer lay inside, but he refused to read it. He tossed the envelope onto the wobbly chair, looped his suspenders over his arms, and went downstairs for a drink.

As stated in the letter, the elders from the Providence Christian Church intended to convene on the fifth of October to discuss the question of Owen's membership. He'd been accused of "improper conduct" by more than one congregant, causing the elders to start formal proceedings for removal. Considering all that he and his family had gone through in the previous months, the men were hesitant to act without offering Owen the opportunity to repent. After all, these were Christian men, many of who were burdened with their own troubles.

Davyd Leas remembered a time when he himself had turned to liquor during the mine strike of 1902. He knew what hardship could do to a man. He headed over to Burke's, hoping to talk Owen into giving up the drink and going back home.

"What's the good word?" Davyd asked, dragging a chair toward Owen's table, kicking up sawdust along the way. Unlike the other miners at Burke's, Davyd took an hour to bathe and change before stepping inside the tavern, but he knew as soon as he sat that the stench of sweat and ale would stick to him long after he departed.

Owen looked up from his glass and snorted. "Last man I expected to see in a gin mill."

"Is that so, my brother?" Davyd reached out and patted Owen's shoulder.

Owen leaned back, balancing his chair on two legs, out of arm's reach. "What is it you want with me?"

"There's some in the church that's asked you be removed from the rolls."

"On what grounds?"

Davyd tipped his head in the direction of Owen's glass. "And abandonment."

"So be it," Owen said, finishing his beer and standing to leave. "I'll not dispute the truth." He stumbled outside and upstairs to his room.

Owen lay down on his bed but couldn't sleep. He kept seeing the look on Grace's face the moment he'd struck her. What kind of a man takes a hand to his wife? he thought. The kind that can't be trusted with anyone's life but his own. That put him in mind of his one true friend, Graham.

Having worked in the mines all his life, Owen never had a formal education, but thanks to a determined mother, he'd certainly had a proper one. Each morning he'd go off to the mine with the other boys to pick slate, and each evening he'd study his lessons by candlelight. He could read and write Welsh by the time he advanced to mule driver, and had a solid command of English before he made inside crew.

Daisy's birth had only increased Owen's desire to learn and improve his circumstances. He enrolled in a series of mining engineering courses at the International Correspondence School in Scranton, locally known as the ICS. First he tackled the position of hoistman where he operated the cage, raising and lowering men and coal to any one of the vertical mine's four levels. The other men couldn't understand why he'd take a cut in pay to work outside the mine, especially with a family to support, but Owen wanted to be skilled in every position, so that one day, when he made mine superintendent, he'd understand the needs of all his workers.

Although Graham lacked Owen's natural tendency toward education, he followed along in the path Owen had carved out for them. Once they both became hoistmen, they worked opposite shifts but overlapped for a time each day so Owen could help his friend with his studies. On one particular October night in 1909, Graham climbed the steps and entered the hoistman's house an hour early for his shift.

"Don't like the look of them clouds," Graham said, pointing south through the open door. "Storms and electricity don't mix." He nodded at the metal levers and ropes used to operate the wooden cage. Graham had never been totally convinced of the benefits of learning the hoistman position, and he had expressed his doubts to Owen.

Owen nodded from his wooden seat in front of the electrical panel. "Now let's see. We left off at hydromechanics and the formulas for the flow of water through pipes."

"Sounds about right," Graham said, still standing in the doorway, staring up at the sky.

Owen thumbed through the little red ICS book in search of the page. "*Q equals the amount of water in cubic feet per—*"

An explosion sounded somewhere deep inside the mine, followed by three urgent whistles. Owen grabbed the controls to pull his men to safety. Graham swung around, watching so intently that he never noticed as the hair on his head and arms stood on end. Lightning hit the roof of the building and shot in several directions. An errant bolt burned into Graham's neck and out the left foot, knocking him forward at first, then back toward the open door. The thick odor of seared flesh filled the small space.

Graham toppled down the steps to the ground below. Owen started toward him, but when three short whistles sounded again, he succumbed to duty. He left his friend writhing on the ground, yelling for help, and turned his attention toward the men in the mine. He hoisted them to safety just as a second pocket of methane exploded inside. With everyone accounted for, Owen scrambled down to Graham whose broken body now lay motionless. Too late to save him, Owen cradled his friend and wept. Days after the incident, Owen would be hailed as a hero for saving the lives of the men on his watch, but he would never forgive himself for sacrificing Graham.

As the horses pulled the ambulance up Spring Street in the opposite direction from the hospitals, the women stepped out onto their porches, knowing that the man inside would be deposited at one of their doorsteps, either already dead or near enough. Grace and Louise met on the sidewalk and held hands. A minute later the ambulance stopped where the two women stood. Owen got out, carrying his best friend in his arms. Ashamed of himself, Owen looked past Louise as he headed up her front porch steps and into her parlor. Louise collapsed at Grace's feet.

A week after his father's death, eight-year-old Tommy Davies stood on the sidewalk in front of the Morgan house and sang out in a high voice, "Hel-lo for O-wen," as if calling for a friend to play. Owen came out and rubbed the boy's head. "You're here bright and early."

"I'm the man of the house now," Tommy said with what sounded like a mix of pride and trepidation. As the eldest son, it was his duty to take his father's place at the mine; otherwise, Mr. Sherman, like any other mine owner, would put the family out of the company house by month's end.

Owen eyed the boy's attire, his father's denim trousers, tied with a rope and cut down in length, one of his work shirts with the sleeves rolled over the wrists, and a brown peaked cap. Graham's old dinner pail dangled from his hand, dragging on the ground. Owen took the pail, patted Tommy's head, and the pair set off on foot for the boy's first day at the mine.

Owen got up from his bed and took a gulp of whiskey, holding the last little bit at the back of his throat, allowing the sting to linger. Something to burn off the coal dust. He swallowed the rest. Something to burn off the guilt he carried over Graham. Standing at the dresser, he opened the top drawer and pulled out his ICS book on mining. Although he'd quit the program after Graham's death, he'd continued carrying the book with him, a reminder of their friendship and youthful dreams. Other than the clothes on his back, it was the only belonging he'd had with him the night he'd left home. Owen pocketed the book and took another drink. Something to burn off the shame of leaving his family. And his church. He picked up the letter and pocketed it too. Just as well, he thought. He'd given up on God the day they'd buried Daisy. Another drink. A long one. No sense in God sticking with him. The last sip, a warm embrace. Something to burn off the pain the way the sun burned off the morning dew. Day after day after day. Grace had been his sun. Before. Not after. Not now.

Owen shuffled downstairs and into the bar, toward a

freshly stoked potbellied stove. First, he burned the church's letter, then, one by one, he ripped the pages out of the book and fed them to the blue flames.

CHAPTER TWELVE

VIOLET ARRIVED HOME ON THE SECOND FRIDAY in October to find her mother and Miss Reese sitting side by side on the couch in front of the parlor window. Violet's breath hardened and stuck in her throat. She slid along the wall till she butted up against the Tom Thumb piano. Without looking, she reached underneath, pulled out the piano stool, and took a seat.

"Your teacher wants to know if I can spare you this Wednesday for a picnic up at Gracye Farms Dairy." Her mother's tone was syrupy, and therefore suspect. "I told her no reason why I couldn't spare you this Wednesday," she paused, "or any other Wednesday she had in mind."

Violet dropped her head and pressed her toes into the floor.

"She tells me she worries about you," Grace paused again, giving her words their full weight, "spending all your time tending to my needs." She turned toward the visitor. "Now isn't that right, Miss Reese?"

The teacher twisted and all the prettiness drained out of her face. "What do you have to say for yourself, young lady?"

Violet studied the stool. Brass talons gripped glass balls at the base of each leg. Instinct told her to say something—make an excuse, find a lie—but her tongue would not cooperate.

This was not the first time she'd found herself at a loss for words.

They'd left her all alone in the yard that day. Mother. Father. Daisy. Violet struggled to move, but her legs were two slabs of stone. Myrtle Evans and her sister Mildred watched from their back porch, shaking their heads.

"Why don't you go in and see about Daisy?" Myrtle yelled over. "Something wrong with you, child?"

"I think she's touched in the head," Mildred said loud enough for anyone outside to hear. "Considering what she did."

"Wouldn't surprise me. The grandmother was . . . you know . . . on Grace's side."

Violet remained planted. She squeezed her eyes shut, trying to make the women disappear.

"Afraid to see what you've done? Is that it?" said Myrtle.

What I've done? She gasped, sucking in charred whispers of air. The oppressive sun glared down on her. What have I done?

Louise Davies slammed down the Morgans' porch steps, into the backyard, and yelled, "You should be ashamed of yourselves, talking to a little girl like that!" She crossed the yard. "Poor dear," she said, covering Violet's ears. "More than likely lost her only sister." Violet's eyes sprang open, and her head shook loose of Louise's grip.

"She'll have to live with that," Myrtle countered as the neighbors went back into the house.

Miss Reese collected her gloves, marched over to Violet at the piano, and thumped her on the chest. "I'll expect to see you in school on Monday morning," she said in a voice oiled with authority.

"And every day thereafter," her mother added with a

smile that looked to take some effort. "You can be assured of it." Grace stood up and moved toward the door. "I do appreciate your concern, Miss Reese. I'll make sure Violet understands the seriousness of her actions." She held the door open.

"Goodbye, then." Miss Reese turned to leave.

Violet waited for what came next. The switch? A tongue-lashing? Something worse?

Grace skirted the piano, shuffled into her bedroom, dropped to the bed, and wept.

With her eyes still closed, Violet swiveled back and forth on the stool, wondering how she should feel—about the teacher, about the tears. It was her fault, of course. Skipping school. Upsetting Mother. But nothing she felt seemed right anymore. Like the morning she'd started smiling at the memory of how her sister used to dawdle at breakfast, building hills and valleys with her oats. When she had tried to cheer her mother with that story, Aunt Hattie had scolded her for not respecting the dead. Violet hadn't meant to be disrespectful. Remembering just came to her, like sleep or hunger. How could she make their bed without picturing her sister pulling up the blankets on her side? Or sit in that classroom without wondering if the *D* carved into the desk next to hers stood for *Daisy*? Or pass by the dandelions that had gone to seed without thinking of her sister plucking bouquets of them for wishes.

Violet threw herself into a spin, swiveling down on the stool as she circled.

None of that mattered now. And she was to blame—for all of it. Making Mother sick. Driving Father out of the house.

Killing Daisy.

When she opened her eyes, she was facing the piano.

Daisy's singing had begun quietly that day. Her song

escaped into the yard, from the open bedroom window, and Violet had turned to listen.

Jesus wants me for a sunbeam . . .

They'd learned the song in Sunday school with all the accompanying hand gestures.

To shine for Him each day . . .

Violet imagined Daisy's fingers twitching, remembering a duty they needed to perform, forgetting their misfortune.

In ev'ry way try to please Him . . .
At home, at school, at play.

Daisy's had always been what choir director Betty Leas called a sterling voice, sweet, pure, clean of affectations, remarkable for a child her age.

A sunbeam, a sunbeam,
Jesus wants me for a sunbeam.
A sunbeam, a sunbeam
I'll be a sunbeam for Him.

Violet stepped around the burned patch of grass and crossed the yard. Through the window, she saw the adults, some standing, others sitting, all listening intently to Doc Rodham, so she entered the house through the front door.

The piano stood at attention on the opposite end of the parlor. Someone had moved the stool, but Violet would worry about that later. She grabbed hold of the left side of the little Tom Thumb and pulled it away from the wall. She tugged the right side in the same direction and repeated the process until the instrument pointed toward the hallway. Tiny globes of sweat dropped onto the red lacquered surface and rolled toward the keys.

Positioning herself at the far end of the piano, Violet caught her breath and started to push. The wheels over hardwood sounded like boots on gravel, but no one in the kitchen seemed to notice. No one came running to help. Daisy's singing had softened, but Violet could still hear her voice between pushes.

Softly and tenderly Jesus is calling,
Calling for you and for me . . .

Once she arrived at her sister's door, Violet saw the problem—not enough leeway to turn the piano. She mopped up her sweat with the skirt of her dress and considered her options. Up ahead on the left, her parents' bedroom door was open. She pushed the Tom Thumb deeper into the hall and, after much effort, directed it toward their room. She worked at the other end, aiming it toward Daisy. She pushed and pulled and shoved and tugged, until the piano finally cleared the opening. She rolled it into the room and up against the opposite wall, next to the window. Without looking at her sister, she grabbed the stool alongside the bed, sat down at the piano, and started to play the refrain.

Come home, come home,
Ye who are weary come home . . .

Daisy's voice remained steady, either unaware of the accompaniment, or taking it for granted.

Come home, come home,
Calling all sinners come home . . .

Sinner. The word ricocheted in Violet's head throughout the entire second verse and exited out her windpipe with a gasp.

Violet focused on her hands and realized she was rushing the notes, the only criticism her mother ever made of her playing. "Feel the music," she'd say with eyes closed, head swaying. As the third verse approached, Violet slowed her fingers and rested her foot atop the damper.

Time is now fleeting,
The moments are passing . . .

Violet stretched the notes, inviting each to settle in for a short visit.

Passing from you and from me . . .

Her mother and father entered the sickroom with Reverend Halloway in tow.

Daisy's song continued, unstrained, purposeful, necessary.

Shadows are gathering . . .

With an audience, Violet felt both conspicuous and cornered. At least her back was to them. At least she didn't have to look them in the eyes.

Deathbeds are coming . . .

She wished she could melt into the floor and seep between the boards into the cool dark earth below. She wanted to run into her mother's arms, to sit on her father's lap, and tell them she was not a jealous girl no matter what they thought—but she could do none of these things. All she could do was play.

Coming for you and for me . . .

Did they blame her? Could they even see her? All the while, her fingers continued their dance across the keys, despite the heaviness of her heart. At once she realized that if she stopped—that is, if she could choose to stop—the silence would give her up. And so she continued to play.

She played through the doses of laudanum every two hours. She played as their mother placed chips of ice on Daisy's tongue; the ice that had been intended for ice cream at the church picnic.

"Stop now, Violet," her mother had said at one point. "Your sister needs her rest."

"No," said Daisy. "Let her play."

So she played whether her sister sang or rested, prattled or whimpered. She played long after she was told to go sleep in her parents' room.

Three days in all, Violet played all the hymns she knew, until her fingers blistered, then bled, then finally calloused. She played on the second day when Doc Rodham soaked the bandages, peeled them away, and dressed the wounds all over again. She played through the choking smell of infection mixed with the perfume of sweet peas from the open window. Through her mother's tears, her father's prayers, and her sister's singing.

And then Violet remembered another song. Daisy immediately recognized the tune.

Away in the manger,
No crib for a bed.

The little Lord Jesus
Lay down His sweet head . . .

Violet stared at the wall and took in the sounds. Her sister's voice. The groan of her mother's rocker. The *tap, tap, tap* of a boot too quick to be interested in keeping time.

Daisy sang. The first verse, the second verse, and finally the third.

Be near me, Lord Jesus,
I ask Thee to stay . . .

Her voice was fragile but steadfast, like a crocus poking its head through a spring snow.

Close by me forever,
And love me I pray . . .

For the third day in a row, Reverend Halloway called on the Morgans.

Bless all the dear children
In Thy tender care . . .

The adults took one breath and held it, as if by agreement, in anticipation of the final lines.

And take us to heaven,
To live with Thee there.

Daisy's voice, a whisper. "I want to look brave when I meet Him."

"A finer soul He'll never see," her mother assured.

"I'm ready," Daisy said, and breathed no more. Without

turning, Violet knew to close the lid over the piano keys.

One long savage wail escaped from the darkest part of her mother's soul. No other sound was heard until the preacher finally said, "She's in the Almighty's choir now."

"Small comfort," her father muttered from the other side of the room.

CHAPTER THIRTEEN

HATTIE FUMED AS SHE STARTED UP SPRING STREET to see about Grace and Violet. The "good Christian women" of Providence Christian had wasted no time that morning filling her in on Miss Reese's recent visit to the Morgan house. Yes, Hattie was concerned that the teacher had stopped by, and yes, Violet did need more supervision than Grace seemed able to provide, but why did she have to hear about it from Myrtle Evans and her lot?

Hattie continued up the street, wondering what she could do to help. Grace refused to move into the boarding house, and Hattie couldn't afford to move to the Providence section of town.

Assuming she'd find Grace in the kitchen, Hattie went around to the side door. As she put her hand on the knob, the door flung open.

"I was just telling Grace we'd probably be seeing you today," Myrtle said with a smile as she waved her in.

Hattie's attention flew to Grace who sat at the table, her head in her hand, with her blouse half-buttoned over what looked like a nightgown. "What's going on?"

"I've solved our problem!" Myrtle announced. "And everyone's on board." She patted Grace's limp hand.

Myrtle's solution came in the form of a rather corpulent missionary, who stood huffing and puffing, her white-knuckled hand gripping the back of a chair.

Forty-three-year-old Adelaide Humphreys had been raised on a Guatemalan mission field until the age of ten. She and her father, Reverend Howard Humphreys, had returned to the States after her mother contracted and subsequently succumbed to malaria. Intent on carrying God's message to anyone who had an ear for it, her father joined the Circuit Riders, a group of Methodist preachers spreading the word on horseback in those godless settlements out west. Adelaide traveled a separate circuit, bouncing from one church family to the next until she reached adulthood. Since she only knew how to depend on others for her keep, she naturally became a missionary herself.

Once a year, Adelaide spent the better part of a month in Scranton, reporting on her work to the members of the Providence Christian Church, who supported her mission out west. Though Adelaide never actually lied about how far west she'd traveled, Hattie had been surprised to learn from a visiting evangelist that Adelaide never made it any farther than Pittsburgh.

"I tell you, these children out west would burn in the fires of hell if it weren't for your generosity," Adelaide would explain at the start of each visit. "Some never even heard of Jesus Christ our Lord and Savior. Can you imagine?"

Murmurs of disbelief would pass through the Women's Bible Study Group, the Christian Endeavor Society, or the congregation at large.

"They'll say to me, *Sister Adelaide, who is this Jesus fellow?*"

Heads would shake in horror.

"Without God's Word, their little souls would go unsaved." She'd raise a hand and shout, "Thanks be to God for the support you have given thus far!"

A rousing "Amen!" would sweep through the congregants.

"But there are still more children, bellies to fill, hearts to be won for Jesus."

Those in the audience would start digging in their pockets. The deacons would advance along the pews, passing the collection plates up and down the aisles.

"Dear Lord," she'd drop her head in prayer, and a wattle of flesh would sag at her neck like a silk balloon in need of gas, "may these fine Christians ask themselves, *Have I given enough to the service of the Lord? Have I sacrificed enough in His name?*"

A few hands would reach back into their pockets in search of their own salvation.

"Father, let them consider whether that extra sweet or finger of whiskey," she'd open her eyes and let them settle on the well-fed woman or bulbous-nosed man she'd spied in advance, "is worth a few lost souls."

More hands would scavenge for coins intended for other, less noble purposes. The men taking up the collection would circle back, smile broadly, and pass their plates a second time.

"Thanks be to God," she'd say, and signal the deacons to hoist her to her feet.

Adelaide Humphreys had arrived at the Morgan household with more suitcases than seemed necessary for a missionary, in Hattie's opinion. Grace managed a weak smile from her seat at the kitchen table while Hattie stood, appalled, in the doorway.

"If you'll be so kind as to show me to my room," Adelaide said pointedly to Violet. Violet started toward her bedroom when Sister Adelaide cleared her throat and tipped her head in the direction of the suitcases. "Milk leg's acting up, and the doctor advised me to avoid strain."

Violet took hold of the largest suitcase and dragged it down the hallway. Adelaide trailed, unimpeded.

"What in the world is going on, Grace?" murmured Hattie.

"I'll be off then," said Myrtle, squeezing by Hattie in the doorway and hurrying out.

"I'm not feeling well," Grace said, standing slowly. "I'm going back to bed."

"That's a good girl," Adelaide Humphreys said when she reached Violet's room. "You can get the others once I'm settled in."

Violet entered first and started to clear her half of the bed.

"This will be fine," Adelaide said as she patted the mattress and sat down. "And where do you sleep?"

"I'm partial to the right side, but I can make do with the left."

"No need for that." Adelaide smiled. "That's a good sleeping couch out in the parlor. Just your size." She stretched out fully, depositing her girth across both sides of the bed. "Now be a dear girl and bring the rest of my suitcases in before I fall to sleep."

Violet returned to the kitchen to talk to Aunt Hattie, but she had gone, the door slamming shut behind her.

CHAPTER FOURTEEN

After Miss Reese's visit, Violet started attending school on a regular basis. She didn't need anyone to see her off each day, which was just as well, considering her mother usually slept long into the morning, and Adelaide never awakened before noon.

"I don't see why you won't come with me," Violet said to Stanley, who was waiting for her near the elderberry bushes on her first day back to school. "It won't be any fun sitting around by yourself."

"What's the point? Pa says there's work for me at the mine if I'd only sprout up."

"That could take years," Violet said, and Stanley's cheeks reddened. "What I mean is, you should go to school while you're waiting."

"He brought me around last year, but the boss sent me home on account of how little I was. I've grown two inches since then." He stopped, turned around, and stood back to back with Violet. The top of his head landed somewhere around the nape of her neck. He stretched up on his toes and said, "Won't be anytime now."

"How come your pa doesn't make you go to school?"

"Says a boy don't need education, just good sense."

"But you're the smartest boy I know."

Roses bloomed on Stanley's cheeks. "What a thing to

say." The smile on his lips belied his words.

"Of course, I can think of half a dozen girls brighter than you, but you're the smartest *boy* I know." Violet laughed at her joke as they turned the corner. "It's washday. Mother said last night that I'm to come straight home." She entered her yard and started for the side porch. "Getting awful cold for fishing," she called out as she made the corner.

Stanley said nothing as he continued up the street.

The next morning, Stanley stood in front of the Morgans' house and sang, "Hel-lo for Vi-o-let." He rested his elbow on the wooden banister, slick with the season's first frost. He wore a brown corduroy jacket, buttonless and well-worn, a hand-me-down from an older brother who, like the two before him, had long since left Scranton. The coat flapped open in the wind.

Violet peeked out the parlor window and saw a cleaner version of the boy she was used to seeing. It looked as though he'd taken a bath and washed his hair, which surprised her considering Saturday was still four days away. "You'll wake Mother," she scolded as she started down the steps. As she approached him, she noticed his sour smell lingered, in spite of his best effort.

"Let's go, slowpoke." Stanley waved her forward. "Wouldn't want to be late."

Once Stanley started showing up for school, he completed all of the second grade work in a matter of weeks. By the beginning of November, Miss Philips promoted him to third grade.

"Well, don't just stand there," Miss Reese said to Stanley, who waited at the door. "There's an empty seat next to Evan Evans."

"Thank you, ma'am." Stanley tipped an imaginary cap as he sat down.

The teacher glared at the boy before continuing her lesson: "As I was saying . . ."

Stanley looked straight on and smiled broadly.

Miss Reese picked up a ruler and tapped it gently against her hand. "We're fortunate to have a renowned Christian like Mr. Billy Sunday coming to our town. This is someone who turned down a $400-a-week salary as a baseball player," she glanced up and down the rows, "to preach the gospel to the likes of you." She closed her eyes dreamily and added, "Who wouldn't want to meet so fine a man?"

"First player ever to run the bases in fourteen seconds," Stanley blurted.

The teacher's eyes popped open. "That was a rhetorical question, requiring no response." She slapped the ruler against her open palm. "Furthermore, young man, I'll not tolerate speaking out of turn."

"Sorry, ma'am. I just get excited about the White Sox."

"White Stockings," Evan corrected.

"Maybe about ten years ago," Stanley said.

"One more outburst and I'll take a switch to both of you. Is that understood?"

"Yes ma'am," they answered in unison.

Miss Reese eyed the boys and started again. "This tract," she handed a stack of papers to Janie Miller to be passed out, "was printed by the Revival Committee. You're to take it home to your parents. It contains Mr. Sunday's entire seven-week schedule and a list of rules for living a proper," she glanced at Stanley and Evan once more, "Christian life."

Janie finished her task, handed the extra papers to Miss Reese, and sat down.

"No skipping school," Miss Reese said without reading from the pamphlet. Instead she stared at Violet, who tried and failed to find that particular rule on the list. "No dancing," Miss Reese continued. "No talking back to your elders. No vaudeville."

Violet quickly threw a look in Stanley's direction, but he ignored her.

"Study the Bible. Pray much. And shun evil companions. Are there any questions?"

"When . . ." Stanley started, then remembered to raise his hand. "When do we get to meet him?"

"The dates and times are listed on the sheet," Miss Reese answered.

"One of the best outfielders ever," he added.

"A lousy hitter, though," Evan said without waiting for permission. "Besides, it doesn't matter. Billy Sunday's a Christian."

"So?" Stanley waited to hear more.

"Catholics can't go see him."

"That's enough!" Miss Reese shouted. "Up front, both of you."

Stanley and Evan trudged forward and held out their arms.

Miss Reese delivered three sharp blows with her ruler to each pair of hands. "Why is it that empty barrels make the most noise?" she asked. The boys took their seats, knowing enough not to answer a rhetorical question.

"Children, line up for a spelling bee," Miss Reese instructed on a particularly chilly day. With Thanksgiving a week and a half away and a layer of snow dusting the ground, the students were restless. They rushed toward the windows, sneaking peeks outside and trying for positions near the end of the line. "Alphabetical order," Miss Reese explained, and the line slowly rearranged itself. Stanley Adamski found himself at the head of the formation.

"Slumber," Miss Reese said, and a collective gasp rose from the room. She started with a word from their new list, the one she'd only put up the day before.

"That's a dirty trick," one of the boys muttered, "even if it's Stanley." Miss Reese eyed the group and the talking stopped.

"Slumber, S-L-U-M-B-E-R, slumber," Stanley said without hesitation. He looked at the teacher and waited for her nod of approval.

"Let's keep this moving." She motioned Stanley to the end of the line. He smiled at Violet as he passed.

"Wagon," Miss Reese directed toward Emily Bowen. Emily relaxed at such an easy word, spelled it correctly, and took her place behind Stanley.

Only five students remained standing by the end of the fourth round: Stanley, Emily, Violet, and the McGraw twins, Jimmy and Meghan.

Violet stepped forward.

Miss Reese looked at her list. "Prairie."

"P-R-I-A-R-I-E, prairie." Violet started toward the back of the small line when Miss Reese announced, "Incorrect." Only Stanley seemed to notice how the corners of the teacher's mouth lifted when she said it.

Violet continued toward her seat as if that had been her intention all along.

Two rounds later, only Stanley and Meghan remained.

"Hatch," Miss Reese said to Meghan.

"H-A-C-H, hatch."

Meghan stepped to the other side of Stanley. The students waited for Miss Reese's high-pitched, "Incorrect," but she simply said, "Soldier."

Several "buts" rose from the class. Miss Reese silenced them with her eyes.

"Soldier," Stanley said. "S-O-L-D-I-E-R, soldier." He

held his place, forcing Miss Reese to mumble, "Correct," in order to send him to the other side of his opponent.

There were three more rounds before Meghan misspelled again. "Celebrate, C-E-L-A-B-R-A-T-E, celebrate." This time, Miss Reese acknowledged the error but announced, "Stanley still needs to spell one more word correctly, or it's a tie."

"Not fair," someone said, but Stanley stepped forward.

"Deficient," a word no third grader had ever seen on any list.

"Deficient, D-E-F-I-C-I-E-N-T, deficient," said Stanley, "as in, *Everyone thought the boy was deficient, but he turned out to be quite smart.*" Giggles rose from the desks.

"Multiplication tables up to ten, five times each," Miss Reese said, her tone clipped. The students started shuffling through their desks. Meghan took the seat next to her brother, but Stanley refused to budge.

"Sit down, Stanley, and get to work."

Violet spoke up: "You forgot to declare a winner."

Stanley smiled at his friend, threw his shoulders back, and remained standing.

"Talking out of turn. No recess." Miss Reese eyed Stanley. "For either of you. Now take your seat."

The boy bristled but held his ground. Miss Reese grabbed hold of her ruler and started toward Stanley, but stopped as the door to the classroom swung open. All eyes turned to the man in the doorway, broad, muscular, red-faced. "Did my boy do something wrong?" Mr. Adamski stared at Stanley standing against the wall. "I told you I don't want no son of mine going to school. What are you, deaf?"

"Mr. Adamski?" Miss Reese took a step toward him but stopped to set the ruler on the chalkboard. Her students sat up, arrow-straight and mouse-quiet.

Violet opened her mouth but didn't know what to say.

Stanley nodded at his father. "I was just passing time, sir." He squeezed by the man, toward the cloakroom next door. "Never even opened a book." He forced a laugh as he reached for his coat but fell to the floor with his father's first blow.

Across the hall, Miss Philips stepped out of her classroom. "May I hel—"

"This here's a family matter," Mr. Adamski explained, tipping his hat with the fist he had just used on his son. "Now go on back inside."

Miss Philips returned to her classroom but stood facing the intruder. Stanley jumped to his feet and scrambled down the hall and out the door with his father on his heels.

Stanley's left eye swelled completely shut by the time he and his father arrived at the Sherman Mine.

"You're late. The crew already went down." The shift foreman made a notation on his board.

"This here's my boy. Old enough for the breaker. Won't give you no trouble. I'll see to it." He glared at his son.

"I'll give you one more chance, Adamski, but that's it." He pulled the boy toward him. "Let me have a look at you." He circled around him. "Sure he's of age?"

"Give you my word."

"Not worth a plugged nickel," the boss said, as he pulled Stanley's hands toward him and looked at his palms. "A bit scrawny," he paused for a moment, "but he'll do. He can start tomorrow morning, six o'clock. Now get back to work."

"Yes sir." Adamski eyed his son. "You better be home when I get there." He started up to the hoistman's house to see about going down.

On her way home from school, Violet checked the oak tree

and the elderberry bushes for Stanley. His corduroy coat dangled from her arm. When she couldn't find him, she walked home from school alone for the first time that year.

FOR TIRED NERVES

> *If overworked homemakers whose nerves are "worn to frazzle edge" would acquire the habit of sitting or lying absolutely still . . . for five to ten minutes twice a day, they would soon see improvement. The mind must be relaxed, worries dropped, thoughts wandering to pleasant things. You will probably try this several times before you get it right, but after a little practice you will find that it yields large returns, far surpassing the sacrifice of the time it takes. Try it, nervous ones.*
>
> —*Mrs. Joe's Housekeeping Guide,* 1909

A little over three months to go before Billy Sunday arrives. Not much time considering all that needs doing. Seems everyone's helping out, though. Fifty-three churches at last count, plus the Rescue Mission and the Salvation Army. Scranton's never seen the likes of so fine a Christian. We want to do our city proud.

Of course, we can't have a Billy Sunday revival without one of his tabernacles. They're none too fancy, but as we always say, "A blind man would be glad to see it." Mr. Sturges offered a good-sized piece of land toward downtown, between Washington and Wyoming avenues. The men will start building in a month or so. We expect to have most of the money raised by then.

In the meantime, Adelaide Humphreys offered to help organize the Christians in Providence, even though, according to her, it's uncommon for such well-known evangelists to work together. But as she explained, "It'll take more than the likes of Billy to rid this city of sin."

She has a point. All we have to do is open the paper to see it for ourselves. Stories of drunkenness, burglary, suicide. Fourteen murders this year alone! And those brothels sure don't help. There's a sign on top of the Scranton Life Building that spells out, *Watch Scranton Grow,* in great big lightbulbs. A nice sentiment, but some argue it should read, *Watch Scranton Grow More Dangerous.* We're lucky to have someone like Sister Adelaide staying here to help in the fight, especially with all her other obligations.

When asked about her mission out west, all she said was, "Duty keeps me here." When pressed, and only then, she added, "God as my witness, that Violet has the devil himself inside her. Never saw a body more in need of saving and that's the gospel truth. With that momma of hers, and no daddy to speak of, it falls to me."

The woman is a godsend. We all say it. Only wish Grace could see it too. Perhaps it's the grief. Though, more likely, it's her delicate condition.

CHAPTER FIFTEEN

THE DAY BEFORE THANKSGIVING, Hattie walked out to her back porch and found a twenty-pound turkey strung up by the feet. Chester had alerted her to someone in the yard. She yelled, "Much obliged, Owen!" in case he was still within earshot. "Makes it kind of hard to stay mad at you." She waited. "You're welcome to join us tomorrow. Grace'll be here. And Violet too." She pulled a knife from the pocket of her apron and sawed down the bird. "I'll save your place at the table."

Owen waited until Hattie stepped back inside. He didn't want her to see him in the woods at the end of the yard, even if she figured he was out there. After almost three months away, he couldn't imagine what he'd say to her, or her to him for that matter. He hadn't forgotten his obligations, though. Rent, food, chores around the house the few times Grace was off at church, and now the turkey. Hattie would be obligated to mention it to her sister. That had to be enough for now.

Grace hadn't been out of the house in weeks, not even to help Hattie the day before Thanksgiving. And she would have been content to stay home on the holiday itself if it weren't for Adelaide's insistence.

"We could all use a good meal," Adelaide said. She

pushed herself away from the kitchen table, pulled in her stomach, and squeezed two fingers into the waist of her skirt. "I'll have to get everything taken in if this keeps up."

Grace looked down at her own waistline and realized neither of them seemed to be suffering from a lack of sustenance, odd considering the sporadic nature of their meals.

Violet walked into the kitchen, pulled out the flour, and started on the baking.

The missionary held out her cup and saucer. "A bit of advice," Adelaide said. "It takes a generous handful of lard to make a proper biscuit."

"Yes ma'am," Violet said as she stopped what she was doing to pour the coffee.

Grace looked at her daughter. An inch taller, a mite thinner, and a seriousness in her dark eyes that she hadn't noticed before. Grace momentarily wondered at the transformation, but let go of the thought when Grief whispered in her ear.

"What is it you're expected to give thanks for?" He patted her hand with his sweaty palm and dragged his chair closer to hers. Grace watched absently as he sucked the flesh from her fingers and licked the bones clean.

"There's my girl," Hattie announced as Violet bounded through the swinging door into the kitchen. Hattie's hands were starch-covered from peeling potatoes, so she wiped them on a rag before hugging her niece.

"Sister Adelaide sent me in to help. She and Mother are resting in the front parlor."

"Is that so?" Hattie pushed two bunches of carrots toward Violet. "Scrub them real good," she said as she left the room.

Some of the boarders were seated on couches, waiting for their Thanksgiving meal. "If you'd be so kind, my sister and I need a moment." The men nodded, lumbered into the dining room, and pulled the pocket doors shut. When Adelaide didn't budge, Hattie added, "Violet could use a hand in the kitchen."

"It does that child good to feel useful," Adelaide stated, nestling deeper into the couch. "Wouldn't want to take that away from her."

Hattie glared at the missionary, then perched on an ottoman in front of Grace. "I've been worried."

Adelaide nodded as if she and Hattie had somehow been in cahoots on the matter.

A labored sigh preceded Hattie's next words. "Somehow, and I don't pretend to know the answer—with my help, maybe, with God's help, certainly—you will pull yourself together." She cupped Grace's right hand between both of her own. "Daisy's gone, but you're still here." She paused to let her words sink in.

Grace stared past Hattie, to Grief, who'd slipped in without being noticed. He leaned against the opposite wall, his eyes sparkling, his complexion still ruddy from his morning repast.

"You can't just let the pain swallow you," Hattie tried again. "After all, there's Violet to consider."

Adelaide leaned forward and added, "We must be grateful for the blessings God has given us."

Grace's fingers curled into fists, the nails digging into her palms.

Grief chuckled mercilessly from his corner. "Neither of these women knows the loss of a child firsthand."

"We can't begin to understand your pain," Hattie directed at the missionary before turning back to Grace. "But that said, you have to fight. For the sake of Violet, if not your own."

"There's a time to grieve, but there's also a time when

grief becomes an imposition." Adelaide smiled and took a breath. "I was a little girl when my father taught me that," her left cheek twitched faintly, "after my mother passed." She pressed her palm against that side of her face. "We admire people who overcome tragedy. We're not comfortable with those who wallow in it."

"Adelaide!" Hattie said. "I certainly hope you're not putting your own comfort above my sister's."

Grief made his way toward Grace. "What an insufferable—"

"On the contrary," Grace said. "Adelaide is simply expressing what everyone else is too afraid to say." She turned toward the missionary. "They all walk on eggs around me because I lost a child. But not you. Never you."

Adelaide accepted Grace's words as validation and settled in her seat, a large goose smoothing her feathers. Hattie sat still, her mouth in a thin line.

"Look at her," Grief said of the missionary. "Nothing but a fat pig, feeding off your pain. The gall." He leaned against the arm of the couch and ran his fingers through Grace's locks. "She can't see past her own stomach. How could she understand your heartache?" He lifted a handful of Grace's hair to his nose and inhaled. "They don't deserve to share your misery."

In that moment, Grace decided to push her pain down inside, where she alone could touch it, where no one else could taint it with their dirty fingers. She'd get out of bed every morning, dress herself, feed Violet, do all that the world and God required of her. It wouldn't be easy, but she'd find a way. Grace leaned forward and glanced at Violet in the kitchen.

"A handsome enough girl," said Grief, "though without Daisy's shine."

"She's mine," Grace shot at him. "I have to love her."

"Of course you love her," Hattie said. "No one ever thought otherwise." She and Adelaide exchanged nervous glances.

Had she said those words aloud? Grace willed herself to do better. She began with the smile, pushing both ends of her lips up, away from the pain she hid inside. She stood and asked, "How can I help with dinner?"

"That's a fine start," Hattie said, and hugged her. "Let's get that bird on the table."

Grace continued to smile throughout the meal, the clean-up, and the pleasant parlor conversation. She wore her new expression like a corset, cinched at the middle, pinching the heart and lungs. Those who thought grief had a beginning and an end were particularly grateful for her effort. Her smile, or at least the semblance of it, eased their discomfort.

Only Violet found her mother's countenance unnerving. She was reminded of a snake before it strikes.

Owen stood at the edge of the yard, catching glimpses of Grace and Violet as they passed by the open back door. He closed his eyes and breathed in the turkey and all that it promised. A couple slices of gravy-soaked bread, a mound of apple dressing, a chunk of plum pudding. His family around him. For a moment he thought to go inside, but knew the stink of whiskey would upset them and spoil the day.

When they finally returned from Aunt Hattie's, Violet found Stanley sitting on the porch waiting for her.

"I've missed you!" she said.

"It's awfully late for company," Adelaide said, and Stanley stood to leave.

"It's too cold out here." Grace eyed the missionary and

held her new smile in place. "Follow us around to the kitchen. You can visit inside."

Once the women settled into their bedrooms, Violet shoveled more coal into the stove, opened the drafts, and stoked the flame. She grabbed Stanley by the hand, intending to lead him over to the fire, but he yelped so loudly, she let go.

He opened his palms, faceup. Infection oozed from angry wounds sliced across his fingers. "Ain't nothing. All the breaker boys get cut. Can't help it when you're picking slate."

Violet led him by the elbow over to the sink. "I hate your father. What was he thinking, sending you into that mine?"

Stanley yanked his arm away. "Don't go dragging Pa's name through the mud."

The seriousness in his voice surprised her. "I'm sorry," she said. "I . . . I didn't know."

"I'm sorry too." He offered his elbow and a shy smile.

Violet hopped up on a stool and pumped enough water to fill a basin halfway, then poured in half as much kerosene. "Now, soak them," she said, giving him the stool so he could reach.

"Are you trying to kill me?" he gasped at the first sting.

"Do you want to lose your fingers to infection?"

"That's what Tommy Davies asked when he saw me. *Piss on your hands* is what he said. All the breaker boys do. And hand up to God, it helps." Stanley raised his right hand, but Violet dunked it back into the kerosene bath. "For crimony's sake!" He winced in pain.

"That's disgusting!" Violet turned up her nose as she pulled out a bowl from the cupboard.

"Tommy's a mule boy, now," Stanley continued. "Said maybe I could help him tend the animals sometime."

Violet eyed Stanley to make sure he hadn't moved, before trying her hand at a poultice of bread and lard. She rubbed the ingredients between her palms as if making a piecrust, then put the doughy lump aside in the bowl. After half an hour of soaking, Stanley gingerly patted his hands dry. Violet rubbed the paste of bread and lard across his cuts, then wrapped his hands in bandages as best she could. "Mother says this is good for infection."

"Let's hope it works fast. I have to go back to work tomorrow."

The next morning, Stanley carefully unwrapped the bandages and scraped off the bread and lard clumps sticking to his fingers. He looked at his hands, glistening with animal fat, and noticed the infection had calmed some. He placed both poultices into a drawer for later use and headed off to the mine.

Long before Stanley ever worked in the breaker, he used to stand at the square, look down across the Lackawanna River, and picture the Sherman Colliery as a kingdom, as evil as any in Andersen or the Brothers Grimm. It spanned a hefty tract of land between Market and Green Ridge streets, and blackened everything it touched—grass, flowers, trees on both sides of the river, and the river itself. The men took the worst of it, some coated in coal dust, others caked in it. Pitch-dark structures housed blacksmiths and carpenters, powder and steam, ogres and trolls. The breaker, a one-hundred-foot giant made up of windows and stairs and odd-angled stories, sat hungrily in the center waiting to feed, its metal teeth able to chew tons of coal at a sitting.

Stanley looked at his hands, then fell into line with the other boys entering the building. He sat at the third chute, a position assigned to him on his first day, and straddled the boards. The two boys above him picked through the coal, tossing away the largest, most obvious pieces of slate and bone. As the coal passed through Stanley's station, he had to sort more carefully, which was nearly impossible since the coal dust blocked the natural light. He didn't complain, though. The boy at the bottom had it the worst. He was closer to the foreman and his whip.

At mealtime, Tommy found Stanley finishing the last of his cold cabbage. After a week of ten-hour days at the chute, Stanley's back had started to bend like the crook of a pear tree.

"You need to stand up when you can. If not, you'll get stuck that way." Tommy nodded in the direction of several boys who stood upright, yet their backs were rounded like old men. "Come on. The walk will do you good."

Stanley followed Tommy toward a barn about twenty feet to the right of the mine's entrance. Inside, countless bales of hay rested against one another, and one lone mule stood in the last stall.

"Who's that?" Stanley asked, nodding toward the white beast.

"Most cantankerous mule a fellow will ever meet. Refuses to work and that's the end of it. Mr. Sherman paid two hundred dollars for her six months ago, and she's never seen the inside of the mine." Tommy grabbed hold of the plaited whip around his neck, moved toward the stall, and threw a handful of old carrots in her direction. The mule peeled back her lips to expose her teeth and snorted. "Won't let herself be harnessed. Won't let herself be led down." She kicked up her front legs, as if punctuating Tommy's words with her own exclamation points, then turned sideways and ignored him.

Stanley edged up to the gate of the stall and extended his hand for her to sniff. The faint smell of bread and lard still clung in the folds of his palms.

"She'll bite you as quick as look at you," Tommy warned

before turning toward several harnesses hanging from nails on the wall. He fingered each, looking for one not too new or too worn. New leather chafed the necks of the mules causing them to buck. Old leather split easily, causing the car to break away from the animal.

"That's a good girl," Stanley cooed as the mule rubbed her nose across his hand.

"Well, I'll be. How'd you do that?"

"You can't come at her head-on." Stanley gently stroked her snowy neck. "She startles."

"How could you tell?"

"She's been beat." Stanley paused to stare at the beast, and she stared back. "It's in the eyes." He started petting her again. "You want something to eat?" he asked her, bending slowly to retrieve one of the carrots. The mule ate from his hand.

"Think you can get her into the mine? Boss'll make you a nipper for sure. Get you out of that breaker."

Stanley looked at the cuts on his fingers, swollen and oozing again after half a day's work. "Opening doors sounds a hell of a lot better than picking through slate. Give me a week," Stanley said as he strolled out of the barn whistling.

Every day at mealtime, Stanley entered the barn and approached the mule. "Well hello there, Sophie." He named her for a mutt he sometimes played with in the neighborhood. "And how are you today?" He started to pet the side of her head, and introduced the harness by inches. First the smell of it, then the feel of it as he rubbed it along her snout. On the seventh day, Stanley and Sophie sauntered out of the barn and toward the mine's entrance.

"Don't spook her now," Stanley said as he handed the reins to Tommy.

The following day, Stanley was promoted to nipper.

CHAPTER SIXTEEN

GRACE SAT ON THE EDGE OF HER BED, waiting for Adelaide to complete her bedtime ritual of Bible reading and prayer in the room across the hall. If the previous weeks were any indication, she would be asleep ten minutes after what Grace considered to be an overly enthusiastic "Amen." She clutched a handbill that read,

ROSALEE SPEAKS TO THE DEAD
At Poli's Theatre
Performances held in the evening, 7:00 and 10:00
December 6, 1913, in the year of our Lord

The words were centered in a hand-drawn frame of what appeared to be souls in various stages of flight. One picture in particular had caught Grace's attention and compelled her to slip the fly sheet into her pocket when she'd seen it on the counter earlier that day at the company store. In the upper right-hand corner, a small outline of a girl seemed to look off at something beyond her. A sketched bow bloomed from the top of her head. Daisy. Grace knew the child to be her own as soon as she laid eyes on her, and understood what she had to do, in spite of the church's teachings on the subject. She would go that night and speak to her daughter. Grace looked at the drawing again, closed her eyes, and imagined a child, not lost to her forever, but rather sleeping peacefully in the room across the hall. At that very moment, Adelaide's snoring began, shaking Grace out of her reverie.

She put on a broadcloth coat, attempted to button it at the belly, found it had thickened more than she thought reasonable, considering her ongoing dyspepsia, and left it open from the waist down. She pocketed the baptism photograph of Daisy and the almost two dollars in coins from her dresser, a donation from the women's Sunday school class after they'd heard about Owen's sudden departure. What would the ladies say if they knew how Grace intended to spend their money? But she couldn't think about that. Daisy was waiting for her in a theatre downtown.

A minute or two after Grace stepped out the kitchen door, Violet threw off her covers and got up from the couch fully dressed. She'd taken to sleeping that way since her father had left. Someone had to keep an eye on her mother. That's what the neighbor women kept saying, and she knew the duty fell to her. She laced up her boots, put on her coat, and slipped through the front door, into the icy December night. Out on the porch, she looked left and right before noticing her mother's footsteps in a fresh dusting of snow. Violet followed the trail toward North Main Avenue.

The electric lights that made Scranton's downtown famous hadn't yet reached the streets of Providence. Gas-fueled flames flickered overhead, lighting the path of stray snowflakes as they floated easily down to the hard-packed dirt road. Once Violet made the turn onto North Main Avenue from Spring Street, she saw her mother about thirty feet ahead. Grace moved at a good clip and Violet struggled to keep up.

About ten minutes later, when Grace had made the left onto Green Ridge Street, Violet lost sight of her completely. She continued, uncertain and uneasy about her mother's intentions, but determined to follow her nonetheless. Just as Violet rounded the corner onto Green Ridge, she plowed straight into a figure in the shadows. As Violet turned to run, a hand reached out and grabbed her by the back of the coat.

"You're not to tell anyone about this. Is that understood?" her mother said.

Violet responded with a vigorous nod.

"Not Adelaide, not Stanley, not Aunt Hattie, not Father. Understand?"

Violet wondered about her father, whose name hadn't been uttered in the house for some months. She felt sure her mother had forgotten him. Violet remembered hearing the fight that night and tiptoeing out to the kitchen just as the door slammed shut. Her mother had sat stone-eyed at the table, muttering something about God forsaking her. Violet had thought to comfort her, but without turning around, Grace yelled, "Go back to bed!" And then, as if someone else were in the room, she said, "God forgive me. I can't look at her now."

With this new mention of her father, Violet dared to hope.

"Do you understand?" her mother repeated, reminding Violet of the question at hand.

A second quick nod.

Grace took Violet by the coat sleeve and continued toward town.

Wonder temporarily supplanted Violet's anxiety as they approached Wyoming Avenue at night. Electrified bulbs announced *Poli's All-Star Vaudeville* on the theatre's roof and illuminated the plate-glass windows below. An enormous awning curled over doors made of what Violet determined to be pure gold. Once inside the lobby, her mother stepped toward a booth and pushed four dimes across the counter.

"Second door on your right." A white-gloved woman handed two tickets to Grace. "An usher will be there to seat you."

Violet noticed her mother walk away without a word. "Thank you, kindly," she said before scurrying to catch up. Several more white-gloved women sold candy and lemonade under a sign reading, *Refreshments*. The smell of popcorn rose from a red and white pushcart, alerting Violet to a hunger she hadn't noticed before, but she knew better than to ask for a treat.

Violet paused as they entered the theatre through the door to the orchestra section. She instantly recognized the balconies, the velvet curtains, and even the same burgundy-jacketed man, from the day she and Stanley had sneaked in.

"Tickets, please."

An easeled sign advertised the evening's entertainment, a spiritualist named Rosalee who *Specializes in Automatic Writing*. Violet didn't know the meaning of the words, but the same urge to flee that had possessed her when she'd been there with Stanley gripped her again.

"Let's go home, Mother. I'll make you some milk. You like warm milk."

Her mother looked ahead, her eyes searching the crowd.

As the usher led them to their third-row seats, Violet scanned the audience, hoping for a familiar face. She found all sorts of people settled in the anchored rows, all strangers. There were women, powdered and perfumed, draped in silk and topped with feathers, accompanied by gentlemen in dark-colored suits of serge or mohair. They seemed comfortable in such lavish surroundings. There were people like Mother in attendance as well, men and women, whose faces seemed as worn as the coats on their backs.

Grace continued to quietly peer ahead as she settled into her seat.

"Is Father coming?" Violet knew this to be an unlikely possibility, but voiced it just the same. Speaking about her father soothed her somehow.

The question was met with more silence. Violet decided to change her approach. She tugged at her mother's sleeve. "Look," she said, pointing to the plaster cherubs standing watch over the box seats. "So beautiful."

Her mother pulled her arm away abruptly, then seemed to reconsider. "They're lovely," she said, turning her lips into the palatable expression others had grown to appreciate. She held the smile and aimed it at Violet, who recoiled. Grace faced forward again, slipped her hand into her coat pocket, and removed Daisy's baptism picture. She traced the edges of the sun-kissed face, occasionally allowing her finger to tickle Daisy's nose, as if to tease her out of the frame.

Several minutes later, a big-stomached man with a milky right eye sat down next to Grace. "Could never hide her light under a bushel," he said, looking at the photograph, seeming to admire the bow-topped girl staring beyond the camera. "Looks ready to jump first chance she gets."

Grace kept her eyes on the picture, lifted her finger, and waited. Daisy remained fixed in the scene.

The man glanced at the photo, and back at Grace. "She has your eyes." He shifted his gaze forward. "I'm hoping to speak to my dear departed wife. Dead seven years now. Love of my life." He looked down at the floor. "Not sure if I believe, though. And you?"

"My daughter, Daisy." Grace slipped the picture back into her pocket but continued to pet the edges of the frame with her thumb. "Five months this week."

"So unfair." The man tipped his head toward her. "What happened, if you don't mind me asking?"

"An accident." The man nodded but said nothing, obliging her to fill the space. "Fireworks. Nine years old, may she rest in peace."

"Heartbreaking," he said, "just heartbreaking. So sorry for your loss."

"For yours as well," she replied.

"Did she suffer much?"

"Three days."

"The horror of it." He waited.

"Sang hymns. Called out to Jesus. Wanted to look brave for Him."

"One of His angels, no doubt."

"Amen."

Daisy. Violet shuddered at the realization. Her mother had come to the theatre to talk to Daisy. Violet loved her sister and ached to be near her ever since she passed, but the thought of receiving messages from the grave terrified her.

Do nothing that you would not want to be doing when Jesus comes.

Surely speaking to the dead was a far worse sin than sneaking into a minstrel show. Could anything Daisy had to say be worth the risk of eternal damnation? Violet pulled her knees up to her chest, wrapped her arms around them, clasped her hands together, and began to pray. I love my sister, Lord, and miss her dearly, but if it's all the same to You, I'd rather not hear from her. Not tonight. Not this way. Amen.

The electric bulbs dimmed, and the curtains slowly parted, quieting the audience as intended. A gentleman strutted to the center of the stage carrying a lighted taper in his hand. He wore a pencil-striped suit and a dark red bow tie. Without a word, he lit several more candles, all positioned on tables of varying heights behind a bloodred chaise longue suddenly visible in the light. Its angle afforded those seated in front the best view of the bulky wooden legs. Each had a carved face whose stunned countenance suggested the moment of death. Gasps rippled through the first few rows, and two or three people, who seemed frightened or repulsed, stood up to leave.

"Ladies and gentlemen, tonight you'll meet Rosalee, the famous medium known on every continent. She astonishes. She amazes. She speaks to the dead."

Violet grabbed for her mother's hand but found it still stuffed in her pocket. She settled for a fistful of sleeve. "I want to go home."

"It was you who decided to come along," Grace quietly reminded her.

"I changed my mind."

"You can't take a thing back once it's done. You of all people should know that." As soon as the last word landed, Grace covered her mouth. "God, forgive me," she whispered against her hand.

Violet released her mother's sleeve and burrowed into her chair.

"Before Rosalee takes the stage, she's asked me to inform you that in order for her to receive messages from the other side, you must believe. Naysayers agitate the dead and jeopardize communication. She asks that all the Doubting Thomases remove themselves from the theatre at this time."

Three more people slipped up the aisles and out through the doors.

"And a word to the faint of heart. Those who receive Rosalee's gift are often overcome with emotion, some joyful at hearing messages from the dearly departed, others horrified at hearing truth spoken aloud. All who have entered, be warned."

Violet squirmed in her seat, while Grace faced forward, the hand trembling at her mouth. Two or three more people stood up to leave.

"No doubt you are familiar with Spiritualism and its many forms of expression. Tonight you will meet Rosalee, a medium whose psychic magnetism attracts every sort of soul, from the moral to the depraved. She cannot control her spirit influences; she simply receives their messages through the art of automatic writing." The announcer stepped to one of the small tables, pulled it alongside the chaise longue, and picked up a sheaf of blank stationery. He stepped to the front of the stage and held it out for inspection. "As those in the first few rows can attest," he shuffled through the sheets with his thumb, "the pages are empty." He removed a pen and small inkwell from his vest pocket, walked back to the table, and placed all of the items on top. "Without further ado, I give you," he paused for effect, "Ros-a-lee."

With the hem of her golden skirt dusting the floor, Rosalee seemed to glide onto the stage. The man in the pencil-striped suit raced toward her with his arm extended and led her to her seat. She reclined against the tufted arm with her legs stretched across the length of the cushion, and pulled the table toward her as a writing desk.

The announcer bowed once to the psychic and disappeared into the wings, leaving her alone on stage. The crowd held its breath, leaned forward, and waited.

Rosalee set the sheaf of paper onto her lap, dipped the pen in the ink, and, without a word, began to write. After what seemed to be enough time to fill a page, Rosalee pointed a finger and said, "You, in the second row with the silk forget-me-nots in your hair."

A pixie of a girl sat at attention and listened to the psychic's oiled tongue.

"Your name?"

"Eleanor Langan."

"That's right. I've a message for you, Ellie."

"Papa? He's the only one to call me that." Eleanor removed a handkerchief from her sleeve.

"Yes, dear one. A message from Papa. A warning. Stay away from that boy. You know the one." Rosalee watched as the girl's hand briefly touched her head. "Him that gave you the flowers."

"How did you . . . he . . . ?"

"Spare yourself the heartache. Wait for the one who is true."

Rosalee dipped her pen into the inkwell, dropped her head, and started in on writing again. A minute or two later she called out, "Jefferson Lawrence."

A handsome gentleman in the middle of the sixth row sat up.

"Where might you be, Mr. Lawrence?"

"You ought to know," he called out, and the audience laughed nervously. "Perhaps a crystal ball would help!" The timid laughter rose again.

Rosalee looked down and read what she had written. "Quick with the tongue, he is." She looked up. "Or so your dear grandmother says."

"Quick with the tongue? A dead grandmother? You'll have to do better than that."

Rosalee offered a close-mouthed smile, more suggestive of satisfaction than joy. "Such foolishness. Such pride."

"Such rubbish," Mr. Lawrence responded, forcing a chuckle. This time the audience remained silent.

"Your evil ways will take their toll."

"I've had enough," he said as he stood to leave.

"That harlot from the brothel, for one."

He stopped halfway up the aisle and turned toward the stage.

"Did you think I wouldn't see? And now, it courses through your veins, the French Disease, the Great Pox. It'll be the ruin of you."

Every eye fixed itself in Mr. Lawrence's direction. He paused to gather his thoughts and eventually shouted, "All lies!" but his denial came too late to be convincing. He continued up the aisle, yelling, "Lies! Lies! Lies!" as if repetition were a proper substitute for sincerity. His words of protestation could be heard as he stormed out the door and through the lobby. When the audience finally turned back toward the psychic, they found her writing again.

Rosalee called out to a white-haired woman whose husband had been hit by a train. He'd been uncoupling cars at the railroad when the engine backed up over him. The signal man had given the wrong sign to the conductor. Several men dragged him off the track, placed him in a wagon, and carried him to the hospital. As one of the attendants started to cut off his trousers, the woman's husband had warned, "Be careful, boys. My legs are with them," and died. That's how Rosalee told the story, and the man's wife nodded in her seat. Evidently he'd shown up at the theatre to tell her he was sorry for an argument they'd had the morning of the accident.

"It's about time," the woman said, and the crowd laughed. "Wanted to buy us a pair of bicycles. I told him he had another think coming if he thought I'd ever set foot on one."

"He's here now to ask forgiveness," Rosalee explained again.

"Imagine, bicycles at our age!" The woman puffed up and looked around the audience for sympathy.

"And he's sorry for that," the medium said, reading from her paper. "So truly sorry."

"Of all the crazy ideas. No telling what might have happened if—"

Rosalee interrupted: "So will you accept his apology and give him peace in the next world?"

"Well, of course I will. What kind of wife do you think I am? He's my husband, God rest his soul . . . until I get there."

Several other spirits appeared to Rosalee. Among them, a mother who had died in childbirth; a fiancée who'd taken her own life; a son who'd gone out to California in search of his fortune and had not been heard from since.

The candles started to sputter as the performance neared its end. Rosalee thanked the audience for its attention and stood to leave.

Relief washed all traces of dread from Violet's face. She unlocked her arms and dropped her legs to the floor in front of her.

In the midst of deafening applause, Rosalee swooned and fell into the arms of the announcer, who stepped out of the shadows in time to catch her. He immediately laid her back on the chaise longue where she picked up her pen and began writing again. The crowd held its breath. Panicked, Violet folded herself into her seat and braced herself for disaster.

"This is a child spirit," Rosalee announced to the hushed audience.

Grace leaned forward.

"Not fully bloomed."

"My pet!" Grace cried out as if the child were in front of her.

"She's telling me a name." Rosalee went back to writing for a moment, then looked up. "Daisy."

"Yes, yes!" Grace moaned. "My sweet baby!"

Rosalee returned to her paper and read. "*Are you proud of me, Mama?*"

"Yes, yes. Mother is proud of you. I've always been proud of you."

"*I'm with Jesus, Mother. I'm surrounded by love.*"

"Oh, thank God. Thank you, God. My baby is safe with Jesus!" Grace began to cry, and someone a few rows back passed a handkerchief to her. It smelled of lavender, like the scented water used to wash Daisy's body, and Grace sobbed even louder.

"*I don't feel any pain.*"

"Praise be to God!" Grace elbowed Violet. "Her burns are healed." She grabbed hold of her daughter and hugged her hard.

Violet tried to shake the feeling that all of this would come to no good, but fear dug in its heels and refused to move along. Her mother wrapped her arms around her more tightly and pulled her in.

Rosalee looked directly at Grace and recited the words she'd written: "*My death was not an accident.*"

A gasp blew through the auditorium like a wind storm. Rosalee went back to writing. Violet peered up at her mother in horror. Grace dropped her arm from around her daughter's shoulder and hissed, "What did you do?"

Ever since her sister's death, Violet had seen this look in others' eyes, but never recognized it in her own mother. Until that moment, she'd always told herself it was grief she was seeing, not blame. Shuddering, she searched her mother's eyes, hard blue stones, and saw Daisy looking back.

After a minute or so, time enough for the full weight of her words to settle, Rosalee looked up. "*My death was not an accident,*" she repeated. "*It was part of God's plan for me—His intention all along.*"

Confusion settled into the folds of Grace's brow. She stared at Violet, but cocked her ear in Rosalee's direction.

Violet buried her face into the collar of her coat, but she could still see the scorn in her mother's eyes, Daisy's eyes.

Rosalee smiled. "*My death was decided long before I*

was born. No one is to blame. My time on earth was always meant to be brief."

Grace sank back in her seat, exhausted, unable to organize her words into sentences.

Violet tried to grab hold of the absolution Rosalee had offered. *No one is to blame.* It withered and died in her hand.

Rosalee began to sing in a childlike voice that had none of the music of Daisy's:

A sunbeam, a sunbeam,
Jesus wants me for a sunbeam . . .

Violet's eyes sprang open and her hands flew to her ears. Daisy's voice echoed in her head:

A sunbeam, a sunbeam,
I'll be a sunbeam for Him . . .

Grace leaped from her seat and ran onto the stage. She dropped to the floor beside Rosalee and rubbed the hem of her golden skirt against her cheek. "My Daisy," she cried. "My Daisy. My beautiful Daisy."

The announcer rushed forward, took Grace by the hand, and led her back to her seat. Rosalee glanced in the direction of the milky-eyed man who, upon seeing Grace, had stepped deeper into the shadows off stage. Seemingly unfazed, Rosalee smoothed her skirt and picked up her pen for one more message. "She says to name the baby Lily since she'll be born so close to Easter."

"What baby?" asked Grace.

Rosalee nodded.

"A baby?" Grace looked down, placed her hands over her swollen belly, and wept.

Words crashed inside Violet's head. *No one is to blame. Sunbeam. A baby*? She tried to stand up when the others applauded, but her legs gave out and she fainted.

When Violet came to in her mother's arms, the onlookers let out a collective sigh of relief. Grace thanked a doctor who had come forward, placed Violet on her feet, and led her out of the theatre.

CHAPTER SEVENTEEN

ON CHRISTMAS EVE, Owen went back into the mines for the second half of a double shift. The fire boss assigned him and a fellow by the name of John Roberts to the last chamber off to the left of the lowest gangway. Both men had mine butties to assist them, two Lithuanians, a month off the boat, who spoke very little English.

Owen had been working doubles almost every day since Hattie had informed him of Grace's condition.

"Better than five months along," she had said, "as near as Doc Rodham can figure."

Closer to six, Owen had thought, assuming the baby took hold the last time he and Grace had lain together.

Owen had known better than to trouble her that night. She'd had enough to do with Daisy's baptism the following morning and the picnic that afternoon. But he couldn't help himself. Grace looked so pretty standing by the sink, her pale face reflected in the window pane. Such beauty. He never could figure out what a woman like her saw in a man like him. He thanked God every night for his good fortune.

She had been washing the dishes, when he came up behind her and wrapped his arms around her waist.

"The children," she scolded, though Owen could see her smile reflected in the shaving mirror, propped on the window ledge.

He glanced at his pocket watch on the cupboard. "Asleep an hour already." He pressed his body against her back and hugged her longingly. "I mean to take what's mine," he said, "just as the good Lord intended." He reached up and removed the pins from her bun, allowing the dark locks to rest on her shoulders. He buried his face in her curls.

"The good Lord never intended for you to put pleasure before obligation," she chided, but she pushed her hair off to the side, revealing a slice of neck.

Owen grabbed hold of her again, harder this time, and ran his lips down the porcelain flesh. Trembling, she closed her eyes and rested her arms on his. He felt the dampness of her sleeves as his hands traveled up toward her top buttons. He opened one, then another, and before she could gather her thoughts, he cupped her breasts inside each palm and circled her hardened nipples with his thumbs.

"The neighbors!" Grace's eyes flashed open in front of the uncurtained window.

"Then you best follow me, woman," Owen whispered in her ear as he took her hand, and led her toward their bedroom.

And now, six months along, Owen thought as he drove a wooden prop into place between the chamber's ceiling and floor. Pillars of unmined anthracite actually supported the roof, but he knew the props were just as important, since they usually groaned or cracked in advance of a roof squeeze. During a collapse, such warnings spared many a life underground.

With the timbers in place sooner than expected, Owen and John Roberts set about drilling the wall in preparation for the explosives that would loosen the coal.

At seven p.m., parishioners gathered at the Providence Christian Church for the Christmas Eve service. Betty Leas, the director, had been working with the choirs since the Sunday before Thanksgiving, and the music promised to be the high point of the evening.

Much to Violet's surprise, her mother had not required her to participate in the program, in spite of Adelaide's protestations.

"Grief aside, the girl should be doing the Lord's work," the missionary had told Grace.

"When you know my grief, then you can tell me where to place it," Grace had finally said. "Until then, she'll not perform, and that's the end of it."

Adelaide never broached the subject again with Grace, but that didn't keep her from discussing it with anyone else who would listen.

Though gas lights had been installed in the sanctuary years before, each person received an unlit taper upon entering. This had always been a candlelight service, and the elders had decided to continue the tradition, in spite of the building's advancements. Tapers glowed from nests of evergreen branches on windowsills, tabletops, and even the pipe organ. A circle of four advent candles burned brightly on the ledge of the baptistery, symbolizing hope, peace, joy, and love. The Christ Candle stood unlit in the center, ready to announce the birth of Jesus later in the service.

Grace, Violet, and Adelaide made their way down the right side of the church, toward their pew, seventh from the front counting the half-pew squeezed in just before the altar. Hattie had already seated herself and seemed relieved to see her family coming.

"There she is now," Hattie said to Myrtle Evans, who'd just asked whether Grace would be "darkening the church's door" that evening. Hattie slid across the pew to make room for the latecomers. "Merry Christmas," she whispered just as the service began.

Louise leaned forward in her pew and added, "So good to see you here."

"*And it came to pass in those days*," a young boy of ten bellowed from atop a crate behind the podium, "*that there went out a decree from Caesar Augustus that all the world should be taxed*." A miniature Mary and Joseph stepped out from the backroom, into the main part of the sanctuary. The blanketed pair strolled hand in hand toward Alice Harris's two-year-old daughter, already seated in the manger her father had built. An angel, two shepherds, and the Powell triplets with newspaper crowns on their heads joined them up front as the story progressed.

At the conclusion of the play, and after an enthusiastic round of applause, the junior choir stepped forward and began singing, "O Little Town of Bethlehem." Jesus, who'd somehow been forgotten in her manger, climbed out just before the fourth verse and toddled toward the congregation on the words, "*O holy child*." Laughter erupted as Alice Harris ran forward and scooped her daughter into her arms.

John Roberts filled two cardboard tubes with black powder, folded the ends, and handed them to Owen, who tamped them four-and-a-half feet into the boreholes. John motioned to the drills, picks, hammers, shovels, and rods scattered across the floor, and he and the butties carried them off a safe distance away. Before lighting the squib, Owen called out, "Fire, fire, fire!" as a warning to any man happening by, and waited. John yelled, "All clear!" from behind a pillar. Owen touched his lamp to the squib's fuse and headed behind his own pillar a minute or so before twin explosions erupted. A cloud of coal dust rushed toward the miners, who crouched with their faces tucked between their knees. They stayed in that position a few minutes longer, waiting for the debris to settle.

Once the air cleared, all four men returned to the area to see the result. They'd added five or so feet to the length of the chamber, but they would have to mine this vein on their backs. Owen grabbed a crowbar, walked along the front ribs of the room, and tapped the roof for weak spots. Two of the front props groaned under the weight, so Owen and John set about adding additional supports to avoid a squeeze.

At that moment, the men heard, "Fire, fire, fire!" from further up the gangway. With part of their own roof still unstable, Owen yelled back, "Hold off!" a second before the powder exploded, dropping thirty tons of coal in their chamber.

As rehearsed, Flo Watkins lit the Christ Candle at the conclusion of the evening prayer. The Davies boys stepped forward, tipped their candles into Christ's flame, and proceeded up the middle aisle, lighting the candle of the first person in each row. In turn, the flame passed from one pew member to the next, until all in attendance held a glowing taper. The congregation sang their final hymn, "Silent Night," then paused to hear the steeple bells before stepping back out into the cold night air.

Instead, they heard three short whistles—an accident at the mine.

The men jumped up first. Some rushed straight to the mine, others stopped off at their houses to grab picks and shovels. None of them took the time to change out of their church clothes. Seconds counted when it came to the difference between pulling a man out alive or dead.

The women and children moved just as purposefully, but toward a different end. Instinctively, they formed a prayer circle and bowed their heads. Adelaide cleared her throat before opening her mouth, giving Hattie enough time to ask, "Sister Griffin, will you lead us in prayer?"

Jane Griffin, the Sunday school's superintendent, prayed for the fifty or so men working that night—husbands, fathers, brothers, and sons. She prayed for the wives and children standing within eyesight of heartbreak and poverty. She asked the women to call out the names of their loved one if he happened to be working the mine that night. When Grace's turn came, she said, "My husband Owen," in what Myrtle Evans would later describe as an "even tone," which she attributed to "a lack of emotion."

At the prayer's conclusion, the women and children scurried downhill toward the mine, with only the light of their candles to lead the way.

Within an hour, most of the miners were accounted for. Some walked, some crawled, some had to be carried. "A Christmas miracle!" one woman exclaimed as her husband ran to her.

The mine owner, George Sherman, headed toward the crowd of women and children huddled outside, their faces hidden behind thick scarves. Some held candles, others gripped rosary beads, but they all prayed for mercy to the same God.

"It could have been much worse," Mr. Sherman announced. "The damage is limited to the lower gangway, mainly, the last chamber. We should be back up and running in a few days."

"We don't care about the mine!" Louise shouted. "What about the men?"

Harold Bowers, the mine foreman, stepped forward. "Of the fifty-two pegged in at the time of the squeeze, we know of forty-eight souls who survived."

"Thanks be to God!" someone called out, and the crowd repeated the sentiment.

"Of course, four still remain inside," Harold continued, "and we'll not give up till we find them."

Hattie grabbed Grace's hand as Mr. Sherman read the names: "John Roberts, Owen Morgan, and two Poles from the Patch, mining butties who worked alongside them."

"Lithuanians," Harold corrected.

"Same difference," Mr. Sherman replied, and trudged back toward the mine.

Hattie and Louise each took one of Grace's arms. "Let's get you home," Hattie suggested. "This night air's no good in your condition."

Grace pressed both palms on her belly and waited. "My husband's in that mine. I'll not budge till there's word."

Sometime before midnight, the mine foreman suggested that the waiting families move to the above-ground stable. At least they'd be protected from the elements and have a place to sit while they waited. By two in the morning, Louise finally convinced Violet to curl up on a bed of hay in the empty last stall. Grace still refused to sleep but, for the baby's sake, agreed to sit on a makeshift bench with her legs outstretched and her head propped against a beam.

She'd been too harsh with Owen that last night. She knew that now, and frankly, she'd known it then. She'd always thought there would be time. To forgive. To be forgiven. Such foolishness. Soon enough they'd unearth his corpse. She shuddered at the thought of another body to tend.

She remembered sprinkling dried lavender into the basin of water alongside Daisy's bed. Grace closed her eyes and inhaled the scent of early summer.

"Dear Lord . . ." she'd said, more out of reflex than inspiration. When no words followed, she'd abandoned the prayer and turned toward Daisy.

She had dipped the rag into the water and started with Daisy's face, first the brow, then the eyes. Someone had shut her eyes—Owen, if she remembered correctly. Next the cheeks, the nose and lips. The scar on her chin where at three she'd caught the corner of the kitchen cupboard, splitting the skin and toppling a sack of flour. At the time, Daisy had stood in stunned silence, covered from head to toe in the white powder. Grace remembered taking one look at her little snowman, and laughing out loud. That got Daisy laughing so hard, she doubled over, sending a flurry of flour into the air and onto the floor. When she lifted her head, Grace saw the blood for the first time, and started to cry at the sight of it. Frightened, Daisy began sobbing and kicking up an even bigger snowstorm, which sent Grace into a fit of giggles in spite of her best intentions. By the time Owen entered the room, he couldn't tell if they were laughing or crying, and neither could they. For months after, whenever Daisy got near flour, someone would tease, "Feels like snow."

Grace had dabbed the scar one more time, kissed the tip of Daisy's nose, and turned to rinse and wring her cloth. Owen had suggested she let her sister Hattie or her friend Louise help, but she wouldn't hear of it. She'd do for her daughter as long as she could. She rubbed the unblemished skin, then patted and rebandaged the burns, taking great pains not to disturb the unhealed flesh. When she finished, she draped a clean sheet over Daisy's body, up to the neck, and placed a wet lavender-scented rag on her face to keep it fresh.

"Goodbye, my pet." She had kissed the top of her head and breathed her in for the last time. She turned to Owen, pressed into the corner, waiting to bring the body out to Mr. Parker, the undertaker. "Make sure he treats her kindly."

Owen had nodded as he lifted his daughter and carried her out of the room.

Grace remained in the girls' bedroom and took out her sewing. Daisy's only other good church dress needed mending if she was to be buried in it. She'd ripped the stitches in the smocking after an evening church service not two weeks earlier. Unbeknownst to Grace at the time, Daisy had been playing hide-and-seek with Janie Miller and caught the top of her dress on some rough bark as she hid behind an oak tree. Owen had threatened to take a switch to his daughter for not acting like a young lady, but of course he never did.

Hattie had made two matching dresses out of a bolt of robin's egg–blue cotton as birthday presents for the girls. Although Violet was the younger of the two, she had received her dress on February 19, the day she turned eight, almost a week and a half before Daisy, who would turn nine in March. More than once in the stretch between birthdays, Violet told Grace how much the dress meant to her. Familiar with hand-me-downs herself, Grace understood. And she understood Violet's disappointment when, ten days later, Daisy received the same exact dress, just one size bigger. Hattie had meant well, but she should have known to vary the styles.

Once Grace finished the mending, she'd wash, starch, and iron the dresses for both her girls. She'd also have to do up Owen's suit and dye one of her shirtwaists the same shade of black as her good skirt. And then there were boots to polish and baths to take. They'd start viewing the body in the morning, and Grace wanted folks to see she took pride in her family's appearance.

Grace looked around the stable at the other people, all contemplating the fates of their own families. What's to become of us?

Grief poked his head in the stable door and opened his mouth, poised to answer.

"Get away from here!" Grace shouted. When Hattie looked in her direction, Grace swatted at the air, as if shooing a fly.

Hattie turned to Violet, still sleeping on the straw.

"Come home," Grief said, swinging one leg inside and then the other. "It takes days to dig out a body."

"He's not dead yet," Grace whispered sharply before closing her eyes to him.

After nearly six hours of pounding away at an endless wall of anthracite, Harold ordered his men to take a rest. Initially they objected, but eventually the desires of the heart succumbed to the needs of the body. Many of the men hadn't had their evening meal, and had been without sustenance for half a day or longer. Some of the women whose husbands had survived the collapse returned to the mine with supper for them. The men ate greedily, not stopping to talk about what they all feared.

Finally, after about fifteen minutes, Albert Adamski said what many of the others wouldn't dare: "Dead by now, for certain. Air's no good in there." He looked back at the mountain of coal filling the entrance to the chamber. "Never had a chance."

Tommy Davies jumped to his feet. "We'll not give up!" The twelve-year-old eyed the men, daring them to disagree, then began piling rubble into a waiting mine car. The other miners stood up, grabbed picks and crowbars, and started back to work.

About an hour later, Albert unearthed tag number 194, attached to the buttonhole of a torn-off shirt pocket. "Told you," he said, as he waved his find in the air.

Tommy snatched Owen's tag out of Albert's hand and went running for the stable.

* * *

Louise watched her son as he entered the barn. He wore a look she'd seen before, a look no child should ever have. He didn't speak, but simply held out the tag on the torn pocket.

Grace wrapped her arms around her belly, rocking herself, rocking her unborn child. "Shhh," she kept saying, as if to quiet the baby inside. "Mother's here."

Louise held Tommy while Hattie comforted Grace. One of the miners who'd been working on the rescue peered into the barn and asked, "Which of you is the widow Morgan? I'm to see you home."

CHAPTER EIGHTEEN

TEN HOURS AFTER THE ROOF COLLAPSED, John Roberts and his butty broke through the boarded-up entrance of the old, adjacent slope mine. A minute or two later, the second Lithuanian laborer hobbled out on a broken ankle, with Owen beside him as a crutch. The orange sun rose from behind slag mountains, and each of the men squinted at the sight.

Harold was the first to spy them, pillars of coal with breath, eyes half-shut, hands bloodied, but alive. He yelled to the hoistman who signaled the workers, and within minutes, a crowd rose up and overtook them. Melba Roberts pulled her toddler into her arms, ran to her husband, and hugged him with the child pressed between them. Two young women, no more than sixteen, pushed through the people to find their beaux. Upon seeing his sweetheart, the injured Lithuanian nodded his thanks to Owen, and draped his arm around the babushka-topped girl. She smiled as he shifted his weight to her shoulders.

Owen stretched up and searched the crowd. He knew he had no right to, but he'd hoped, if he made it out alive, to find Grace waiting for him. After all, it was her face he had seen in front of him as he crawled blindly on his belly through the old rat-infested tunnels. He and the other men had quickly realized how grim their circumstances were.

Ten minutes into the collapse, they knew they'd die for sure if they had to depend on the rescuers to get them out the way they'd come in. Too much coal had dropped in front of them, and in the case of one of the Lithuanians, a chunk of it had broken his ankle. It was Owen who'd thought of the old adjacent mine. It hadn't been worked in twenty years, but thanks to the blasting they'd done before the squeeze, they were five feet closer to it than anyone on the outside knew. With only enough room for one man, each of them took turns on their backs, picking away at the coal that separated the two mines. Soon enough, Owen noticed the toll the work was taking on the injured Lithuanian, so he took over the man's share of digging to allow him to rest. Once they breeched the wall, they squeezed their way through at some points, and picked their way through at others. About six hours into the collapse, the man with the broken ankle seemed ready to give up. Owen refused to leave him behind. "A few more feet," he'd say, not knowing if the man understood him. "A few more feet." By the time they'd crawled out, their hands and knees were shredded from the jagged rocks.

"Well, I'll be," Bobby Lewis said, slapping Owen on the back. "Thought you were a goner, for sure."

"Grace?" Owen asked the question he did not want answered.

"We gave you up for dead," Bobby said before adding, "Went home sometime this morning. Sure be mighty pleased to see you, though."

Owen closed his eyes and saw her face before him, the face he'd followed out of the darkness, into the light. Her cheeks reddened, her brow dappled with sweat, strands of dark hair falling on her cheeks, rushing into Hattie's dining room that first Thanksgiving. Gave you up for dead. So that was it, he thought. Gave you up.

Owen turned to Bobby and asked, "Where can a fellow get a drink on Christmas morning?"

Bobby laughed. "Let's go see if they'll open up Burke's for a man come back from the dead."

When they reached the square, Owen looked to the right toward his home before Bobby pulled him into the tavern.

As soon as the news hit Spring Street, Myrtle Evans rushed across the yard to Grace's house. "And where is he?" she asked as she pushed through the door.

Both Louise and Hattie looked up from the table, confused.

"Who?" they asked simultaneously.

"Why Owen, of course. Thought he'd be home by now." She looked around the room. "But I must have thought wrong."

"Owen is gone," Grace said as she came into the kitchen, surprising them all. "Owen is gone," she repeated, as if her tongue were trying a new language.

"Anything but," Myrtle explained. "Mrs. Proudlock saw him with her own eyes, black as pitch, but Owen for sure. Near the Christmas tree at the square. Brought the children down to see the—"

"My Owen's alive?" Grace interrupted as Hattie led her to a seat at the table.

"They all are."

"Thanks be to God!" Grace cried, and stood to hug Myrtle.

"Said they worked their own way out. No more than half an hour ago. Naturally, I assumed he'd come straight here."

Grace rushed toward the front door, stepped out on the porch, and peered down the street.

Myrtle followed her outside. "Though come to think of

it, Mrs. Proudlock said he turned left at the corner, into the beer garden. Probably had the stink of whiskey on him too."

Grace stepped back inside and Hattie shut the door with Myrtle still standing on the porch. So that's it, Grace thought.

"He's alive," Hattie said, her voice thick with emotion. "Thank the Lord."

"But married to the drink," Grief called out from the bedroom.

"But he's alive!" Grace yelled back to him.

"That's right," Louise reassured, her troubled eyes darting to Hattie.

Grace looked at both women, studying their expressions. What was it she saw? Relief? Confusion? Worry? Worse, Grace thought. Pity. She shuffled past them and turned toward her bedroom.

Later that morning, Hattie woke Violet with the news of her father's resurrection. Violet decided, in that moment to see him for herself.

"Where are you off to?" Adelaide asked as Violet wrapped a scarf around her neck.

"To visit my father."

Adelaide raised her hand in protest, but Grace simply said, "Let her go," and Hattie nodded.

Violet jumped off the side porch into the yard and collided with Stanley as he turned the corner.

"Heard the news," he said with a great big smile.

"I'm going to see him," Violet said, brushing past the boy. "You can come if you like."

Stanley studied Violet's expression—tightened brow, pursed lips, muscled jaw, all suggesting serious business. He slipped a paper sack into the pocket of his corduroy coat and fell into step alongside her.

Violet headed down Spring Street toward the square. She knew her father had been living at Burke's. She'd heard the talk plenty of times. What she didn't know was what she would say when she saw him.

"A penny for your thoughts." Stanley patted his pocket, making sure the bag was safe inside.

"And where would you get a penny?" Violet heard the tone of her voice and wondered at its meanness.

"I'm a working man now," Stanley reminded her. "Collect my pay like all the other fellows." He threw his shoulders back and pushed his chest forward.

"In time to hand it over to your pa."

Stanley stopped in front of the church, stared straight at Violet, and asked, "Who put the bee in your bonnet?"

"Maybe I don't always want to be seen with Stinky Stanley. Did you ever think of that?" she yelled as she crossed the street to Burke's.

Violet took three deep breaths and wiped her nose on her sleeve before walking through the front door. Several men, coated in coal and linked arm in arm, started in on the chorus of a familiar hymn.

Then sings my soul, my Savior God to Thee
How great Thou art, how great Thou art . . .

The room had the smell of dirty coins and sour sweat. Violet crinkled up her nose, pulled her collar to her face, and breathed into it.

"What's a kid doing here?" the barkeep yelled. "First you make me open on Christmas, now this?" One by one, the men stopped singing and looked at Violet. "The law will be shutting me down for sure."

"Is that my doll baby?" Owen squinted his eyes as if trying to make out the shape of an animal on a dark night. "Is it you?" He set his whiskey on the bar, rubbing the soot off his face before going to her.

Violet started to cry. She ran to her father and threw her arms around his stomach.

"Let me have a look at you." Owen held his daughter out at arm's length. "Is it really you?" He took her in with his eyes. "My sweet doll baby." Owen knelt down and hugged Violet for a full minute. He stood up, grabbed a rag from the bar, and wiped smudges of coal off her face. "So beautiful."

Violet winced at his breath, the smell of metal.

"She don't like the stink of fire water," Bobby Lewis said, and all the men laughed. "Won't give you a minute's trouble, that one."

"This is no place for a kid," the barkeep said again, nodding toward the door.

Owen took Violet's hand, led her outside and up the steps to his room.

The first thing Violet noticed when she entered her father's room was the unmade bed.

"I wasn't expecting company," Owen said as he pulled the blanket across the mattress and smoothed it with the back of his hand.

Violet stayed standing in the middle of the floor. "When are you coming home?" she asked. For a moment, they both seemed to be surprised by the question.

"I almost forgot," Owen finally said, clearing newspapers off his one good chair and motioning for Violet to sit. "I have something for you." He went over to his dresser and removed two packages from the top drawer. "This one's for you." He handed the present to Violet. "Sorry it's not store bought." He sat on the edge of the bed. "Go ahead and open it."

Violet tore off the brown paper and found a cigar box with its lid painted to look like the outside of a two-story house, complete with front porch and rockers. A white picket fence stood in tall grass on all four sides, and bunches of purple flowers bloomed in front.

"It's a playhouse for dolls," Owen turned the box on Violet's lap and lifted the lid, "if you open it away from you."

"It's wonderful," Violet said, studying each detail.

"There's more." Owen turned the box around again.

Her father had painted a kitchen, parlor, and bedroom on the inside of the lid. Lamps shone yellow in each room, waiting to light the way for any who entered. A paper mother, father, two little girls, and a baby lay in the bottom of the box. Owen had cut the figures out of a discarded Sears, Roebuck & Company catalog. He'd pasted the shapes to cardboard and filled each one in with vibrant color.

"I should have chosen an older picture for you," Owen said as he picked up the cutout intended to be Violet. "You've grown like a weed since I last saw you." He dropped the doll back into the box and reached for the one who resembled Daisy. "Wouldn't be much of a family without her," Owen added, defending his decision to include her.

Violet simply nodded, as she sorted through the cutouts to find the father.

"Not much of a family without you, either."

Owen dropped the Daisy doll back into the box, walked over to the dresser, and pulled out a bottle of whiskey. He blew the dust out of a nearby glass and filled it halfway. "Ain't that the truth," he said, holding up his drink before swallowing its contents. "You better head on home. You're mother's probably worried sick by now."

Violet set the cutout of her father on top of his bed before closing the lid to her cigar-box dollhouse.

"Just as well," Owen said as he refilled his glass. "Wish

your mother a Merry Christmas for me, now, won't you?"

Violet nodded curtly as she headed toward the door.

"Wait a minute." He grabbed the second package and handed it to his daughter. "It's for your mother. A button box." Violet took the second cigar box, this one painted with lilacs and morning glories, and left without a word.

When Violet crossed the street toward home, she found Stanley waiting silently for her on the church steps. "I'm so sorry," she whispered, sitting down next to him. Tears rolled down her cheeks. "I don't know what got into me. I didn't mean it, I swear." She raised her right hand to heaven.

Stanley sat and said nothing.

"Please don't be sore at me."

Stanley stewed for another minute. "A penny's nothing to a working man," he finally said. "I could spend a penny right now if I had a mind to."

"I was just feeling mean. I'm sorry."

"If you was to say, *Stanley, let's get ourselves some gumdrops*, why, I'd say, *What color?* without blinking an eye."

"Red, of course," Violet responded nervously, not sure if she'd been forgiven.

Stanley reached into the pocket of his coat, pulled out the paper sack he'd been carrying, and handed it to Violet. "Merry Christmas."

Violet opened the bag and found a whole scoopful of gumdrops, as red as the tips of Stanley's ears. "Stanley Adamski," she pulled out a piece of candy and popped it into her mouth, "this is my best present." She thought about the dollhouse on her lap and hoped her father couldn't hear what she'd just said. "Merry Christmas." She kissed him on the cheek and handed him a gumdrop. "How'd you get old Pickle Puss to let you pick a color?"

"Went in with the widow. She did the asking, but I did the paying."

By the time they reached the top of Spring Street, their bellies were full and the bag was empty.

TO DRIVE AWAY SPARROWS

If bothered with sparrows, put a little molasses on their roosting place and they will leave.

—*Mrs. Joe's Housekeeping Guide,* 1909

Such joy. Every man spared. Seven from our own congregation, if you count Owen Morgan. And what a blessing for his family, considering the shambles he left them in. No two ways about it, Grace couldn't take another tragedy. Feeble-minded, if you ask us. And that child, troubled as she is, needs her daddy. Though we have to wonder how much of an example he can be, living over that beer garden. "The sins of the father," as Adelaide reminds us. Now there's a woman who knows her Bible.

Still, Owen survived, and Violet is back in school. Awful familiar with that Polish boy, though. And now they're spending time with the widow Lankowski. Not our kind, but pleasant enough. Knows how to pinch a penny, that one. Catholics always were cheap, though. Educated too. Quotes Shakespeare like it's the Good Book. A bit uppity for a Pole. As Myrtle Evans always says, "Put shoes on their feet and they think they're swell."

Truth be told, the widow can also be generous in her own way. Sent what she called *halupkies* over to the Morgan house the other day. Some sort of stuffed cabbage, according to Sister Adelaide. No telling what was inside. She couldn't get them past her nose. A nice thought, just the same. Sister Adelaide threw them away, but not before thanking the widow kindly and getting her to say the name a couple times more, so she'd get it right in the retelling.

Of course, there are those who pity the widow. Her husband beat her more than most, God rest his soul. Maybe she needed it. Maybe not. Who are we to judge?

CHAPTER NINETEEN

STANLEY STEPPED INTO THE WOODEN CAGE and stood next to Tommy Davies as he had every morning since he'd become a nipper. Three weeks inside, and Stanley still needed the comfort of a familiar face as the hoistman lowered them into the mine. He closed his eyes, trying to imagine sunshine as he was carried down. Three sixes. Six in the morning until six at night, six days a week. Stanley knew he'd meet the devil here for sure. It was just a matter of when. He blessed himself the way the widow had taught him and counted the days till sunlight. In winter that meant Sunday.

When the floor of the cage hit the floor of the mine, Stanley opened his eyes and got out. He followed the others to an empty mine car, swung his leg over the side, and climbed in. He closed his eyes once more and silently began saying the "Our Father."

"Where'd you come from?"

Stanley jumped at the sound of his father's voice. "Been working as a nipper." When his father said nothing, Stanley added, "Be a month come Friday."

Having worked underground most of his life, Stanley's father could see well in the dark. He looked at his son and asked, "How the hell did that happen?"

"Got that mule," Stanley pointed to Sophie being hitched to another car, "on a harness." He smiled proudly.

"Foolest thing I ever heard. White mule's bad luck. Mark my words. No good'll come from her." Stanley's father turned away, and they rode the rest of the way in silence.

As the miners tumbled out of the car and headed toward the peg-board shanty, Stanley fell into line behind them. The small blue flames on their caps threw shadows on the glistening walls. Electric pumps whirred in the distance, keeping out the flood of water anxious to resume its natural path. Wet boots suggested the men did not put too much faith in the machinery.

As the fire boss gave the assignments for the day, each man pegged in, knowing that if his peg still remained in the board at the end of the shift, someone would come looking for him, hopefully in time.

"Tunnel number nine," the boss said to Stanley. "Mind the doors. And no sleeping."

As a nipper, Stanley spent most of his time waiting in what they called the airshaft, a stretch of tunnel blocked off by doors on either side where large electric fans circulated fresh air throughout portions of the mine. The doors to the shaft were hung in such a way as to close automatically with the air current, but Stanley needed to open them by hand when mine cars came through. There he sat for ten hours a day, almost entirely in darkness. All too often, a nipper fell asleep out of boredom, waking seconds before a car crashed through the doors—or worse. Sometimes a sleepy boy would try to open the door in time, only to be run over where he stood.

Since there were no birds to call in the mine, not even canaries anymore, much to Stanley's disappointment, he kept himself awake by whittling sprags. Tommy had taught him about sprags, a one-foot piece of wood used to brake the mine cars. A mule boy, such as Tommy, would run alongside the car and force a sprag into the spokes of a wheel to stop it. The idea terrified Stanley.

"If you want to be a mule boy someday," Tommy had said, "you'll need to get over that."

What I want is to go back to school, Stanley had thought, but chose to keep the notion to himself.

Stanley sang in between whittling sprags and opening doors. Hearing his own voice echo in the dark made him a little less afraid. Tommy had taught him a better version of a song sung in the schoolyard, and it was Stanley's favorite. He always started his day with it.

My sweetheart's the mule in the mines,
I drive her without any lines . . .

He'd belt out each note and exaggerate each word.

On the bumper I sit . . .

He'd hold that last word, enunciating the "t" into its own syllable.

And I chaw and I spit . . .

He'd wait an extra two beats, sometimes for effect, sometimes to release a giggle.

All over my sweetheart's behind.

When he finished the song, Stanley would laugh and start again, singing a little louder each time.

On the first of January, Stanley pegged in and set about work in the airway chamber of the number nine tunnel. He thought about the new year, 1914, and what it had in store for him. He could think of nothing favorable. He thought about his birthday, a week away, but came up empty again. He ate his meal, two biscuits and cold cabbage, and dropped the crumbs on the ground. He'd learned early on to feed the rats. The men spoke of them with reverence, since a rat could hear the crack of a prop or smell a pocket of gas better than any man. More than one miner had warned Stanley to run if the rats started scurrying.

At the end of his shift, Stanley followed the track up toward the peg-board shanty. He heard Sophie coming behind him, pulling about five tons worth of coal up the slope, so he stopped and waited. "That's my girl," he said, reaching out to pet her. Sophie nudged him away and whimpered. "What's the matter?" he asked. She shook her ears and cried once more as she passed him by.

About twenty feet back, an earth-colored mule pulled a dozen men in Stanley's direction. Albert Adamski was among them. Stanley leaned against one of the coal pillars supporting the roof of the mine, and waited for his pa to catch up.

Worried about Sophie, Stanley turned his eye toward her at the top of the incline a second before he heard the snap of her harness. Five tons of coal hurtled back downhill. Stanley's hands each grabbed a sprag from the ground before alerting his brain to the danger. He tried to focus on the blur of the rear wheel as his right hand shoved a sprag into its spokes. The wheel chomped, chewed, and spit out the wood brake in pieces, slowing the car only long enough to give Stanley one more try. He focused, stretched, and then jammed the other sprag at the front wheel, but his reach landed a few inches beyond his target. The wheel crunched and groaned to a stop, taking Stanley's hand with it.

The men in the car, whose lives Stanley had just saved,

jumped out and rushed toward him. Albert Adamski led the pack, but raced past his son uphill, leaving the others to tend to him. John Roberts ripped off his shirt, grabbed a piece of splintered sprag, and tied a tourniquet near the bottom of the boy's left forearm. Owen Morgan and Evan Evans Sr. positioned themselves at the boy's head and feet and carried him running to the mine hospital, about a half-mile up, near the number five tunnel.

When Stanley's father reached the top of the hill, he slammed Sophie across the back with the handle of his pick. "I knew you were no good!"

Sophie looked back and responded with a kick to the head, instantly killing the man.

CHAPTER TWENTY

TWO JAGGED BONES POKED OUT from the wrist, like bared teeth on a rabid dog. Harold Bowers, the only man on duty with first aid training, propped Stanley's mangled arm up on a rolled blanket. He loosened the boy's clothing, placed two fingers at his neck in search of a pulse, and found it feeble.

"Who's carrying whiskey?" the man yelled to the miners hovering nearby. A half-dozen flasks appeared before him. Harold grabbed the closest one, lifted Stanley's head, and tipped the drink toward his lips. "Don't give up on me now, son." Though seemingly unconscious, the boy managed to swallow a mouthful. Harold lowered Stanley's head back onto the stretcher. "I can't do no more." He shook his head. "He's in God's hands now."

"The wagon's ready up top!" someone yelled from the gangway.

Harold motioned for Owen and John to grab hold of the litter and carry the boy up and out of the mine.

As the wagon pulled in front of the State Hospital for the Northern Anthracite Region, Owen jumped off the back and ran inside ahead of the others. "We need a doctor!" he shouted as he rushed through the doors. "There's a boy out here, lost his hand. Come quick!"

Doc Rodham rushed into the hallway at the sound of the commotion. "What's happened?"

Owen froze for an instant. He hadn't seen the doctor since the day Daisy died.

Doc Rodham had waited in the parlor for the undertaker to arrive, so they could discuss the condition of Daisy's body. Extra measures had to be taken because the death was so traumatic. After carting his embalming equipment into the house, Mr. Parker assured both the doctor and Owen that he'd take the utmost care with the little girl.

While Owen had seen Doc Rodham to the door, the undertaker moved silently into the center of the parlor and opened his portable cooling table like a book. He pulled four wooden legs toward him, locked them into place and set the contraption upright in the middle of the Morgans' parlor. What had looked like a suitcase too thin to be of use opened to a length of six feet, long enough to accommodate the tallest bodies. He adjusted the top portion of the table, so a corpse's head could rest at an upward angle, and draped a gray cotton bed blanket over the caned surface. Looking around the room, past the couch, the two upholstered chairs, and the little red lacquered piano, Mr. Parker spied a gate-leg table in the corner. He pulled it toward him, lifted one leaf, and swung the base into position. With his work area ready, he opened a black valise and placed its contents—formaldehyde, glycerin, sodium borate, boric acid, sodium nitrate, eosin, and assorted tools for drainage and injection—on top.

"Mr. Morgan," Mr. Parker had said, "whenever you're ready." After a moment of silence, the undertaker added, "Please, take what time you need."

"Where's the boy?" Doc Rodham tugged on Owen's arm.

"Outside," Owen said, remembering his purpose, motioning for Doc Rodham to follow.

"Who applied this tourniquet?" the doctor asked as he climbed into the wagon and placed his stethoscope on Stanley's chest.

"That's my doing," John responded from his place near the boy's sweat-soaked head. "Don't know if I—"

"May have saved the boy's life." The doctor motioned the men to carry Stanley inside. "Easy now. Very gentle."

Half an hour later, Evan Evans Sr. arrived at the hospital to check on Stanley. He found Owen and John waiting in the hallway, outside Stanley's room.

The door opened and Doc Rodham asked, "Has someone notified his kin?" Inside the room, Stanley lay on a bed, dimly conscious.

Evan Sr. peeled off his cap and started fingering the brim. "Don't have none," he said. "His ma's dead." He picked up his head, eyes darting from Owen to John and back to the doctor before adding solemnly, "And his pa was killed at the Sherman this very morning."

Shock crossed Owen and John's faces as they turned toward Stanley, who gave no sign of distress or understanding.

"I see." Doc Rodham looked back at the boy and pulled the door closed. "The lad's condition is grave. He's in need of an operation. Blood vessels have to be tied off. Bones need to be shaved to keep from pushing through. Flesh should be trimmed and stitched if he's to have any chance at all."

"Maybe we should tell the widow Lankowski," Evan Sr. suggested.

"Is she related?" the doctor asked.

"No, but my missus seen her take the boy to Polish church for the last few months."

"That Myrtle always seems to get an eyeful," Owen said. Then he added, "I'll go and fetch the widow."

Owen stepped off the streetcar and headed toward Spring Street to deliver the news. He could offer the widow Lankowski honesty or hope, but not both. Which one would be more merciful? He needed to give her a fair evaluation of Stanley's condition, but every time he tried to picture the boy and his injuries, he saw Daisy on that bed.

After Grace had finished bathing her, Owen lifted Daisy and carried her down the hall. The sheet, still draped over her body, fluttered as he walked back into the parlor. He stopped in front of the cooling table, laid Daisy out, and arranged her body in a state of repose.

Mr. Parker stepped over to the front window and drew the curtains. The family's official grieving period had begun. As was the custom, a mourning wreath already hung on the front door. Though it was afternoon, the undertaker lit two oil lamps, so he could set about his work in the darkened room. He took a step or two toward Owen and Daisy, and waited.

Owen had started to tremble from the inside out. Mr. Parker grabbed a kitchen chair in time to catch him in mid fall. Every part of Owen shook violently, desperately. He set his hands on the lip of the table to steady himself, but pulled them back as soon as he noticed Daisy's body quivering because of his shakes.

"I'll take it from here." Mr. Parker had lifted Owen gently by the shoulders.

"Not Daisy, God. Not my Daisy." Owen's voice shook in tandem with his body. "Why not me, Lord?" He paused for a moment in the doorway. "Take me. Anybody but Daisy." He grabbed a shovel from the cellarway, hitched his horse to the wagon, and went off without a word. Owen traveled up Spring Street, past the No. 25 School, which Daisy and Violet had both attended, and headed toward the old cemetery on Shady Lane in Chinchilla. Along the way, he saw neighbor children cooling off in Leggett's Creek, while their mothers swept or nursed or hung up the wash. Scrubbed fathers made their way to the mines while blackened ones returned. Life hadn't stopped after all, much to Owen's surprise.

When he'd arrived, he found several of the church men with shirtsleeves rolled and collars opened, already digging the small grave. "Much obliged," Owen said, piercing the earth with his shovel. The unforgiving July sun beat down on them.

A gust of January's frozen wind reminded Owen of his obligation. He glanced across the street at his own house before climbing the widow's front steps.

The widow Lankowski sat in one of ten chairs lined up along the tiled wall of the hospital's white hallway. A string of wooden beads, rough-hewn at their inception, worn smooth by years of prayer, pooled in the middle of her broad lap. Gnarled hands, mapped with rivers of veins, cradled a pitted silver crucifix. She made the Sign of the Cross, an automatic gesture for the fifty-year-old woman who'd grown up in the Polish National Catholic Church, and mouthed the words to the Apostles' Creed in her native tongue, "*Wierze w Boga, Ojca Wszechmogacego Stworzyciela nieba i ziemi, I w Jezusa Chrystusa . . .*" Thus began her nineteenth recitation of the rosary, three hours worth and counting.

She began a Hail Mary, "*Zdrowaś Mario, łaskiś pełna Pan z Toba*," as Doc Rodham entered the hallway with rolled white sleeves and a bloodstained apron. Owen and John, who had stepped out for a drink sometime during the second hour of surgery, came around the corner at that moment.

"He's holding his own," Doc Rodham said.

The widow kissed her crucifix and held it up to heaven.

"Can't ask for more than that." He paused. "Not out of the woods, though, by any means. Lost lots of blood. And if infection sets in," he shook his head, "we could still lose him. We've done all we can." Glancing at the rosary beads threaded between the widow's fingers, he added, "Medically speaking."

Owen took the doctor's hand and looked him in the eye. "Thank you. For today. For everything." He dropped his eyes. "I never did have a chance to thank you proper."

"We'll see how the boy fares. At least he has a chance. We're not always so lucky, but I don't have to tell you that."

"How long will he be here?" John asked.

"Weeks. Months. Time will tell." Doc Rodham unrolled his sleeves.

"And after that?"

"The Home for the Friendless, I suppose."

The widow shot out of her seat, her rosary dropping to the floor. "Not while I'm breathing," she said, bending down to scoop up the beads. "Not *mój drogi*, not my dear Stanley. He'll come home with me."

CHAPTER TWENTY-ONE

"THERE'S BEEN AN ACCIDENT," Violet's mother said to her that night. "Your little friend. The one who came around on Thanksgiving night."

Violet shot up from the couch. "Stanley? You don't mean Stanley?" She started to tremble.

"He's quite grave, I'm afraid. Lost his hand in the mine." Grace picked up the blanket that had fallen to the floor and draped it around Violet's shoulders. "I'm sorry. Truly." She closed her eyes. "So much pain for those who least deserve it." She shook her head and plodded toward her bedroom. "You'll want to include him in your prayers," she called back before stepping inside and shutting the door.

The next day, everyone in school knew about Stanley's accident. "I wonder if he'll still be able to play stickball," the boys said, as if they'd ever asked Stanley to play any game with them before. The girls took turns crying and comforting one another, as if Stanley had been the secret sweetheart of them all.

"Where were you when he needed a friend?" Violet yelled at Olive Manley who seemed particularly broken up. Olive simply cried louder, compelling Miss Reese to hold Violet inside during recess.

* * *

Just before lunch, Olive leaned over to Violet and whispered, "If you're such a good friend, why aren't you with Stanley?"

Because it's my fault he's dying.

The thought slammed into Violet's brain like the coal car that had taken Stanley's hand, unearthing other words buried along its track. Daisy. Father. Mother. And now Stanley.

The Fourth of July. That was the start of it. But what had she done to make God so angry? Jealousy. Was that it? "Nothing more disappointing than a jealous child." Her father had said so that very day when he sent Violet and Daisy into the yard. And she was. Jealous of Daisy's store-bought dress, her baptism, her long hair. Could jealousy ignite a sparkler? And Stanley. The widow took him to church, went with him to buy the gumdrops. She favored him. Had Violet been jealous? The thought soured in her stomach. "A jealous child." She knew truth when she heard it.

With only her right hand, the widow dipped a cloth into a basin of cool water, squeezed most of the water out, and placed it on Stanley's forehead. Her left arm dangled at her side. She needed to see what a person could do one-handed.

It had been three days since the accident, and the boy remained in a sort of limbo, a half-coma, eyes open but empty, lips moving without sound. "How soon before the fever breaks?" she asked.

The nurse, a stout woman who moved languidly through the twenty-bed ward, simply shook her head. She placed a glass bottle and several lengths of cotton batting on a small side table.

"Show me how," the widow said. "I'll need to do for him once I get him home."

"It's different with an amputee." She pulled small scissors out of her apron pocket to cut off the old dressing of cyanide gauze and salicylic wool. "You have to wrap the bandages to shape the stump."

The first snip unloosed a smell so foul, both the widow and the nurse choked on the fetid air.

"Get the doctor!" the nurse yelled in the direction of the door. A pair of feet ran down the hallway, and in less than a minute, Doc Rodham arrived at Stanley's bedside.

"I was afraid of this." He slowly peeled back the dressing. "Acute inflammation. Happens in such cases." He poked at a pocket of angry flesh. "Pus needs draining." He lifted the swollen limb. "No line of demarcation. Not gangrenous yet." He placed the arm back on the pillow. "Not a stone's throw away from it, though."

The doctor continued his examination. Temperature, 103 degrees. Pulse rate, rapid, 112. Tongue, furred and milky. When he finished, he announced his course of action to the nurse: "Drainage and bloodletting." Turning to the widow he added, "And prayer."

The nurse scampered out the door and down the hall, faster than the widow had ever seen her move.

"It's best if you step out," Doc Rodham said, "so I can tend to him here."

"My place is with the boy." The widow peered out the window, settled in a nearby chair, and pulled her beads out of her pocket. "I'll not get in your way." She glanced outside once more and wondered momentarily if Tommy Davies would show up this time with Violet. The widow had asked him every day since the accident, knowing how good she'd be for Stanley. She looked again and saw Tommy turning the corner, alone. Perhaps it's best for now, considering Stanley's condition, she thought, as she crossed herself and started in on the Apostles' Creed.

The nurse reappeared with all the necessary tools: anesthesia, forceps, scalpel, tubing, needle and thread, milk, and a small glass cylinder. She had the table set up by the time the doctor returned with the jar of leeches.

Doc Rodham poured an ounce of ether, half the amount given to surgical patients, into the chamber of the inhaler, since the boy was already in a semi-unconscious state and the cutting would be minimal. He placed the facepiece over Stanley's mouth and nose, and after he took a few breaths, his body seemed to relax.

The doctor sliced into two abscesses, and soaked up a dark, foul-smelling fluid before stitching drainage tubes into the incisions. Next, he rubbed the milk around the circumference of the stump while the nurse plucked one of the leeches with the forceps and dropped it in the narrow cylinder, tail first. She handed the container to the doctor, who tipped it over, placing the mouth of it against Stanley's skin. The doctor held it there until the leech latched on, sucking out the bad blood, then he handed it to the nurse to be filled again.

On Monday afternoon, Violet set out for the hospital after school. It had been four days since Stanley's accident, and three since she'd realized her part in it, but she couldn't stay away any longer. She had to see him for herself.

Violet headed down School Street and over to North Main Avenue. She intended to keep walking toward downtown until she reached the State Hospital, where she'd heard Stanley had been taken.

When she reached the square, she froze in front of the church, listening to the whistle of the finch. She thought of all the birdcalls that required two hands, sat down on the steps, and sobbed.

Half an hour later, Violet turned around and headed back up and over to Spring Street. She looked at her own house with its curtains drawn against the day, crossed over to the widow's place, and let herself in the back door. She shoveled just enough coal into the stove to throw a little warmth in her direction. She couldn't go, not today. "So much pain, for those who least deserve it," her mother had said. How true, Violet thought, as she rested her head in her arms. If anyone deserved to suffer, it was she, not Stanley. And certainly not Daisy.

People had come from all over town to view Daisy's body. Some knew the family and wanted to pay their respects. Others had read about the accident in the papers and wanted to see the little girl who sang hymns as she lay dying. Mr. Edward Baker Sturges added extra trolley runs on the Providence line to accommodate the number of riders going to and from the Morgans' house. Though he'd never met the family, George W. Bowen, the poet, came over from Wayne Avenue to, as he put it, "see one of God's angels." There had even been talk that Mr. Sherman would shut down the mine for the day of the burial, but that never happened.

Several of Daisy's friends showed up accompanied by their parents. On their way up to the porch, some of the mothers could be overheard reminding their children of the dangers of fireworks and matches, and of not minding their elders. Others kissed the heads of sons and daughters, muttering, "There but by the grace of God," as they opened the screen door and stepped inside.

Flowers had occupied every corner of the modest parlor. A painted banner with the words *Beloved Daughter* stretched across a wreath of Shasta daisies propped up in front of the coffin. Their yellow eyes watched from white-petaled lashes as people stepped forward to pay their respects. All manner of fragrant flowers bloomed from vases, pots, and any container that could hold water. The cloying scents of roses, phlox, and daylilies mingled with the rising smell of decay.

A fine layer of netting stretched across the top of the casket, inviting mourners to view Daisy without touching her. As Mr. Parker had explained, "It's best, considering the condition of the body." Neither parent had objected.

Her mother and father stood in front of the coffin to receive condolences and stand watch over their daughter. Even with the netting, Mother said she could still think of a handful of people who might try to get at the child. Some folks believed they had to touch a body to grieve it.

The casket itself lay atop a wooden stand of Mr. Parker's design in front of the parlor window. What furniture there was had been pushed flush against the opposite wall, like condemned prisoners awaiting execution. Even so, there was hardly enough room for the number of people who showed, and most who chose to stay made their way out to one or the other of the porches.

Flo Watkins, Ruth Jones, Marion Thomas, Janie Miller, and Susie Hopkins, all friends of Daisy's who'd been baptized the same day, arrived together. They stood in the line for almost forty-five minutes before moving inside, their Sunday dresses dripping and clinging from the savage heat. They had waited about twenty minutes more before stepping forward, to allow Myrtle Evans and her sister Mildred a wide enough berth for their grief. The sisters held their ground at the coffin, wailing in tandem as if rehearsed. The performance had ended with Mr. Parker thanking the women for coming as he ushered them past Owen and Grace, into the kitchen.

The girls took their turn before the coffin. A white slumber blanket that looked to be silk covered Daisy to the chest. Her blue capped shoulders and hand-smocked neckline hinted at the dress underneath. The face had already begun to turn like an overcast day before a storm, though anyone who knew the girl could still make her out. Mr. Parker had managed to set her features in a natural expression, a difficult task considering the body's condition. Someone had plucked a flower from the wreath and tucked it behind Daisy's right ear before the official viewing, before the netting was set in place. Mr. Parker had placed blocks of cedar under the coffin lining, so the sharp smell of fresh-cut wood wafted up into the girls' noses.

"Move along," Myrtle Evans waved from the kitchen. "Give someone else a turn, why don't you."

Startled, the girls stepped forward, toward Violet's parents. "Sorry for your trouble," Flo managed, while shifting her weight from one foot to the other. "We best be going. Tell Violet we're sorry we missed her."

At the other end of the room, Violet sat tucked under the little piano with the stool pulled in against the pedals, her matching blue dress a wrinkled mess from the close heat and her cramped position. She'd seen her sister laid out in the coffin the night before when she and Aunt Hattie sat vigil. That was enough looking for her.

"You always sit with a body," Aunt Hattie had explained, "out of respect for the dead."

The dead were the last people who needed respecting, Violet thought, but she'd known better than to share her opinion with her mother's sister. After all, Aunt Hattie had practically raised her mother, so she knew a thing or two about the ways of the world.

Their watch over Daisy had been shrouded in darkness, save for the light from an oil lamp on the stove. Every now and then, Violet would excuse herself, move to the kitchen, and stare into the flame. Alone, her eight-year-old mind would try to make sense of all that had happened.

Why did Daisy have to die?

When would she see her again?

Did Father mean it when he said, "Anybody but Daisy"?

So many questions raced inside her head but the important ones turned tail before crossing the finish line.

"Mrs. McGraw asked why we didn't get baptized together," Violet said as she came back into the room. "She lives over on Oak Street. I go to school with her kids."

Aunt Hattie tipped her head and squeezed her eyes. "Something wrong with you, child?"

The same question Myrtle Evans had asked her in the yard. Violet decided to shut her mind to questions she could not answer. "Irish twins is what she called us, being born so close." She leaned in toward the coffin to check for movement. "Mother told her there was no need for name calling." She settled back into her chair but kept an eye toward her sister. "I agreed, us being Welsh and all."

"Nonsense," Aunt Hattie had whispered, so as not to disturb the dead. "Maureen McGraw is Irish herself. And bog Irish at that."

Violet climbed her front porch steps, mad at herself for not having the courage to go see Stanley. She pictured him in that hospital, all alone. I know what that feels like, she thought, and closed her eyes and wished with her whole heart for Daisy to come back to be with her, to stand with her so she wouldn't be so alone. When she opened her eyes, she saw Adelaide pulling back the curtain. "Grab the bucket," she called through the glass. "We're going to need more coal for the supper." Violet dabbed at her eyes with the sleeve of her coat before picking up the empty pail and heading inside.

By the fifth day, Stanley's fever broke, the infection subsided, but the boy had yet to stir. When Doc Rodham came by to remove the drainage tubes, the widow asked him when Stanley would wake up. "He doesn't even mutter anymore. It's like the light's gone out of him."

"The body has its own timetable for healing," was all the doctor could think to say.

Tommy Davies removed his cap and knocked on the Morgans' front door as he'd done for the last six evenings. "Sorry to bother you again, but I'm going to the State Hospital to see Stanley, and wondered if Violet might come along. I'd keep a good eye on her."

Grace stood at the door without saying a word.

"The widow's sure he'd wake up for Violet," he added as he rolled and unrolled the hat in his hands.

Grace smiled as if she understood but shook her head.

"Sorry to trouble you," Tommy said on his way down the steps. He turned back to say he'd take out the ashes when he got home, but the door had already been shut against him.

Grace shoveled more coal into the stove and poured herself some tea. She felt for Stanley, but she had no intention of sending Violet down there, no matter who was laid up inside. No good ever came out of a hospital that she could tell. Hospitals were for the dying, and her family had seen enough of that already.

Adelaide patted Grace's hand, and held out her own empty cup. "You're right not to let her go. No sense encouraging those two."

Grace slammed the teapot on the table between them and took her cup and saucer into the bedroom.

In the parlor, Violet pulled her knees in closer, so her mother wouldn't see her folded under the little piano. *The widow's sure he'd wake up for Violet*. Tommy's words squeezed into her head and sidled up against the others. *It's my fault he's dying*. Each truth stepped back to size up the other. Both seemed to be of equal weight. Violet knew the blame was hers, but she also knew the widow never lied. He's dying, she thought. He'll wake. She closed her eyes and folded her hands in prayer. Please, God, spare Stanley. Either way, come morning she was going to see him and his fate would be decided.

CHAPTER TWENTY-TWO

VIOLET WRAPPED A RED WOOLEN SCARF around her neck, tucked the cigar-box dollhouse under her arm, and stepped out into the biting January morning. She hadn't skipped school since Miss Reese's home visit in October, but she decided the whipping she'd surely get would be easier than another day of uncertainty. A few inches of snow had fallen overnight, and as she started down the hill, she placed her feet inside the tracks made by the miners before sunrise.

When Violet reached the bottom of Spring Street, she turned right, toward the square. Having been to Poli's Theatre twice, she knew how to make her way downtown in the direction of the State Hospital. Scranton had already had its share of weather that season, but it hadn't had any new snow until now for at least a week. Violet marveled at the snow's ability to transform the city. Tree limbs curtsied under its weight; lampposts donned hats of it.

Once Violet crossed over to Murray's, where she and Stanley had bought their gumdrops so long ago, she found that most of the storekeepers had already thrown ashes on their sidewalks to keep customers from slipping, though foot traffic still seemed light for that hour of the morning. She continued on her way, down to Green Ridge Street, toward Penn Avenue. She knew the hospital to be a straight shot after that.

Violet noticed the storeowners, driving their wagons toward town. She remembered the day she and Stanley had seen the Billy Sunday signs on their way to the Wholesale District. And how later that afternoon, they tried unsuccessfully to see a minstrel show. Stanley still called her a baby whenever he thought of her dragging him out of the theatre. She'd done it to protect their souls. Did it matter now?

Still four blocks away, the hospital loomed, like Goliath before the Israelites. Violet's heart began to pound as she imagined poor Stanley, lying helpless in a hospital bed. Would he wake for her? Was he already dead? It's my fault—the one truth she remembered in the morning light. If only Daisy were here to walk with her, to hold her hand. Violet's legs kept moving forward, but her thoughts circled round, in search of answers.

"If you're not a sight for sore eyes," Doc Rodham said when he and Violet nearly collided on the sidewalk. He took her hand warmly and led her inside.

The widow's faith began to falter. She placed her hand on the boy's forehead and erupted into sobs. "*Mój Bóg, dlaczego ma ty opuszczony mi?*"

"What's wrong? What are you saying?" Violet asked as she ran the length of the ward toward Stanley's bed. "Is he dead too?"

"No, no, my sweet." The widow reached out, pulled the girl in before helping her off with her scarf and coat. Violet kept a firm hold on the cigar box. "I thought that God had forsaken me," the widow explained, "and I foolishly asked him why. I see now He never left me. He sent an angel." She rubbed Violet's arms briskly to warm her and whispered, "*Ojciec przebaczać mi*," and then in English for the benefit of Violet, "Father, forgive me."

Violet turned to Stanley to look him over. She noted

how small he seemed in the center of the hospital bed. She scooted around to his left side, grabbed hold of the blanket, and asked, "Can I?"

The widow nodded.

Slowly, Violet lifted the blanket to reveal the injured limb, shorter than before though wider with the bandages wrapped around it. She studied it for a long moment. "Something's not right." She put the cover back in place.

"The hand couldn't be saved," the widow said, surprised to have to tell her.

"I don't mean that." Violet looked at him again.

"Then what?"

Violet paused for a moment, and leaned in close. "His smell," she said. "He lost his smell."

Confusion settled on the widow's face.

"The sour smell," Violet explained, "that stuck to him—his hair and clothes. It's gone."

The widow broke into a smile. "Cooked cabbage. Only thing his *tata* knew to make, God rest his soul. Eat it pretty regular myself."

"But you don't smell."

"Add a crust of stale bread to the cabbage pot. Soaks up the odor. Keeps it from clinging to you. And throw a handful of whortleberries on the stove to sweeten the—"

"Why doesn't he wake up?"

"He will," the widow answered, and she meant it. "I'm certain of it. He'll wake for you." She remembered the beads in her pocket and fingered them.

"I brought you something," Violet said to Stanley. She swung around and set the dollhouse on the bed, near his good right hand. She opened it, removed the mother, Daisy, and Violet dolls her father had made, and placed them on the little table. Next, she reached for two more cutouts, crudely drawn in her own hand. They looked to be a father and son, or, more precisely, her father and Stanley. She set these next to the others and went back to the box again. Inside lay at least twenty birds, some drawn by the same childish hand as the male cutouts, and others torn from a seed catalog Violet had found near the schoolyard. "I've been practicing," she said, pulling out a penned blue jay and placing it on the blanket. "*Twee-dle-dee, twee-dle-dee, twee-dle-dee.*" She dropped her head. "Doesn't sound as good as yours. I still need teaching." She looked straight at Stanley, but he didn't respond.

She pulled out a smaller bird and whistled again, this time the saw of the wren. Her call went unheeded.

On her fifth try, the *chip, chip, chip* of the red cardinal, Stanley began to stir.

"*Wychwalają Boga*!" the widow shouted. "Praise God!"

The nurse, at the other end of the ward pushed decorum aside and yelled, "Our Stanley?" in a high-pitched voice, startling several patients around her. When Violet nodded back, the nurse ran into the hall for the doctor.

"You best take the little one out," Doc Rodham said to the widow, "and let me examine the boy."

Violet grabbed hold of Stanley's good hand with both of hers. "But he just now woke up. I don't want to leave him." Stanley's eyelids fluttered open and he half-smiled.

The widow crossed herself and offered a prayer of thanks before gently pulling on Violet's shoulders and pointing her toward the door. "Doc Rodham won't let any harm come to him. Besides, we have to do what we're told, or they won't let us stay."

Violet held her ground.

"There are rules in hospitals," the widow explained. "Especially about children. We don't want them to remember you're too young to be here."

"A hospital's no place for the sick," Violet said to Doc Rodham before heading toward the hallway.

"That's just her mother talking." The widow followed behind. She guided Violet toward the wooden chairs alongside the windows. The late-morning sun squeezed through slats on the open blinds. "A January thaw," the widow said, aware of a world outside for the first time since Stanley's accident. "Lucky we don't have too much snow on the ground. One warm day is all it takes to flood the cellar."

Violet dropped her head into her hands.

"Of course, it's probably much colder out than it looks." The widow turned her chair and faced Violet. "He'll be home in no time. I promise." She pulled the girl onto her lap and rocked her.

"I tried to come sooner." Tears dripped down Violet's cheeks. "It's my fault he's here."

"What silliness! He's alive. That's your doing, and the good Lord's." She hugged Violet tighter and started to cry herself. "I should have come for you, but I was afraid to leave him."

Violet opened her eyes and stroked the widow's cheek. "You were right to stay. You're all he has now."

"*We're* who he has now. And don't you forget it." The widow reached into her sleeve and pulled out a handkerchief. "Now blow."

An hour later, a nurse led Violet and the widow back into the room.

"My stomach thinks my throat's been cut," Stanley said, his voice shaky but resolute.

"The lad's hungry," Doc Rodham said with a wide smile. "A good sign. A good sign, indeed."

CHAPTER TWENTY-THREE

DUSK HAD FALLEN BY THE TIME Tommy Davies showed up once again at the State Hospital. As was his custom, he kept his head bowed, eyes to the floor, while he walked the length of the ward. He'd seen enough suffering in his twelve years, and didn't need to catch sight of more. It only made a person feel helpless, and that didn't do anyone any good.

"Would you look what the cat dragged in?" Stanley said, loud enough to be heard across the room.

"Crimonies!" Tommy's head popped up. He rushed forward and stopped at the foot of Stanley's bed. "You scared the heart out of me!" He grabbed ahold of his friend's feet.

"Be careful, now," the widow warned. She stood on Stanley's right, holding a cup of beef tea in her hands.

Tommy gave the feet another squeeze, gentler this time, and rested his hands on the iron footboard.

"One more sip," the widow said, holding the cup to Stanley's lips. "Only way to get your strength back."

Tommy turned to Violet, who stood on Stanley's left. "When did he wake?"

"Late this morning. Just in time for his birthday!" she answered, turning to pick up an empty milk tumbler from the bedside table. "Should I get more?" she asked the widow, but Stanley waved them both away.

"A fellow can't take all this fussing."

"You stay with him," the widow said to Violet, as she gathered the cups. "I'll be right back."

Stanley looked up at Tommy and asked, "How's Sophie?"

The widow paused about four beds away to listen.

Tommy looked down at his feet and curled and uncurled the cap in his hands. "So how long you think you'll be laid up?"

Stanley pushed himself up on his right arm and asked about Sophie again.

Tommy shook his head. "Won't work. Won't eat. Just pining away, if you ask me."

Stanley dropped back on his pillow. "What will they do with her?"

"Mr. Evans says she's no good, oughta be shot for what she . . ." Tommy swallowed the last word, suddenly aware of its implication. He took a breath and started again. "Don't fret. Mr. Sherman never put down a mule, and he's not about to start now. She cost him two hundred dollars, after all."

The widow continued down the ward and out the door. A minute later she returned to Stanley's side with a damp rag in one hand and a tin cup in the other. She reached over the boy to Violet. "Set this water on the table in case he gets thirsty."

"Anyhow, Sophie'll pick up," Tommy said, still tangled in the same conversation, "as soon as you're strong enough to get back to work."

The widow looked directly at Tommy. "He'll not go back in that mine, not ever." She placed the rag on Stanley's forehead. "As soon as he's well, he's off to school."

"I'll have to think on that," Stanley said, pushing the rag away.

"Think all you want, young man, but as long as I have breath in me, you're getting an education."

Stanley eyed the trio surrounding him. "Pa don't believe in school. Never did."

Tommy and Violet looked to the widow for direction.

"Don't believe in hospitals neither." Stanley moved his lips, as if trying out his next line before releasing it. "I figure that's why he's not here." He eyed his friends to see how the words landed.

"Oh, my boy," the widow said, as she turned the rag. Your father, *Niech spoczywa w pokoju*," then in English, "God rest his soul, has gone home to be with the Lord."

"How?" Stanley asked, his voice cracking.

"Killed at the mine," the widow said. "Same day you lost your hand."

"I'm so sorry," Tommy said, dropping his head.

"Me too," Violet added, and they stood in silence.

"I'm tired now." Stanley turned his head toward the wall.

The widow motioned for Violet and Tommy to leave.

"I'll see you tomorrow." Violet gave Stanley's hand one last squeeze.

"Good night," Tommy said, and they walked toward the door.

The widow wiped her damp cloth across Stanley's closed, moist eyes. "Sleep, my child. *Spać*."

Tommy held the door open for Violet as they went out into the sharp January night.

"I guess he really loved him," Violet said, and shoved her hands into her pockets.

"Who?" Tommy asked, buttoning his coat to the neck.

"His father. Don't know why it surprises me. Just can't understand how anyone could love someone so mean."

"A boy always loves his dad." Tommy looked up at the falling snowflakes, illuminated by the electric lights. He stopped for a moment, opened his mouth, and caught some on his tongue. "A boy always loves his dad," he repeated, and winked toward the sky.

As the pair continued down Penn Avenue in silence, Violet tried to reconcile the emotions springing up inside her. She felt sorry for Stanley. He'd lost his hand and his father, even if no one liked the man. Yet, at the same time, she felt great joy. Her friend had not been taken from her. She hadn't killed him after all. And now he would be free of the mine. Still, Stanley's pain made her joy seem childish, even selfish, and she struggled to understand her own confusion.

When Violet and Tommy reached Green Ridge Street, they crossed over and started up the hill. Just as they reached North Main Avenue, a horse pulled up alongside them and stopped abruptly.

"Where have you been?" Owen hollered as he jumped out of the saddle. He tied the leather reins on the closest hitching post and grabbed hold of his daughter's arm. He pulled her in and walloped her on the behind with great force. "You scared us to death!" he yelled, then hugged her hard. He gripped her hands, held her at arm's length, and looked her in the eye. "I thought I lost you," he said in a quiet voice, and hugged her again.

Violet did not return the embrace. Tears of embarrassment rolled down her cheeks as she tried to find words. She'd been with Stanley. He needed her. He woke up for her. And how could her father hit her, especially in front of Tommy? "You don't care about me," she finally managed. "You left us, remember?"

Owen let go of his daughter, untied the reins, and handed them to Tommy. "See Violet home for me, will you?" Before Tommy had a chance to answer, Owen started toward Providence Square on foot.

"Praise God!" Hattie shouted as Tommy slid Violet off the horse and down to the ground. She ran and scooped the girl into her arms and carried her inside. "She's home! Praise

God!" Hattie brought Violet straight into the kitchen before setting her on her feet.

Violet locked eyes with Grace, sitting on a chair pulled close to the stove. Grace wore a vacant expression, but her arms shot out in an automatic gesture. Relief washed over Violet as she rushed toward her mother. She longed to be held in those arms. Too late she realized the impracticality of an embrace with a swollen belly between them. Grace caressed Violet's cheek and finger-combed her hair.

"And just where did you get to?" Adelaide asked as she buttered a muffin from the dozen Louise had brought over that afternoon. There were only eight left, and no one but Adelaide had eaten.

Tommy tramped into the kitchen after hitching the horse. "Stanley woke up for her," he directed toward his mother Louise, who stood behind Adelaide. He turned to Grace. "The widow called her an angel."

Violet didn't remember hearing the compliment, but she took it in just the same.

"Everyone is safe," Louise said. "That's all that matters."

"You gave us a fright, young lady," Adelaide said with her mouth still full. "I'll probably suffer all night with this indigestion."

CHAPTER TWENTY-FOUR

OWEN'S FROZEN BREATH CHARGED ahead of him as he traveled back to Burke's on foot. Violet was safe. Tommy had seen to that. But Owen was her father. It was his job to protect her. To protect them all. He'd failed tonight. He'd failed with Graham. And, worst of all, he'd failed with Daisy.

The night before Daisy's funeral, Reverend Halloway had determined that the church would be the best place for the service. He knew of at least fifty souls who planned to attend, and the Morgans' parlor would hold a quarter of that number. People knew by word of mouth to line their wagons up along North Main Avenue no later than eight o'clock in the morning. Frankly, after three days of viewing, the body stank and needed to be buried before the noonday sun.

Isabelle Lumley, Maude Babcock, and Dorcus Proudlock, Sunday school teachers at the Christian Church, and Jane Griffin, Sunday school superintendent, had offered to serve as pallbearers. Initially, Reverend Halloway had objected to the idea, but Grace thought the notion of women carrying a child so simple, so pure, she insisted he reconsider. Jane also suggested that the smaller boys from the Sunday school be used as flower bearers. Grace's favorable response caused the reverend to find merit in the idea.

Owen had lain awake that morning listening to Grace starting her biscuits in spite of the mountain of other people's food in her kitchen. He hadn't the strength to face her or the day impatient to break over the slag horizon. Culm fires with their rotten-egg smell glowed in the distance. Like everything else, they would burn themselves out. "God . . ." he said aloud. "God . . ." he began his prayer again. When no words followed, he rolled over and faced the window. The rising sun split the sky, alerting all who were awake to the start of another day. "God . . ." he tried a final time, but the word soured and spoiled on his tongue. Owen tumbled out of bed, washed his face in the basin, and headed for the parlor.

Louise Davies, who had nodded off at some point during her overnight vigil, shot straight up when Owen came in. "Just resting my eyes," she said, pushing tendrils of red hair into her bun. She shoved the chair back to make room for him by the coffin.

He stepped toward Daisy. "A darker day I'll never know." He lightly touched his lips to the netting over her face.

Louise fussed with the chrysanthemums, removing the dead ones, reorganizing those that were still fresh.

Owen went over to a shelf on the wall and took down the family Bible, the one his mam had used to teach him how to read and write, Welsh on one side, English on the other. The words *Holy Bible* had been pressed and burned into the brown leather cover. The first page read,

The Old and New Testaments
Translated Out of the Original Tongues

Owen had placed the Bible on the gate-leg table, grabbed pen and ink, and pulled up a chair. He opened the book and turned to the section sandwiched between Malachi and Matthew, the Old and New Testaments. Gilded letters announced the purpose of each page.

Bonds of Holy Matrimony
Marriages
Births
Deaths
Family Temperance Pledge

He turned to *Births* and ran his finger across the ornate heading first, then the words written in his own hand.

Daisy Morgan
Born in the year of our Lord
March 1, 1904
At five o'clock in the morning

He traced each letter of her name, from the *D*'s swollen belly to the *Y*'s joyful flourish.

"You don't have to do this just now." Louise watched as he slid his finger across to the opposite page.

Deaths.

He dipped his pen into the ink and paused long enough to read the only entry he'd written there.

Rose Morgan
Stillborn in the year of our Lord
October 11, 1912
At half past ten

He tapped his pen against the rim of the inkwell and began to write.

Daisy Morgan
Died in the year of our Lord
July 7, 1913
At 3 o'clock in the afternoon

He blew lightly on the page until the ink was dry, closed the Bible, and dropped his head into his hands.

Later that morning, as the horses pulled up along the road to the church, the number of people who turned out had astounded even Reverend Halloway. A weekday funeral, even for a child, was not usually attended by more than just the family and close friends. Somehow, perhaps through newspapers or the grapevine, Daisy's story had captivated the residents of Scranton. The legend had already been told, polished, and told again. The child not only sang hymns for three days, she sang them nonstop, without a word of complaint or a minute's rest. Any possible suffering had been removed from the tale, shelved out of reach. And at the moment of her death, the very moment, clouds had pushed the sun back and darkened the afternoon sky. Even those who hadn't known the little girl noted how the sun stopped shining and wondered at its meaning.

Reverend Halloway had approached the undertaker's horse-drawn funeral hearse and helped Grace and Violet as they stepped out from under the folding top and over the side of the wagon. Owen had waited in the carriage until Daisy's Sunday school teachers assumed responsibility for the child-sized coffin in back. Three women on either side gently carried it into the church and down the aisle. On a silent count of three, they lifted the casket onto a table in front. Flowers surrounded the altar, blanketing it with their perfume. The women took their seats in the second row. Grace, Owen, and Violet followed, heads bowed, arms interlocked, and sat in the first pew. Reverend Halloway cleared his throat to signal his flock.

"Brothers and sisters in Christ, we gather this day to mourn the loss of Daisy Morgan, precious daughter of Grace and Owen, loving sister." He tilted his head toward Violet, causing many eyes to settle in her direction, some in sympathy, others trying for it. "While our hearts are heavy, we take comfort in the knowledge that Daisy died happy in faith. Our loss is her eternal gain, for on the very day of this child's tragedy, she accepted Jesus as her Lord and Savior after a profession of faith."

Owen broke into choking sobs. Eyes moved toward the grieving father.

"Now, brethren, heed the lesson found in the early flight of Daisy Morgan . . ."

Owen's mind slipped its moorings and floated away. He had not heard another word until the reverend's voice rose as if in admonition of the crowd. "Her sudden death should serve as a loud call that we may also be ready, for according to Matthew, *The Son of man is coming at an hour you do not expect*. In Proverbs we are warned, *Do not boast about tomorrow, for you do not know what a day may bring forth*. Are you ready to meet the Lord?"

A few muffled "Amens" rose from the pews.

He started again with more authority. "Is your heart free from the sin of this world?"

The crowd caught up with the preacher's expectation. "Amen!" they shouted.

"Have you accepted Jesus as your personal Savior?"

"Amen!"

"Do honor to this child's memory. Get right with the Lord and serve Him each day as though it were your last."

At the cemetery, Daisy's Sunday school teachers carried her

to a level spot next to the hole the men had dug a few days earlier. A series of braided ropes lay on the ground underneath, ready to be of use. Grace, Owen, and Violet stood in front of the coffin, and the rest of the mourners began to fill in the space behind and around.

James Harris pushed through the crowd, and gave Owen's shoulder a squeeze before stepping forward to nail the lid on the casket he'd built. He slid his calloused hand along the wood he'd planed so lovingly. Grace dropped her head but jumped involuntarily with each thud of the hammer. Owen tried to put his arm around her, but she pulled away. Violet closed her eyes and counted on her fingers, three strikes for each nail head, six nails in all, eighteen blows in total.

With a nudge from Jane Griffin, the young flower bearers inched forward and placed handfuls of daisies on top of the coffin. Four of the elders approached, lifted the pine box, and lowered it on ropes into the grave. As was required by custom, and only for that reason, Owen threw a shovelful of dirt into the opening. The junior choir started in on "Rock of Ages," and the mourners gradually joined in.

Rock of ages, cleft for me,
Let me hide myself in Thee . . .

Owen stood in front of Burke's, breathing in the icy January air, hoping to numb that part of his brain where "Rock of Ages" resided, but the silence only seemed to amplify the sound inside his head. Outside the gin mill's door, footprints of sawdust and mud fanned out in the gleaming white snow.

Let the water and the blood,
From Thy wounded side which flowed,

Be of sin the double cure;
Save from wrath and make me pure . . .

Make me pure. Owen brushed the snow off his coat, thinking about Grace and how she'd made him pure when he'd married her, or so he thought. Even after Graham's death—especially then. He'd longed to drink, and she knew it, but he held onto Grace and his little family—or, rather, they held onto him. And it had worked. For a while. Then Daisy, his beautiful sweet girl. When the ground opens up and swallows a man whole like it did the day they'd buried that coffin, he grabs hold of whatever he can find in the dark.

Owen walked into the gin mill and threw back a whiskey to quiet his mind.

PART TWO

Little Billy Sunday's come to our town to stay
An' drive the Devil out o' here, an' make him keep away,
An' kick the stuffin' out o' booze an' swat all kinds o' vice,
An' hammer sin an' pull the mask from everythin' not nice.
Folks sez they're not afraid to go, an' hear him preach the word;
Course I don't know if what he does is right, but this I've heard:
You feel yerself a slippin' when he begins to shout—
An' Billy Sunday'll git you, if you don't watch out!

—Charles B. Stevens

SEA AND CAR SICKNESS

> *Sea sickness and also car sickness can be avoided by the liberal eating of well-salted popcorn. This has been tried many times, with success, and is a very simple remedy.*
>
> —*Mrs. Joe's Housekeeping Guide,* 1909

A.P. Gill, Billy Sunday's architect and advance man, arrived yesterday by train. Seven weeks and a day before the evangelist himself. Same amount of time it took our resurrected Savior to appear before His Apostles, as Sister Adelaide reminded us. Fitting, since Mr. Sunday's visit promises to be about as miraculous as Pentecost.

Billy Sunday always leaves a town in better condition than he finds it. Churches filled to the rafters. Beer gardens boarded up. Why, just last year, he inspired a group of gentlemen from Wilkes-Barre to turn their monthly poker games into prayer meetings. Expect to see that same spirit here. And we're not alone. According to the *Times*, a fellow from Johnstown, New York, asked Mr. Sunday to find him a wife here in Scranton, a Christian woman who can keep him from backsliding. Several women in our own congregation took note of the article. Some a little too enthusiastically.

As for Mr. Gill, we had the pleasure of his company in service this morning. He's preaching around the city, preparing people for the revival. A fine-looking man, though he put Pearl Williams in mind of that louse who abandoned her. Same dimples. Same thick head of hair. Fortunately, Mr. Gill's voice is high-pitched, so Pearl just shut her eyes and listened.

We're to start holding prayer meetings in each other's houses every Tuesday and Friday, beginning in February. After church, Adelaide took charge of organizing the folks around Providence Square. Said she'd offer Grace's home if it weren't so small. Isabelle Lumley volunteered her house. Reminded us it has two stories. "With the staircase on the outside, as I recall," Adelaide said, knocking her down a peg or two. Someone else suggested the Rockwell place, but we had to refuse. His people are Baptists. Closet drinkers. Not our kind.

When enough moneyed members finally came forward, Adelaide moved on to news about the tabernacle. Seems they need volunteers to saw boards and drive nails. James Harris asked about union carpenters, but Sister Adelaide turned a deaf ear. Didn't want to borrow trouble before the revival even starts. Can't blame her. We all want to make a good impression. Besides, James earns enough to keep his family going all winter. Makes furniture in that barn of his. No reason for him to get folks riled up. As we always say, the more you stir the pot, the worse it stinks.

CHAPTER TWENTY-FIVE

STANLEY SQUIRMED IN HIS HOSPITAL BED as the widow Lankowski deftly cut the bandages away from his forearm.

"Careful," Doc Rodham warned. "And remember to check for swelling."

The widow stopped, one snip away from completing the task. She eyed the doctor, then turned her attention back to the boy.

"I think she's trying to tell us you're in capable hands." Doc Rodham smiled at Stanley. "And I agree."

The widow threw the used dressing into a basin, and inspected the injured area. A thick mound of fibrous tissue covered the truncated limb. She lifted it gently, noting its colorless appearance, like flesh too long in water. "No sign of infection," she said. "*Bogu dzięki*." Thank God.

Doc Rodham watched as she tended to the arm. "Now remember, meats of any kind. We want him to build up his strength. And vegetables in small amounts, especially cauliflower and turnips."

"What about cabbage?" she asked.

"And cabbage," the doctor replied. "But keep him away from fruit, potatoes, tapioca, and sugar."

"Sugar?" The widow's head popped up. "It's the first I've heard of that."

"Oh," he said, as if remembering something. "A little

sugar won't hurt. Not to worry. Just don't let him overdo it."

Relieved, she finished bandaging the limb. "And you spoke to Tommy Davies?"

"Took care of the matter this morning."

"Thank you for that." The widow reached across the bed and held the man's hand in both of hers. "Thank you so much for everything."

"My pleasure." Doc Rodham dropped his arm and turned to Stanley. "I suppose that's it, then. I have to let you go home."

"Home? Today?" Stanley said. "Truly?"

"Unless you'd like to stay a few more weeks. I could still use some help with those birdcalls."

"Sorry," Stanley responded, kicking off the woolen blanket. "I'm leaving."

"Tell you what. When I stop by to check on that arm, you can finish teaching me."

Stanley nodded and swung his legs over the side of the bed, poised to hop down. The widow eyed him, and he swung his legs back in place.

"Of course, there is one problem," the doctor said. "How to get you home?"

"We have money enough for the streetcar," the widow said. "It drops us right on the square, two blocks from Spring Street. We'll ride shank's mare after that," she laughed, slapping the sides of her legs. "The walk will do us both good. I won't let him overdo it."

The doctor shook his head. "I'm afraid that won't work." When Stanley and the widow started protesting, he added, "Have you ever ridden in an automobile, son?"

"Never!"

"Well, this is your lucky day."

* * *

Doc Rodham palmed the crank at the front of the Model T with Stanley standing a few feet behind him. "You never want to grab hold with your fingers." The doctor turned the handle and started the engine. "You'll break your wrist," he called out over the roar of the motor, "if she kicks back in the opposite direction. From now on, you'll have to be especially careful with your good arm."

Stanley nodded solemnly, memorizing every detail of this spectacular event. The widow watched from the safety of the sidewalk.

"Everyone in!" Doc Rodham yelled. At first, Stanley settled into the roadster's uncovered backseat, but Doc Rodham and the widow quickly overruled him.

"There's room in front if we squeeze together," she said. Stanley slowly climbed over and sat in the middle.

Doc Rodham drove up Vine Street and over to North Washington Avenue. "What do you think?"

Stanley smiled as the wind blew across his face, but the widow pursed her lips. "Hold onto me, Stanley. *Boże. Boże.* Lord. A little fast, don't you think?"

A few blocks down the road, A.P. Gill, Billy Sunday's architect and advance agent, stood in front of the new tabernacle, speaking to reporters from Scranton's three newspapers, the *Truth*, the *Republican*, and the *Times*. George Sherman, Colonel Watres, and E.B. Sturges were among the dignitaries who had accompanied him to the location.

From the outside, the building looked like an organized shantytown, with its rough-hewn wood and abundant entrances. Windows dotted each of the four exterior walls and poked through the top of a turtle-back roof designed to carry Mr. Sunday's voice to every corner of the place. Smoke curled from fifteen metal chimneys attached to fifteen stoves inside. They'd been fired up since the previous morning. The workmen needed to dry out the ground in time to install the seats.

"You may not think she looks like much," Gill said to the reporters, "but that just puts me in mind of Matthew, Chapter 6, verses 28 through 29. *And why take ye thought for raiment? Consider the lilies of the field, how they grow; they toil not, neither do they spin. And yet I say unto you, that even Solomon in all his glory was not arrayed like one of these.*"

"So true," Sherman said, though his befuddled expression suggested he was still trying to decipher the meaning of the passage.

"And how many will it seat?" the *Truth*'s reporter asked.

"Twelve thousand," Gill paused for effect, "and one, counting Billy Sunday, of course." Everyone chuckled. "We have our work cut out for us, though. Especially since we've increased the choir space to fourteen hundred and sixty."

"How's that?" the *Republican*'s man asked.

"Just last year, a group from Scranton performed in Indiana, Billy's home state. That's when he discovered that your fair city is the musical center of the North. So, naturally, Billy insisted we increase capacity here."

The *Times* reporter broke in: "About Mr. Sunday's work with the poor—"

"That's enough for now, boys," Watres cut in, not seeing the need to let someone from the *Times*, the only paper he didn't own, ask a question. "We have plenty of work ahead of us."

"Last one," Gill said, holding up his index finger. "And I'm glad you asked, son, because Billy Sunday is very committed to working with the downtrodden. After all, we're told in Proverbs, Chapter 19, verse 17, *He that hath pity upon the poor lendeth unto the Lord; and that which he hath given will He pay him again.*"

"Just so," the reporter looked up from his pad and locked eyes with Gill, "I believe it's that same book that tells us, *He who oppresses the poor reproaches his Maker, but he who is gracious to the needy honors Him.*"

"Good to see you know your Bible, boy." Gill's smile flattened. "Now, what is it you're after?"

"Why hasn't Mr. Sunday hired union laborers to build his tabernacle?"

"I figured as much," Gill chortled, but his face reddened. "I'm not afraid of labor unions. There is no man who will do union labor as much good as Billy Sunday." The businessmen flanking Gill nodded in agreement.

"With all due respect, sir, at last count two hundred carpenters remain idle in the city. One man I spoke to worked only five days in the last six weeks. And he knows of others who are worse off."

"We're finished here," Sturges said as he took Gill by the arm and pulled him toward the tabernacle's main entrance. "Please accept my sincerest apologies."

The *Times* reporter kept pace with the dignitaries. "Only twelve union carpenters have been hired by Mr. Sunday even though he'll raise more than enough money to pay a hundred times that number. It's my understanding the rest are unpaid workers organized by the same churches that promised to use union labor." Gill and his entourage reached the doors. The pressman shouted, "Aren't you taking the bread out of—"

"Barroom bums!" Gill exploded. "The barroom bum who doesn't know how to hold a job, who never held a steady job, who never did work all the time, is the only man who is shooting the hot air. Loafers! That's all they are!"

"There's talk the union members, those *loafers*, if you will, may boycott the Sunday revival meetings. What then?"

Gill opened the door and eyed the reporters. "Good day,

all. We have work to do." He drew in a breath and glared at the man from the *Times*. "The Lord's work."

Sturges put his hand on the small of Gill's back and led him inside. Watres and Sherman followed without a word.

"Thought you might like to see the tabernacle, since it's on the way home." The doctor pressed on his brake pedal, pulled over to the side of the road, and drew the floor lever back until they came to a complete stop. He slid out of the car, but the widow stayed seated to catch her breath, so Stanley slipped out of the driver's side.

"I heard they build one just like it wherever he goes," Stanley said.

"This one's bigger," the doctor explained. "Wants room for every singer in the town."

"No doubt, with all the Welshmen." The widow came up behind them, patting her face with a handkerchief. "They have such beautiful voices."

Stanley remembered something he'd heard in the mines. "What happens when two Welshmen meet on the road?" He waited, then answered, "They form a choir."

Doc Rodham laughed, surprising Stanley, who hadn't realized he'd told a joke. "Here's a riddle for you," the doctor said. "What's five feet tall and a mile long?"

"I give up. What is it?"

"A Welsh parade." They both laughed this time

"Don't encourage the boy," the widow scolded from behind, where they couldn't see her smile. She pulled up her skirt, stepped on the wooden sidewalk, and headed toward the structure.

Doc Rodham bent down, pulled Stanley onto his back, and carried him over to one of the windows. They spotted a group of well-dressed men surveying the open, unfinished interior. For now, the inside looked like an oversized pole-barn, with its bare beams and rafters. Cords of wire stretched across the ceiling. "Bet they'll light the place with electricity before they're finished," Stanley called back to the widow, who was still making her way through a bit of snow left from the previous evening.

"Is that so?"

"How long will he be here?" Stanley asked.

"Seven weeks," the doctor said, "so you'll be sure to see him."

"Evan Two-Times said Catholics aren't allowed," Stanley ventured.

"What a thing to say," the widow responded. "We pray to the same Holy Father as the Protestants. Don't listen to such nonsense. That's his mother talking." The widow stood next to them and crossed herself. "Lord, help me. I certainly have my work cut out." She opened her eyes, smiled at Stanley, and crossed herself again. "Amen."

Once they were back in the automobile, the widow thanked the doctor for stopping. "When the time comes, I'd like to take the boy, if he's up to it."

"I don't see why not," Doc Rodham said, as he turned the corner onto Sanderson Avenue. "Mark my word. He'll be running races before long."

She glanced at a lever on the steering wheel. "Then perhaps we should slow down a bit, and get him home in one piece."

Doc Rodham stepped on the pedal and pulled back on the throttle. He grinned at Stanley. "Don't argue with a woman, my boy. You'll never win."

Violet wandered over to the front window and pulled back the curtain for the third time in an hour.

"You'll wear a hole in that rug, with all your pacing," Adelaide called out from the couch. "Haven't you anything better to do?"

Violet dropped the curtain and went back into the kitchen. "Can I help yet?"

Grace inhaled, held the breath, and exhaled slowly. "Almost," she said, gesturing for Violet to sit. A little more than six months along, a swollen Grace moved carefully about the room. She headed to the stove with a couple of clean broom straws in hand, tied a loop in one of them, and dipped it into a pot. When the white boiled icing coated the circle completely, Grace blew in the center. A perfect bubble formed, indicating the frosting had finished cooking. She lifted the pot off the burner and placed it on the stove's shelf to cool. Next, she grabbed dry towels from the sink and pulled the oven door open. She poked the centers of two small cakes with the other straw. When it came out clean both times, she removed the cakes and tipped them facedown on wire racks in the middle of the table.

Violet took the towels, wet them in the sink, and draped them over the exposed bottoms of the pans, one of the many lessons she'd learned from watching her mother in the kitchen. The coolness of the damp rags would help to loosen the cakes.

"Thank you." Grace lifted her eyes and pressed her lips together, not quite a smile, but a definite expression of gratitude.

Violet sighed with relief. Today would be a good day after all.

About ten minutes later, Grace slowly lifted the pans, revealing two eight-inch round chocolate cakes. Violet went to the cupboard, took out the Haviland dinner plate with hand-painted flowers and coin-gold edges, and placed it on the table. It had been a wedding present to her mother from Aunt Hattie, one of the few mementos salvaged from their childhood and reserved for special occasions.

After a minute or two, her mother set the icing, a large

spoon, and a dull knife in front of her daughter. "Me?" Violet asked, surprised to be given such responsibility. "By myself?"

Grace nodded as she filled the kettle and set it on the stove to boil.

Violet placed the first cake upside down on the plate, then dropped a spoonful of frosting into the middle and spread it evenly over the surface. Next, she placed the second layer right-side up, on top of the first, so the flat bottoms pressed together. That way, the second cake wouldn't slide off, another lesson learned at her mother's side. She added more icing and fanned it out across the top and down the sides. When she finished, she waited for her mother's inspection.

Grace pulled the plate around to see the cake from all angles. "Stanley will be quite pleased," she finally announced, and stood slowly to make the tea.

Violet examined the cake once more and smiled at her effort. She licked the spoon and scraped the pot before setting them in the sink to soak.

"He's home!" Violet shouted, as she looked out the window and across the street. The gray late-afternoon sky stood in contrast to her delight. "And in an automobile!"

This last detail prompted even Adelaide to drag herself off the couch and over to the window. "Well I'll be," she said. "Shouldn't spoil a child like that, though. He'll just start expecting more out of this world."

Violet put on her coat and carefully picked up the cake. Grace threw her coat over her shoulders and held the door open.

"Aren't you coming with us?" Violet asked Adelaide.

"I'll be there shortly," she said. "Make sure you save me a piece of cake."

* * *

"Now who could that be?" the widow said to Stanley, who was seated in a tufted chair with a bed quilt wrapped around his legs. She winked at Doc Rodham and opened the door.

"Happy Birthday!" they all shouted as Violet entered.

"*Wszystkiego najlepszego w dniu urodzin*," the widow added.

"But my birthday's long gone," he said, as he waved his friend to sit down next to him.

"We know," the widow replied. "Three weeks today."

"You woke up for me on your birthday, remember?" Violet said, and Stanley grinned.

"Well, I didn't want to miss my party," he joked. "That's some cake. Did you make it yourself?"

"Mother made the cake, but I iced it." Violet looked around for her, eager to share the limelight.

"She never came in," the widow said gently. "Too much excitement, I suppose. We'll save her a piece."

Grace sat at the edge of her bed, shivering, her coat still draped around her shoulders.

"You were right not to go." Grief strolled toward the bed and dropped alongside her. "We don't need anyone else." He stroked her arm. "Certainly not the girl."

Grace bristled, intending to object, but surrendered to his caress. She couldn't step into that party any more than she could carry on with this charade. No longer would she pretend that life went on—without Daisy, without Owen, with only Violet to . . . what, to love? She stared down the hall at the other bedroom, bereft at the emptiness of it, and wondered what was to become of her.

About half an hour after Violet arrived, someone knocked on the widow's back door.

"It's your home now too. You may as well see who it is."

The widow took Stanley's plate and lifted the quilt. "You'll help him, Violet, won't you?"

Violet jumped up and led Stanley into the kitchen by his good arm. The widow and Doc Rodham followed closely behind.

"It's Tommy Davies," Violet announced as she pulled open the door.

"Tell him to come in," Stanley said, turning to sit down.

Violet's eyes widened. "I think you better see this for yourself."

Stanley moved toward the door, stepped out on the porch, and froze. He couldn't move. He tried, but it just wouldn't happen. Only his mouth succumbed to his will. "My Sophie!" he cried. "Is it really you?" He remained there a minute more, then leaped so quickly, Violet had to grab hold of the banister as he passed. "I've never seen such a beautiful sight in all my days!"

Violet rushed into the house, calling for her mother, yelling something about a mule.

"Finally," Adelaide said. "I've been sitting here for over two hours waiting for my cake." She held out an empty milk glass.

"Where's Mother?" Violet asked, glancing in the parlor, and back into the kitchen. "Can you believe it?" she shouted, anxious to share the news, even with the missionary. The words knocked up against each other, like agates in a game of marbles. "Mr. Sherman, he sold her the mule, the widow, he can keep her, Stanley, in Mr. Harris's barn, for now!"

"What?" Adelaide pounded the table. "Are you telling me she bought a mule for a useless cripple?"

Violet bristled. "A what?"

"I never heard of such a thing," Adelaide went on. "Well,

he's hers to spoil, I suppose. No one else would take him in." She shook her head. "Now, where's that cake?"

"I left it for Stanley!" Violet stormed into the parlor and over to the Tom Thumb piano. She sat on the stool and began to run her fingers over the dust-covered lid.

"You what?" Adelaide shouted, loud enough to be heard in the bedrooms.

Violet measured out her words without looking up. "I-left-the-cake-for-Stanley," she said. "It was his birthday."

The blow to the cheek landed so swiftly, it knocked Violet off her perch and onto the floor. "You'll think twice before you try that tone with me again. You may have the others fooled," Adelaide hissed down at the child, "but have no doubt, I can see the blackness in your soul."

Violet's eyes darted around the room, yet no one rushed in to save her. "Then you best watch out," Violet said, in a voice foreign even to her own ear. She grabbed hold of the little piano, pulled herself up, and stormed down the hall. "And that's a good sleeping couch. Just your size!" she yelled, before slamming the door to her bedroom. Once inside, she collapsed on the floor, shuddering at the boldness of her words.

Grace remained seated on the edge of her bed and listened as Adelaide stomped toward the room. "I'll not put up with such insolence," she warbled in her most evangelical voice through the half-open door.

Grief sighed audibly from his chair in the corner.

"Nor should you have to," Grace said, hands folded, head bowed. "The matter will be handled by morning."

"See to it, then," Adelaide pointed her voice toward Violet's door, "or I will." She stood at the threshold a moment longer, before marching back out to the parlor.

As daylight announced itself at the window, Violet awoke

from the soundest sleep she'd had in months. She snuggled deeper into her bed, wondering about the trouble she was in. If she never opened her eyes, she'd never have to face her mother or Adelaide; yet, if she waited for them to come in, her punishment might be worse. Finally, she shook off her covers in one quick motion, and padded down the hall. All the while, the voice repeated in her head, *You best watch out*, sounding more familiar each time.

"I trust you'll have no problem finding a more suitable arrangement," Grace was saying as Violet slipped into the parlor.

Adelaide sat on the couch, gaping at the suitcases Grace had packed and lined up at the door.

"Perhaps a family without children," Grace suggested. She eyed the plate of sugar cookies on the woman's broad lap. "Or a baker." She looked up and noticed Violet in the doorway. "And why aren't you dressed for school?"

Violet hesitated.

Adelaide sat there for a long time, wide-eyed, searching for her voice. "You're out of your mind," she finally managed. "Completely out of your mind."

Violet stepped forward as if to defend her mother, but Grace shooed her away. "I'll not have you late for school."

Violet turned back to her bedroom. A row of packed suitcases. Adelaide, stunned into silence. She couldn't be sure; it had been so long, but just for a moment, she thought, surely this is what hope looks like.

When everyone had gone, Violet to school, Adelaide to Lord knows where, Grace sat at the kitchen table, trembling.

"What made you do it?" Grief bounded into the room and pulled up a chair.

She eyed him closely. He seemed to be a study in contradictions. Rawboned, but hearty. Hollow-cheeked, but robust. He smiled broadly, revealing a piece of flesh caught in his front teeth. "You've developed quite an appetite," she finally said.

"Insatiable." He kissed her hand.

She breathed more evenly, and the trembling stopped.

Grief leaned in toward her cheek.

She nudged him away, but without conviction. "A mother's instinct," she said, finally. "You wouldn't understand."

"Come now." He sucked his teeth and laughed. "You'll have to do better than that."

She shrugged. "I'm just as surprised as you are."

Grief reached up and traced the furrows on her brow. "No matter," he assured them both. "She's gone. That's what's important." He let his finger trail down her face to the cleft of flesh between the nose and upper lip. "So tantalizing," he squealed. "It's hardly fair." He pulled her close and whispered, "Now, we just have to get rid of the girl." He took his bite. "Then we can truly be alone."

CHAPTER TWENTY-SIX

WHEN ADELAIDE LANDED on her doorstep, Myrtle Evans's curiosity ruled her tongue. "Look no further," she told the missionary, inviting her to stay as long as she liked. The story of those suitcases out on the front porch was far too tempting to pass up.

"God as my witness," Adelaide explained, holding out her cup for more coffee, "it wouldn't be overstating the truth to say I barely escaped with my life." She pointed a forkful of boiled cake in Myrtle's direction. "Not to be indelicate," she said, scraping the crumbs off her plate and into her mouth with a plump finger, "but I can hold my tongue no longer. She's off her nut. And that child of hers is no better."

Myrtle leaned forward and cut another piece of cake. The smell of cloves, cinnamon, and nutmeg filled the space between the women.

Adelaide caught a raisin as it rolled off the cake plate, onto the table, and popped it in her mouth. "Not another bite," she said, pushing her dish in Myrtle's direction.

"You've had quite a shock to your system." Myrtle served the second slice. "A little sustenance is what's needed. Now, unburden yourself. Tell me every word."

"If you insist." Adelaide shoveled an ample chunk of cake past her lips. "God as my witness," she raised her unoccupied hand, "all of this over a simple inquiry." Myrtle nudged her forward with her eyes, though the missionary hardly needed the encouragement. "I asked—out of concern, of course—how that poor crippled child would be able to ride a mule in his condition."

"A fair question." In fact, Myrtle had posed the same one to her sister Mildred the previous evening.

"I was only thinking of the boy."

"Naturally."

"Well, if that didn't set Violet off into one of her rages, screaming and kicking like a savage Indian." Adelaide belched before taking her last sip of coffee. "And that mother. Forgive me, but she lost her backbone when she lost Daisy. Never once stood up to Violet the whole time I stayed there. I'm not one to carry tales, mind you, but that woman spends her days staring off with what can best be described as a moony expression on her face. Has more bats in her belfry than the Presbyterians, and that's the truth."

Adelaide repeated her story several more times, as Myrtle seemed to have a steady stream of neighbors passing through her kitchen for a bit of conversation. After a lunch of beef and potato meat pies, Adelaide exclaimed, "Haven't had a pastie that moist since my last trip out west. It's as if Grace purposely asks the butcher for a cut of meat without any fat."

When it came time for the missionary's afternoon nap, she asked Myrtle to fetch her bags. "Milk leg's acting up," she explained, before lumbering down the hall toward the bedrooms.

On the last Friday in January, Owen collected his pay envelope, minus the rents and the family's tab at the company store, and headed home to the square without a single nickel left for beer. Knowing that Burke's didn't operate on credit—

he'd actually seen Bobby Lewis thrown out of the place for asking—Owen continued up West Market Street to a beer garden called Stirna's, five doors away from the church, right next to the Masonic Lodge. Mike Stirna, the owner, was a Lithuanian fellow, but that wouldn't keep Owen from trying it out. Joey and Bobby Lewis had both heard that a miner's first drink at the little gin mill was always free. Of course, they'd never stepped foot inside themselves, seeing that they were such good Welshmen. Buying drink from the Irish was sin enough; no need to throw good money at the Lithuanians. With that foreign tongue of theirs, not even the Poles understood them half the time. "What next," Bobby had joked, "liquor with the Turks over in Westside? Booze with the coloreds downtown?"

It made no difference to Owen. A drink was a drink, and a generous barkeep was a godsend. He wandered into the place and headed for the bar. Mike Stirna stood waiting, his muscled arms folded over his chest. Behind him, several photographs showed a younger version of the man in various boxer poses. Mike took one look at Owen, caked with coal dust and fresh snow, poured a jigger of whiskey, and slid it toward him.

"On the house. Clean out lungs."

"Much obliged," Owen said, as he wiped his mouth with the back of his blackened hand. "Any chance an honest man might get a drink or two on credit?"

Mike pulled a red ledger out from under the bar and carefully wrote the name *Owen Morgan* with a bit of pencil.

"Do I know you?" Owen asked, pushing his empty glass forward.

"Algird!" Mike yelled behind him as he refilled the whiskey. "First two drinks always on house for Mr. Owen Morgan of the Sherman Mine. After that, settle your account on payday."

Owen started, "I'm not sure I . . ." but stopped when he saw a tall man with a hitch in his gait coming down a set of steps toward him.

"A few more feet," the man said with a smile, his accent thick but understandable.

"Well, I'll be," Owen said as he threw back his drink. He hadn't seen his mine butty since they'd crawled out of the Sherman on Christmas morning.

The two men embraced, and, after some thought, Algird managed the words, "Thank you."

"My nephew," Mike said. "Still working on his English. Told me you save him. Say you no leave him behind, even with broke ankle. We always be grateful."

Owen listened as Algird spoke to Mike in his native tongue.

Mike poured a beer and handed it to Owen. "This one on Al."

Owen nodded his thanks and the men embraced once more before Algird shuffled back upstairs.

Four beers later, Owen decided he'd prefer to take his drinks at Stirna's all the time. Free drinks aside, Mike treated his customers fairly, and people kept to themselves. Owen even inquired about renting one of the rooms over the bar, but with a man like Mike running the place, they were already full-up.

"Thanks again," Owen said, as he turned to leave.

"Be seeing you tomorrow." Mike waved, and headed over to another miner who'd just walked in, fresh off the late shift. The barkeep poured a jigger of whiskey and pushed it forward. "On the house. Clean out lungs."

"Many thanks."

Recognizing the voice, Owen swung around in time to see Bobby Lewis throwing back his free drink. "And will your brother Joey be joining you?" Owen asked with a smile, knowing the two were inseparable.

"What's that?" A red-faced Bobby slid his empty glass toward Mike.

"Good to see you," Owen said, patting the man's shoulder. He ambled out of the bar into the cold January night.

Next door, the Masons were leaving for home. "Never noticed the full moon," Owen said to no one in particular. Since the Masonic brothers established the Moon Lodge in Providence long before gaslights had been in use, their meetings were traditionally held on nights when the moon was full. That way, the men would have light to guide them home.

"A fine night for a meeting," Warren Maxsom, the lodge's Worshipful Master, answered. "Good evening," he tipped his hat, "and God bless."

Owen stood in front of the building a moment longer, staring up at the plump moon.

"I'm the last one out, again." Davyd Leas smiled as he pulled shut the door to the Masonic Lodge. "How's Grace these days?" He put his arm around Owen's shoulder, an easy gesture, one that suggested talk of wives and children was a daily occurrence between the two.

Owen dropped down to adjust his boot laces, effectively freeing himself from the man's hold. He hadn't seen Davyd since the day he showed up at Burke's to talk about the elders' intention to remove him from the church rolls. Owen hadn't wanted to see him then, and he didn't want to see him now. "Grace's needs are met. Violet's too. About all I can say on the matter."

"Her time's coming soon."

"Beginning of April, near as I can figure." Owen stood, but kept his eyes to the ground.

"Heard she finally gave that missionary the boot."

Owen looked up, surprised by this bit of news. "How's that?"

"You need to look after her," Davyd said, now that he had his attention. "You're the only one who can. And you're too good of a man not to."

Owen struggled for words, but couldn't find any that fit.

"It's not right," Davyd continued, "her being alone. She needs you." He slapped Owen on the back and turned for home. "You're duty-bound," he called out, before disappearing into his house at the crest of the hill.

Owen stayed in place a moment longer, then continued down West Market Street. He got as far as the church, started toward Burke's, glanced at the full moon, and thought, Just maybe it's guiding me home.

Owen slipped around back, afraid the moon would give him away to his neighbors. He glanced past a gossamer-covered window and into the girls' room. Violet was snuggled in for the night curled on her side, Daisy's half of the bed unused. He thought of the last time he saw Violet. *You left us, remember*? And he had, no doubt about it. He couldn't blame his daughter for speaking the truth.

Ten o'clock, he thought, as he trekked to the far side of the house. Would Grace even be awake at this hour? He moved over to the window alongside the rain barrel and peered into the kitchen. From this vantage point, he could make out the right side of the room: part of the stove, half the kitchen table, and a good portion of the wall leading to the parlor. An oil lamp flickered from an unseen perch, casting shadows on a bit of ceiling.

He waited. A shadow passed across the wall. Grace was near. Owen closed his eyes, breathed in, and for moment thought he was catching the scent of lilacs in spring. When he looked again, he saw Grace, sitting at the table, a steaming cup before her. So beautiful, he thought. She dropped her head into her hands. So fragile. He wanted to go in. He willed his legs to move, but stood, frozen to the earth. *You're duty-bound*. And he was; yet duty alone could not propel him forward.

There she sat, eyes bluer than he dared to remember. Ringlets of dark hair fell around her face; a white embroidered blouse stretched over her growing breasts. She peered toward the window. Owen's heart pounded in his chest. Could she see him? Did she know he was standing just feet away? She stood up, holding her cup, and padded in the direction of the sink. He saw her swollen belly, his child growing inside her. A part of him. Did that part still exist, or had the bitterness and the whiskey killed it off? Only one way to know, he thought, and just like that, he walked up to the kitchen door and held out his fist to knock.

"What I want is to be left alone," Grace said, loud enough to be heard outside.

Does she know I'm here? Owen wondered. Is there someone else inside? He waited.

"Stop sulking," Grace said. "It doesn't become you."

Owen stood on the porch a moment longer and listened.

"It's just that I'm tired of going round and round," she said.

Owen went down the steps and back to the window. He watched as Grace grabbed hold of the oil lamp. He couldn't see anyone else inside, but he didn't have a clear view of the whole room.

"I'm going to bed." Grace turned down the wick on the lamp, extinguishing both its light and Owen's hope.

He hurried out to Spring Street and back toward his room at Burke's.

Grace sat down on her bed and stared into the dark. These

nightly go-arounds with Grief exhausted her. "Lord help me," she whispered as she curled up under the covers. "Lord forgive me." She waited with her eyes open.

After a time, she heard Grief making his way toward the bedroom. Grace lifted the blanket, inviting him in, as they both knew she would.

TO DRIVE AWAY RATS

> *Fill their holes and run-ways as fast as discovered with chloride of lime or concentrated lye. Their feet get sore and they will seek other quarters.*
>
> —*Mrs. Joe's Housekeeping Guide,* 1909

Sister Adelaide wore out her welcome, is all. Can't blame Myrtle for wanting her house back. Two weeks of waiting on someone hand and foot takes its toll. Especially when you have your own family to tend. Sometimes godly folks are harder to please than the rest of us. Not always, mind you, but more often than not, in our experience. We should know, having put up our fair share of missionaries over the years.

Can't find fault with Grace either, God bless her. Lord knows, as strange as she is these days, she did try in her own way. Suffered with Adelaide even longer than Myrtle, and that's a fact. Just wish she didn't keep to herself so much. It's not natural.

Of course, with Sister Adelaide gone west, Reverend Halloway took charge of organizing the residents of Providence for Billy Sunday's revival. The choir's been practicing three nights a week, and the elders have been calling on backsliders. The men's Sunday school class is up to two hundred, and the evening prayer meetings are going as planned. We're hoping to make an impressive showing on Mr. Sunday's first day here. We want him to think back fondly on the members of the Providence Christian Church.

And we're not the only ones excited about the campaign. All sorts of people are getting in on the act. Even Mr. Murray from the dry goods store. He's been advertising in the *Truth*. Have the paper right here.

Billy Sunday's got one month
Before converting as many men and women
From the downward path
As will be attracted
By his magnetic power.
His mission is to save souls.
Our Mission is to save you money.

A little inappropriate, if you ask us, but who are we to judge?

CHAPTER TWENTY-SEVEN

THE DAY BEFORE VIOLET'S BIRTHDAY, the widow assessed Stanley, who was finishing his lunch of kielbasa and pierogi, and asked, "You're sure you'll be all right?" Much to her amazement, Stanley had adapted quite well to life with one hand, but she still worried about him.

He wiped his mouth with a sleeve sewn closed at the end of a handless forearm and nodded. "I'll be fine. Now go. You want to get there before they close, don't you?" He took another forkful of the smoked sausage. "And remember to get the red gumdrops. Red are her favorite. And the makings for a chocolate cake. That's everyone's favorite." He took a swig of milk and laughed. When some of the milk shot out of his nose, he blotted his face with the already stained sleeve.

The widow threw extra coal into the stove, kissed the boy's head, and took her coat from the chair. "*Mój drogi*, I won't be more than an hour." She headed out the door.

She walked around to the street, still fretting over Violet's ninth birthday. She stopped in front of her statue of the Virgin Mary. Stanley had asked her repeatedly if they could have a cake ready on the exact day, February 19, in case Violet's mother wasn't up to it. He hated to think of his friend being disappointed, especially after all the trouble she went to for his party. Of course, the widow would bake a cake for Violet, but she couldn't help thinking it would mean so much more to the little girl if it were her own mother making the fuss. The widow had prayed daily on the matter, asking God if she should speak to Grace or hold her tongue, but when no answer came by the eighteenth of the month, she decided to make a trip to Murray's.

The widow offered one more prayer, this time to the Virgin. She turned around just as Grace came out on her porch with a galvanized coal bucket. "I think I have my sign," she whispered to the statue, and crossed the street.

"Let me get that for you," the widow called to Grace, taking the pail and scattering the ashes on the ice-covered steps and sidewalk. "Last thing you need to do is take a fall in your condition."

"Thank you." Grace turned to head back inside.

"Before you go," the widow said, "I'm on my way to Murray's, but I'd be happy to stop at the company store to save you a trip."

"That's very kind," Grace replied, pulling her coat closed over her belly, so the widow Lankowski couldn't see the nightgown underneath. "I have all I need, thank you."

"Thought you might be short on something for tomorrow." The widow climbed the steps, handing over the empty container. She glanced back at the Virgin Mary, took in a deep breath, and asked, "So, what is it you're doing for Violet's birthday?"

Grace grabbed the bucket and crossed the threshold.

"I'm only asking on account of Stanley," the widow quickly added. "He was so pleased with his party, he wants to make sure Violet has one of her own. He even asked me to make her a cake."

Grace stood at the door but said nothing.

The widow rushed on: "I told him I'd be happy to, but I needed to check with you first."

"I have to go now," Grace said, shutting the door.

The widow stood on the sidewalk another moment before heading down Spring Street toward the square, wondering what she would tell Stanley.

"A birthday!" Grief shouted from his place at the parlor window. "Ha! I'll give Violet what she deserves." He sliced a bony finger across his neck, and turned as if to see whether Grace had caught the gesture. She sat at the kitchen table, brow furrowed, eyes downcast. He glanced back out the window and watched as the widow turned right at the end of the block. "And if she's so concerned," he sauntered into the kitchen, "let her take the girl off our hands."

Grace lifted her head to listen.

Grief stopped halfway across the room and leaned on a chair. "Hmmm. Now there's an idea." He dropped down next to Grace and stroked her thigh. "Anything to be alone with my Gracie."

Grace shot up, as if trying to shake off a nightmare. She glared at Owen's pocket watch on the cupboard. Two o'clock. Every night, he'd placed it in the same spot, and she hadn't moved it since he'd left, except to wind it each evening before bed. I have to make the effort, she reminded herself. That's what a mother does. She moved toward the sink. "Day's half over," she said loudly, pumping water to wash up. Owen's shaving glass caught her attention, and she peered into it, searching for a familiar face. A stranger stared back at her. Pouches of dark flesh puckered under her eyes; a patch of gray hair striped the front of her head. "I've never seen this woman," Grace lamented, squinting. "Such cold eyes." She shivered. "You can't trust someone with cold eyes."

"Of course you can." Grief laughed. "I certainly do."

"I'll not look at her again," she muttered, yanking the

mirror off the window sill and sliding it behind a row of bottles on a nearby shelf. She stood there, staring absently at the polishes for furniture, stoves, and pianos. And the washday soaps for disinfecting, cleaning, and bluing. And the tin of concentrated lye. Where did that come from? she wondered, as she picked it up. Owen, of course. She shook the container. Empty. Definitely Owen. He saved everything, finding a purpose for what was used up, like making dollhouses and button holders out of cast-off cigar boxes. She looked at the can more closely. *Guaranteed to rid a house of rats, mice, cockroaches, and all kinds of troublesome vermin*. Now there's a thought. She set the container back in its spot on the bowed shelf and almost smiled.

The next morning, Violet woke with a start. Her birthday. The weight of it squeezed the air from her lungs. Nine years old. The same as Daisy. The age for baptism and junior choir. Violet had managed the impossible. She'd caught up with her sister, at least for now, but someday she'd turn ten and eleven and twelve, running ahead, leaving Daisy behind.

Violet pulled the covers over her face, blocking the sunrise, delaying the day. My ninth birthday. The sickening thought found its way to her in the dark. She threw off the quilt, but stayed in bed a few minutes longer, thinking about last year, how Father came in singing the birthday song, waking both girls before he left for work. And how Mother made two plates of *pice ar y maen*, Violet's favorite, for breakfast. Every time their mother made the little Welsh cakes, she'd tell them the story of Old Home Week, the day she'd met their father. "Couldn't speak a word, and that's the truth," she'd say, and the three of them would laugh themselves to tears.

Violet wiped her eyes on the sheet and climbed out of bed. Just then, she heard a snowball splattering against the window, and boots crunching their way through the yard. Startled, she pulled back the gossamer curtain and found Stanley pressing the words *Happy Birthday* into a fresh layer of snow. His brown corduroy jacket covered the gray union suit he wore for sleeping. Unable to pry open the frozen window, Violet pressed her face against the glass. When Stanley finished the tail of the *y*, he looked up, grinned, and waved goodbye. Violet waved back, until Stanley disappeared around the corner of the house. She ran to the side window, but he'd already passed by, leaving a crooked-winged snow angel behind. Violet smiled as she crossed the room to get ready for school.

Grace was up and dressed by nine thirty, an hour after Violet had gone, but still earlier than any other morning in months. "I'm hungry," she said, as she cooked some collar bacon and fried two eggs in the drippings.

"Something's different," Grief said, watching from his place at the table.

When Grace finished breakfast, she announced, "I'm off to call on the widow Lankowski. After that, the company store. Come if you like." She wrapped a woolen scarf around her neck and pulled on her coat.

Grief's eyes darted back and forth, following Grace's movements, but he said nothing. His cheeks faded to the color of chalk.

"I'd like to apologize for my behavior yesterday," Grace said as the widow opened the door.

"No need." The widow waved her inside.

"I can't stay but a minute." She stepped into the front room.

Grief remained on the porch and listened from the doorway.

Grace immediately noticed the elaborate lace antimacassars draped over the tops of the couch and chairs. "Your handiwork?" she asked, momentarily distracted from her purpose.

The widow nodded. "A skill from the old country."

"How lovely." Grace wandered over to an upholstered rocker and fingered one of the lace cloths. "So beautiful." When she looked up, she spied the cake under glass on a buffet. Chocolate frosting rose and fell in perfect peaks and valleys. "Oh dear," she said. "I'm too late. I wanted to invite you and Stanley over for cake, but I see—"

"What a relief," the widow said. "Mine came out so dry, no amount of icing could fix it. I wouldn't even feed it to Sophie."

"You're too kind. But you don't have to—"

"Not another word." The widow patted Grace's hand. "And I'll tell Stanley about the party as soon as he wakes. He went back to bed after breakfast this morning. Can't imagine why he's so tired." She nodded toward a tower of books and laughed. "Maybe I'm pushing him a little too hard. I just don't want him to get behind in school."

"That's admirable," Grace said, picking up a copy of *Adventures of Huckleberry Finn* and thumbing through it. She returned it to the top of the pile. "Five o'clock then?"

"Yes, and thank you." The widow smiled.

"No, thank you. I thought a great deal on your visit yesterday, and after that, something lifted inside me. I know how fond you are of Violet. Your being there for her is a great comfort." The women embraced, and the baby kicked, giving them both a start. "This one will always be with me," Grace said, rubbing her belly. She waved goodbye and headed over to the company store on Wayne Avenue.

"All is not as it appears," Grief called out. "A little over seven months along, and you're moving faster than I am today." When Grace didn't respond, he added, "Like it or not, I'm still here." He paused to catch his breath while Grace stood waiting for him in front of the store.

Adam Bonser, the storekeeper, pulled a ledger and pen from under the counter. "Good to see you, Mrs. Morgan. What'll it be today?" he asked, wiping his hands on his white apron. "I have some nice liver in back."

"Not today," Grace responded. "Four squares of chocolate, if you'll be so kind. It's my Violet's birthday."

"They grow up so fast." Mr. Bonser climbed a ladder and grabbed a box labeled *Iris Premium Chocolate* from an upper shelf.

"Not fast enough," Grief said, perching his withering frame on a pile of roofing shingles to the right of the door.

Grace threw a look in his direction, and turned back to Mr. Bonser. "It's for a marble cake," she explained. "Violet's favorite."

"I'm sure she'll be pleased." He returned to the counter, broke off four pieces, and wrapped them in brown paper.

Grace's eyes darted around the store.

"Something else I can get for you?"

"A nickel's worth of those peppermints." She bit her lower lip. "Why not spoil the birthday girl?"

"Give her what she deserves," Grief mumbled, and turned away from the pair.

Mr. Bonser scooped half a dozen pieces into a sack before recording the chocolate and the candy in his book.

"I almost forgot." Grace took a deep breath before the words tumbled out. "A tin of lye. Concentrated." And then quickly, as if an afterthought, "For the rats."

Grief turned to listen, suddenly interested again.

"This time of year?" the storekeeper asked, reaching under the counter.

Grace had gone too far and she knew it.

"Better to lay it down before winter sets in." He wrote the words *concentrated lye* in his book and handed the can across the counter. "Rats look for a warm place to cozy up just after the snow starts falling."

She pressed her lips into a smile. "Always good to have some on hand in case of an early spring thaw."

Grief chuckled, rose, and sidled up to Grace.

"I suppose," Mr. Bonser answered, "but just the same."

"Thank you," Grace said, hurriedly gathering her packages.

"See you soon, Mrs. Morgan."

She nodded and turned to go.

"Lord willing," he said, "and the creeks don't rise."

"Lord willing," she called back as she walked out the door.

CHAPTER TWENTY-EIGHT

GRACE MADE A SIMPLE WHITE CAKE BATTER and poured two-thirds of it into a pair of greased and floured pans while her baking chocolate melted in a double boiler on top of the stove. She scraped the chocolate into the remaining batter, stirred it through, and dropped spoonfuls of the mixture into the partially filled cake pans. Next, she took a knife and cut the chocolate batter into the white, to create the marbleized effect. When she was satisfied with the design, she tapped the bottoms of the pans on the kitchen table, breaking any air bubbles that might have formed inside. As she slid the cakes into the oven, Violet walked through the door.

"You're just in time," Grace said, pushing the bowl and spoon toward her daughter. "I thought I'd have to lick them myself." She held out her arms.

Confusion settled on Violet's face.

"I know, I haven't been myself lately. But that's all done with now." Grace raised her arms again.

This time Violet moved forward.

"And happy birthday, my sweet."

Grief started humming the birthday song from his overstuffed chair in the next room, but Grace ignored him.

Tears filled Violet's eyes as she awkwardly hugged her mother around the belly.

"No time for crying," Grace said, wiping Violet's face with a corner of her skirt. "Stanley and Mrs. Lankowski will be coming soon." She looked over at the cupboard to see the time, and found Owen's watch missing. Grace's heart raced. He was here. She took a breath. No matter, she reminded herself, eyeing the new tin of lye on the shelf.

"Awfully quiet out there!" Grief yelled from the parlor. "Does my Gracie need saving?" He chuckled, but stayed seated in his chair.

Grace shivered as she fought the urge to call back to him. Instead, she turned to Violet. "Wash the bowl when you're through and I'll start the icing."

When Violet was at the sink, she noticed a small purple draw-string pouch dangling from the nail that still held one of Daisy's hair ribbons. She turned questioningly toward her mother.

So that's what he was up to, Grace thought, glancing once more at the empty spot on the cupboard. "A gift," she said, "from your father, I expect." She reached over Violet's head, unhooked the tiny sack, and handed it to her daughter, wondering if Owen had made a good trade.

"Are you sure?" Violet asked, afraid to hope.

"Only one way to know."

Violet carefully loosened the fabric at the neck and pulled out a round gold locket with a matching rope chain. When she turned it around in her palm, she discovered a bunch of miniature gold violets affixed to a mother-of-pearl face. Her mouth dropped as she held out her hand to show her mother.

"It's lovely," Grace said, her voice low. "Worth every penny." She noted the joy on her daughter's face. "Open it."

Violet slid her thumbnail between both halves and carefully split them apart. She found a small piece of paper inside and unfolded it with trembling hands. She read aloud.

"*Happy birthday, doll baby. You'll always be my girl.*" Violet's eyes filled with tears once more. "He remembered," she said, tucking the note back where she found it. She handed the necklace to her mother and turned around.

Grace fastened the locket around her daughter's neck. "It's perfect." She grabbed the shaving mirror from behind the bottles. "See?"

Violet admired herself in the glass for a moment, and twirled through the kitchen. "He remembered," she said again, falling into a chair.

Stanley and the widow arrived at exactly five o'clock. "Happy birthday!" they both yelled when Violet opened the door to the parlor.

"Look," she said, holding up the necklace. "A gift from my father. He remembered!"

"Of course he did," the widow said. "He loves you." She lifted the locket and admired it from all angles. "*Piękny*. Beautiful. Treasure it always." She glanced into the kitchen at Grace and added, "He's a good man."

Grace smiled as she finished icing the cake. "And how's our Stanley?" she asked, handing the boy one of two frosting-covered spoons. "His color's good."

"And his appetite." The widow laughed. "Suffering a bit, though. Doc Rodham calls it *phantom limb*."

Grace passed the other spoon to Violet, who asked, "What's that?"

"Ain't nothing," Stanley said, licking the last of his icing.

"Isn't," the widow corrected.

"Sometimes I'd swear my hand was still there." He swatted the air over his stump with the spoon. "Gets mighty itchy. And more than once I've tried to scratch my head with it." He laughed. "Ain't nothing," he said again.

The widow smiled. "I don't know what I'm going to do

with him." She turned to Grace. "And how are you? Back on your feet, it seems."

"I've found peace." Grace watched both children laughing at the table, now eating red gumdrops out of a paper sack. "Everything is going to be fine."

After they'd eaten half the cake, two pieces each for everyone, the widow grabbed a package from the parlor and handed it to Violet. "From me and Stanley. I hope you like it."

Violet ripped open the brown paper wrapping and found a delicate white shawl inside.

"Look," Stanley said, grabbing one corner while Violet held onto the other. "They were my idea." Small lace birds, connected by the smoothest cotton threads, stood in profile along the shawl's border.

Violet sat, speechless.

"Don't you like it?" Stanley asked, handing his end back to her.

"Where are your manners?" Grace scolded. "I've never seen anything so fine."

"It's . . . it's too beautiful," Violet finally managed, and tears sprang to her eyes.

"No more beautiful than the girl sitting before me." The widow lifted Violet's chin. "Remember that." She took the wrap, unfolded it, and draped it around the girl's shoulders. "So beautiful," she said, and Grace smiled dreamily.

Later that night, as the neighborhood slept, Violet stood in front of her bedroom window, studying her shawled reflection. When she swayed back and forth, the lace birds took flight and her gold-trimmed locket winked at the quarter-moon. A few inches to the left, and two necklaces appeared in the thickest part of the glass. A phantom locket—like Stanley's hand. She bent down to see her face reflected twice. A phantom sister. That's how it was with Daisy. Violet still reached out for her when she was lonely or scared or had a story to tell. But then she remembered. She hated the remembering.

Standing up, she pressed her hand against the one reflected in the window and held it there for some time.

Around eleven o'clock, Owen staggered up the steps to his room, steadying himself on the banisters. He unlooped his suspenders and dropped into bed with his boots still on. "Happy birthday, doll baby," the closest words to prayer he'd uttered in months. "I miss you more than you'll ever know." He mumbled something about forgiveness into the pillow, and fell into a restless sleep.

Daisy and Violet came to him in a dream, beautiful in matching white dresses. Each took a hand, as he led them up a cool, green mountain, with hundreds of pine trees lining a well-worn path. Light poked through the branches, casting long shadows behind them. The girls prattled on, adding their voices to the chorus of squirrels and birds.

As they drew closer to the top, the tree line started thinning. Unimpeded, the orange sun blazed overhead, tiring the children, quieting them. Flies, gnats, and mosquitoes buzzed all around.

The three dropped, exhausted, when they reached the crest, and slept. Owen woke atop a smoldering mountain of slag, the smell of brimstone filling his nose. "Daisy," he yelled, "Violet!" suddenly aware of their absence. "Someone help me!"

Later that night, Grace also appeared to Owen. She kneeled on the ground, a spade in one hand and seeds in the other. "Let's see how high the sweet peas grow this year." She smiled at him, squinting into the glaring sun. Grace stood up, revealing the wooden cross Owen had planted at Daisy's grave.

He cried out, "Don't look back!"

She started forward, but turned to the cross. The orange flame erupted, swallowing Grace with its intensity.

Before morning, Graham visited Owen's dreams too, growler in one hand, pickax in the other. "Don't like the look of them clouds," he said.

"Stay," Owen begged.

"You know better than that."

"Then take me with you."

"And who do you suppose will look after Grace?" Graham pulled himself free, but Owen grabbed him, and the two men wrestled.

"Deliver me," Owen yelled out, "I pray thee!" He loosened his hold.

Graham rose up, turning toward the colliery.

The bright sun appeared again, this time in the mouth of the mine, illuminating Grace, Violet, and Daisy, waiting in front as Graham approached. Owen tried to move, but discovered his legs had turned to stone. He tried to call out to them, but no one answered. When they all looked at Owen, he noticed a pale figure enveloping Grace with his ropy arms. As Owen squinted, orange fire burst all around them. Daisy screamed, "Father!" and Owen woke, covered in sweat.

Owen tipped his cap when he saw Tommy Davies waiting on the stoop. "Couldn't get started this morning. Sorry if I held you up."

"No problem," the boy said, waving his hand. "Better get down the hill."

The two walked in silence until they turned right, toward the mine.

"Heard Grace got rid of that missionary," Owen said, eyes to the ground.

"Heard the same thing myself." Tommy crossed over toward the above-ground stable.

"Anybody else staying with her now?" Owen called after him.

"I wouldn't know," Tommy responded before heading inside.

Who was she talking to so late? Owen had wanted to ask the boy, but he couldn't get the words out. He knew he didn't deserve an answer. A better man would have gone inside that night to find out for himself.

At the end of his shift, Owen stood in line at the pay station off the main gangway to pick up his envelope. Same routine every two weeks.

"Number?" the pay master would ask, even though he knew Owen by name.

"One ninety-four," Owen would answer, and wait for the man to search through a wooden file box on top of the small desk.

With a few men still ahead of him, Owen mentally tabulated his earnings. He'd filled eighty of the five-ton wagons, so his pay should be forty-eight dollars before deductions, a decent wage if he actually took all of it home.

"Number?"

Owen stepped forward and answered.

The paymaster handed over an envelope without looking up. "Number?" he shouted again, as the next man moved ahead.

Owen shuffled toward the wooden cage, checking the calculations on the front of the envelope. Rent, fourteen dollars; company store, seventeen dollars; tool sharpening, one dollar—leaving him with a balance of sixteen dollars for food, drink, and his room at Burke's. He hadn't had his pay in hand five minutes yet, and he already knew he'd have to go back into debt to make it through the next two weeks. If he were allowed to shop at Murray's, he might have a chance of getting ahead, since their prices were almost a third less than those at the company store. But Owen knew that was impossible. Mine owners made it clear that if you wanted to keep your job, you'd shop in their stores.

Owen headed up the hill toward Providence Square, past Burke's on one side of the street, Stirna's on the other, and continued along West Market to Wayne Avenue. He was low on black powder and knew he'd need more before the end of the month, as they were about to start blasting a new chamber. I'll have to go on the books soon enough, Owen thought. Today I'll pay cash like a respectable man.

"I'll be right with you," Adam Bonser yelled down from the ladder as Owen entered.

"Take your time," Owen replied, looking at the picks and shovels along the wall. "I'm in no hurry."

The storekeeper returned to the counter with a box of washing powder in hand. "Now what is it you were saying, Mrs. Evans?" he asked, recording the item in his ledger.

Myrtle Evans glared at Owen. "That every man in this town needs to hear Mr. Sunday's message." She watched as Owen crossed over to look at hoes and seeds. "Backsliders in particular. Those who have taken to the drink."

Mr. Bonser nodded. "And is there anything else I can get you today?"

Myrtle looked down at her list. "Four cans of mock turtle soup."

"Be right back," he said, disappearing behind a curtain.

"Yes sir," Myrtle continued in spite of Mr. Bonser's temporary absence, "Billy Sunday's crusade may be just the answer for some folks." She turned quickly to watch Owen's reaction. She saw none. "I hear they're just about finished with the tabernacle," she said, stepping closer, trying to catch his attention. "Installed electric lights, chairs, a platform for the choir, and a pulpit in front."

Finally, Owen nodded out of politeness, which Myrtle mistook for interest. "All that's left is to lay the sawdust on the aisles, so sinners can *hit the sawdust trail,* as Mr. Sunday is so fond of saying."

When Mr. Bonser returned with the soup, Myrtle checked her list. "Two yeast cakes and a package of currants ought to do me for the week."

Mr. Bonser recorded the additional items, then climbed back up the ladder.

"According to the *Times*," Myrtle went on, "Billy Sunday will be arriving at the Lackawanna train station next Saturday, but he won't start preaching till Sunday morning."

Owen stepped up to the counter, carrying his black powder.

"And will we be seeing you there, Mr. Morgan?" Myrtle asked.

"We?"

"The good Christians of this fair city, of course. We're trying to make sure Mr. Sunday's crusade is well-attended."

"I'm sure a man like Sunday won't have any problem filling the pews. And besides, with good Christians like yourself, there won't be any room left for an honest sinner like me."

Myrtle ignored Owen's remark, and turned back to Mr. Bonser. "It's a seven-week campaign, but if you ask me, that first Sunday is most important. Everyone from Providence Christian will certainly be there. Members in good standing, that is." She gathered her packages. "And since you're closed on Sundays, you'll have no problem making at least one of the three services planned that day."

Mr. Bonser nodded. "I'll try my best." He turned away

from her. "Now what can I do for you, Owen?"

Myrtle started for the door, pausing briefly to look at flower seeds on a shelf. "Grace always has such a colorful garden. Just hope she can pull herself together enough to tend it this spring. Poor thing. Always talking to herself."

Owen shot around. "With all due respect, Myrtle, Grace is none of your concern."

"Then whose concern is she?" Myrtle held onto him with her eyes. "Certainly not yours, Owen Morgan. Certainly not yours." She turned on her heel and left the store.

Owen looked back at Mr. Bonser who was busying himself with his ledger. "What do I owe?" he asked, pulling the pay envelope from his pocket.

"A dollar fifty for the powder." The storekeeper flipped through his book till he found the letter *M*. "Plus thirty-five cents for Mrs. Morgan's purchases." He ran his finger down the page. "Peppermints, baking chocolate, lye."

Owen plucked two one-dollar bills from his envelope.

"Did Violet enjoy her party?" Mr. Bonser slid the book back under the counter and pulled out a cigar box to make change. He pushed fifteen cents across the counter, as Alice Harris came into the store with her little girl. "Be right with you," Mr. Bonser said.

Owen pocketed the change but stayed put. "Lye?"

"For the rats."

"What rats?"

"Can't say exactly." Mr. Bonser tucked the cigar box under the counter. "She seemed to be worried, though. Something about a spring thaw. I told her better to put lye before the first snow."

"I did that," Owen commented to himself. "Are you sure you heard her right?"

"Yes sir. Said so herself." He pulled out his ledger again. "Oh well, you know women. Always making a problem when they can't seem to find one." He laughed, then caught himself. "Pardon me, Owen. No harm intended. My tongue gets away from me sometimes." He blushed as he hurried over to Mrs. Harris. "What can I get for you today?"

Owen tipped his hat in Alice's direction, and walked out the door. The thought of the lye nagged at him all the way over to Market Street and down the hill. Laying down lye this time of year would be like throwing money away. Not that money was the problem. No. He was the problem. If he wasn't drinking, he could be there to take care of the rats, and that was the truth. But knowing a thing and acting on it were about as different as watching a bird soar and being able to fly. Grace doesn't know any better, he told himself, as he pulled open the door to Stirna's.

CHAPTER TWENTY-NINE

ON SATURDAY MORNING, February 28, Betty Leas and the entire choir from the Providence Christian Church took the streetcar to the tabernacle downtown. This would be their last group rehearsal before the official opening of the Billy Sunday campaign the following day. Banners announcing, *Scranton for Christ*, *Get Right with God*, and *To-day is the Day of Salvation* stretched across the wall. Red, white, and blue buntings and American flags decorated the wooden poles supporting the building's unfinished ceiling. Betty pointed to the bare lightbulbs strung along the rafters. "I see the electricity's finally working."

"By the grace of God," Mr. Gill said and smiled.

Mr. Gill led the singers down aisles of sawdust to their seats up front where D.D. Ackley, the official pianist, and Homer Rodeheaver, the music director, waited for all the choirs from around the city to come together. Betty counted heads one last time to make sure everyone from Providence Christian had made it. Forty-five. She offered up a silent prayer of thanks. After yesterday's dressing down, no one wanted to be late. When several women from the Methodist church had tried to sneak in after the appointed hour, Mr. Rodeheaver had stopped the rehearsal and warned, "You've got to be Johnny-on-the-spot if you want to be part of Mr. Sunday's choir! There are others ready to take your place. I only need to ask."

After all the people had assembled in front, Mr. Rodeheaver thanked them for their punctuality. He tapped his baton, looked over at Mr. Ackley, and said, "'I'm Bound for the Promised Land.' Let's begin."

"I wish you'd reconsider," Louise said to Grace over an afternoon cup of tea. "I don't like the thought of leaving you, so close to your time." Grace tried to wave her off, but Louise continued: "There's too many of us planning to go see Billy Sunday tomorrow. Won't even be a service at the church."

"I'll be around in the morning and afternoon," Hattie said, entering the kitchen without knocking. "Don't want to hear another word about it."

"Then I'll stay back in the evening," Louise said. "No need to go to all the revival meetings in a day, anyhow."

"The whole congregation will be attending tomorrow, and I'll not have the two of you staying behind on account of me." Grace stood up, poured another cup of tea, and set it out for her sister.

"But if we're all downtown," Hattie said, dusting a few errant snowflakes off her coat before sitting, "no one will be around to look after you."

"She has me," Grief said, pulling off his tie and tucking it into his coat pocket.

Grace stood up with her hand on her back and added a shovel of coal to the stove. "I'm a month out, and I've never gone before my time. Besides, I won't be alone. Violet will be here with me."

"And what can a child do if the baby comes early?" Hattie asked as she warmed her hands on the cup.

"Fetch the doctor," Grace answered. "If need be."

Violet walked into the kitchen looking for her cigar-box dollhouse.

"Speak of the devil," Grief said, and laughed.

"Hello, sweetheart." Hattie stretched out her hands. "How's my girl?" She hugged Violet, pushed her back, and held her at arm's length. "Let me look at you." She twirled her around and peered at Louise. "Can you believe she's nine years old already? Where does the time go?"

"And so beautiful," Louise said. "Now Violet, do you think you're old enough to keep an eye on your mother tomorrow?"

"Yes ma'am," she said, finding the box on the cupboard and tucking it under her arm.

"And you'll see that she gets her sleep?" Hattie added.

Violet glanced at her mother for some indication of how to answer. It had never occurred to her to tell her mother when to go to bed.

"Not to worry," Grace said. "I'll be sound asleep by nightfall."

"We'll both be," Grief chimed in, glancing at the lye on the shelf before slipping out of the room.

As was his custom, Billy Sunday arrived at the Lackawanna train station with little fanfare. He always liked to slip into a city before dusk on a Saturday, saving most of the excitement for the revival itself. Sturges and Sherman were among the handful of dignitaries who met his train, eager to see the man who preached a message of "subservience on earth for rewards in heaven." Such notions served the purposes of businessmen eager to quell the rumblings of the working class. And Sunday's natural sincerity only made his words that much more effective.

Those waiting for the evangelist spotted him easily as he stepped down from the train. Though in his early fifties, Sunday still had the broad chest and narrow hips of an athlete. He often credited his years as a professional baseball player for the stamina he displayed at the pulpit.

"Neat as a pin," Sturges remarked as Sunday approached. He wore a fur-trimmed coat and a Dakota hat, similar to a fedora but with a higher crown and curled brim.

"A pleasure to finally meet you," George Sherman said, stretching out his hand.

"Always a pleasure to do the Lord's work," Sunday returned with a smile.

Once a porter secured Sunday's bags, the men ushered him inside the train station, where a pressman from the *Truth* stood waiting. "Welcome to the Electric City," he called out. "Cleanest town around."

"Glad to hear it," Sunday said, turning to get a good look at the grand lobby with its mosaic floors, marble walls, and vaulted stained-glass ceiling. "A mighty fine structure."

"Five stories high," Sturges said. "We're quite proud of her."

"Can't say I blame you." Sunday took off his hat. "Imagine the sermons I could preach here." All of the men smiled.

The reporter glanced at his tablet. "If I may, sir, where will you be staying while you're with us?

"Over on Monroe Avenue. The Christys, one of Scranton's finest families, have invited me to share their home."

"And what is it you hope to accomplish during your Scranton campaign?"

"Well, son, I'm here to assault evil." Billy Sunday set his hat on a bench and threw a fist into his open palm. "I'd like to see every booze fighter get on the water wagon." He took off his jacket, swung a leg up on the seat, and leaned in. "Every sinner hit the sawdust trail."

A passerby yelled, "Amen, brother!"

Travelers made their way over to listen.

"You know," Sunday said, looking around at the gathering crowd, "I am familiar to some extent with the people of this fair city. You are a zealous, earnest bunch, and I know you will fight for the Lord."

A ticket agent, caught up in the excitement, shouted, "Jesus saves!" from his booth to the right of the entrance.

Sunday cupped his ear. "Do you hear that? The Lord is working already." He loosened his tie. "I've just come off my campaign in Pittsburgh, and it seems to me that there is a great big wave sweeping across this state. A great big thirst for the Gospel. Now is the accepted time. Today is the day of Salvation. *Believe in the Lord Jesus Christ and ye shall be saved.*" Sunday dropped his foot, put on his jacket, pushed up the knot on his tie, and asked, "Does that answer your question?"

Everyone around him applauded.

"Sorry about that, son. I'm a little enthusiastic when it comes to serving our Lord." He laughed. "Anything else you need to know?"

The journalist looked back at his tablet. "Your plans for tomorrow?"

"Three services. Ten, two, and seven thirty. That gives everyone a chance to come." Sunday waited, allowing the man to take down the information, before beginning again. "Folks can expect rousing sermons and the most inspiring music on the Atlantic Coast. Best choirs yet, according to my song director. Had sixteen hundred and sixty singers show up, but we only have capacity for fourteen sixty. Actually had to turn two hundred away. That's a first for Billy Sunday."

"And any advice for those who will be attending?"

"No children in arms. That's why we set up a nursery at the YWCA. And it's hats off starting tomorrow. The ladies may wear veils, but that's it. Don't want to block anyone's view with all those feathers and such."

"Anything else?" the reporter joked.

"Well, as long as you're asking, tell your readers that I require the utmost silence and quiet during my sermons. I like to give everyone a chance to hear. I must therefore ask people to refrain from coughing. If you have to cough, place your handkerchief over your mouth."

The reporter looked up quizzically. "I see." He decided to change the subject. "And when might we expect to see Mrs. Sunday?"

"Well now, you have me there. Ma Sunday is supposed to be here tomorrow, but I heard a few of the old timers talking about snow, so we'll have to wait and see," Sunday said, putting his hat on.

"That's enough for now," Sturges said, placing his hand on the evangelist's back. "We have a police escort waiting out front. Mr. Sunday needs his rest if he's to start preaching tomorrow." All of the men nodded as Sturges led the guest out through a pair of twelve-foot-tall mahogany-framed doors.

Owen rested his foot on the railing while Mike Stirna poured him another shot.

"To early spring," Mike said, pushing the whiskey forward. "Can't hardly believe tomorrow is first of March. The robins will sing before we know."

"Let's have a drink!" a customer yelled from the opposite end of the room.

"Hold your horses!" Mike shouted back, returning a bottle of Old Forester to its shelf. "In hurry to nowhere," he said to Owen. "Salesmen. They all same." He headed down the bar and asked, "Now, what'll it be?"

The first of March. The words were a blow to Owen's gut. How can that be? He tried to steady his trembling hand long enough to grab hold of his drink. Daisy's birthday! He spilled his whiskey across the marble-topped surface.

"Sorry," he called down to Mike, who came running with a towel.

"No problem," Mike said, wiping down the bar. "Just give me minute, and I'll get you another."

Owen held up his hand. "No thanks." He turned to leave.

"Everything all right, Mr. Morgan?"

Owen left without another word.

Grace, he thought, as he lay on his bed. What must she be going through tonight? Owen stood up, went over to his dresser, and grabbed the cardboard cutout Violet had left behind on Christmas morning. A father, dressed in a paper suit and tie, clean shaven, smiling, dependable. I've let them down, he thought. He crumpled the doll and threw it across the room. His legs quivered and gave out, sending him to his knees. Suddenly aware of his position, he bowed his head and clasped his hands in front of him. When the words refused to follow, he collapsed in a heap on the floor.

Grief slipped into the kitchen, pausing a moment to gaze at Grace. "You seem troubled," he said, curling a lock of her hair around his finger.

Grace stood up to bank the fire before going to bed. "How is it that none of them remembered?"

"I remembered," Grief said, coming up behind her, smelling her hair. "I always remember." He lifted the strands and sliced them across his teeth.

Grace returned to the table and caressed the gilded frame that held Daisy's baptism picture. "Just as well."

"They don't deserve her," Grief said. "We both know it's true."

Grace kissed two fingers and pressed them on Daisy's cheek. They'd be together soon enough.

Grief stepped back to look at Grace. "Now, just what kind of ideas are you spinning in that pretty head of yours?"

She stared straight into his eyes. "I thought you could see all my fears."

"That's precisely the problem." He lifted the oil lamp to her face, and watched her lips press into a smile. "You no longer have any fears."

Grace erupted into unbridled laughter. "If you only knew."

Violet sat in bed with her knees folded into her chest, the blanket pulled up to her chin, listening to her mother cackle in the kitchen. What's going on with her? A chilling silence supplanted the maniacal laughter, as if daring Violet to ask again. Terrified, she buried herself under the covers till morning.

EGGSHELLS TO CLEAN BOTTLES

Eggshells dried and crushed are the very best bottle cleaner for a baby's bottle; use rain water and soap or hard water and soda.

—*Mrs. Joe's Housekeeping Guide,* 1909

Grace seems to be getting on. Won't be any time now. You just have to look at her to know she's having another girl. Dark circles under the eyes, hollow cheeks, spotty complexion. Daughters steal your beauty when you're carrying them. We can all see it when we look at her, especially Pearl Williams, though she's only birthed boys.

Lucky for us, Pearl happened to be at the train station when Mr. Sunday pulled into Scranton. Had to pick up that sister of hers from upstate New York. A pretty enough girl, even with the clubfoot. She's the one who got herself in trouble with that boy from Henryville, not that it's our business. Pearl said Sunday's face shone about as bright as those patent-leather shoes he wears. And he has himself a great big smile—the kind that lets a man get away with a thing or two. That's probably how he got so many converts. Thank goodness for us he's a man of the cloth.

Don't imagine Grace will be in any condition to go see Mr. Sunday. Seems a shame. He'd do her good, most likely. Leastways, it couldn't hurt. Lord knows we've tried to bring her around. Keep coming up empty-handed. Maybe Mr. Sunday would have better luck. Then again, as Mildred reminded us,

"God helps those who help themselves." Claimed to be quoting the Bible, but we know better. Still, she has a point.

Grace does need to straighten up. We've all said it. Not to Grace, of course. She wouldn't listen. Keeps to herself most days. Talks to the air as near as we can figure. Stopped going to church altogether. We pity her, truly, but she has to mend her ways before it's too late. If she keeps knocking at the devil's door, someone's bound to answer.

CHAPTER THIRTY

OWEN WOKE TO THE PEAL of the church bell, the same one that had tolled Daisy's death. He sat up on the wooden floor, leaned against the dresser, and shook the numbness out of his left arm. What have I become? he thought, pulling himself up. He shuffled over to the uncurtained window and tipped his head toward a clear blue sky. More like the first of May, not March. The bell rang a second time, demanding his attention. He looked across the street at Providence Christian Church. Grace. Will she be there today? Below the steeple, a perfect circle of stained glass beckoned him with fingers of morning sun. He walked back to his dresser, took out the suit of clothes he'd gotten from the house the day he'd picked up his watch, and went over to the basin to wash up.

Owen turned the handle on the large wooden church door and entered the sanctuary. The sun burned through the jewel-colored windows, lighting up the empty pews. Confused, he ambled back outside, sat down on the steps, and started to snicker. "Well, isn't that something?" he said aloud to himself. "I finally show up and no one's home. God sure does have himself a sense of humor." He pondered the empty church a moment longer.

"Everyone's downtown," Evan Evans Sr. yelled from the

front of his wagon, as he pulled up alongside the church. Myrtle, her sister Mildred, and young Evan sat in back. "Billy Sunday's preaching."

"Will Grace be there?" Owen called down.

"Yours is the last face that woman needs to see, today of all days!" Myrtle shouted, before slapping her husband on the back and making him pull away.

She's right, Owen thought as he stood up. He glanced over at Burke's, then up at Stirna's. "Sunday blue laws," he said to himself, and started for town in search of a speakeasy willing to serve him on the Lord's Day.

"You'll find out soon enough," Grace said, pointing her spoon toward an empty chair. "How many times do I have to tell you that patience is a virtue?"

Violet watched the one-sided conversation from the doorway. Dread soured in her stomach and rose up in her throat. She shuffled into the kitchen and sat down without saying a word.

"You startled me." Grace turned to her daughter and smiled. "I never heard you come in." She stood up, poured a glass of milk, and slid it toward Violet. "I have a surprise for you," she said, grabbing a towel-covered plate. "I made them this morning while you were sleeping."

Violet removed the cover and found a dozen Welsh cakes stacked in front of her. "Thank you," she managed as fear coursed through her belly. "I'll have one in a minute."

"I remember the day I met your father . . ." Grace looked over at the empty chair and her voice trailed off. She stepped over to the shelf, lifted the tin labeled, *Concentrated Lye*, and set it back in its place. "Plenty of time," she said, shaking her head.

"For what?" Violet asked.

"For anything. Your heart's desire. What is it you'd like

to do today?" Grace poured herself a cup of tea and sat down at the table. "Of course, with me being this far along, whatever it is will have to be close to home. It would've been nice to see Billy Sunday, though. Won't get that chance again." She spooned cream off the top of the milk and stirred it into her cup. White foam bubbled on top. "That's money in your pocket," she said and laughed. "Learned that from your father." She paused. "Did I ever tell you?"

Violet shook her head.

"Something his mother taught him. Your grandmother, God rest her soul. Don't know why. Just the same." She scooped the foam and handed the spoon to Violet. "That's money in your pocket." Grace sat quietly for a minute, looking off, through the window. "He's a good man," she finally said, "your father. We must always remember that, no matter what happens."

The widow took Stanley's hand and led him toward the tabernacle. They fell into step with all the other folks making their way in to see Billy Sunday's first service. The blazing sun melted what little snow was left on the ground, and mud oozed up between the wooden sidewalks. "A glorious day," the widow remarked as Myrtle Evans and her family approached.

"What a pleasant surprise," Myrtle said. "Nice to see you're not tied to some pope over in Italy when it comes to Christian activities."

Mildred nodded. "Especially since Mr. Sunday seems to be so tolerant of you Catholics."

"*Zeby cie kaczka kopnęła*," the widow replied. She had always liked this particular expression from the old country: *Let a duck kick you*. It was mild enough to suggest no real harm, yet pointed enough to be satisfying.

Myrtle noticed Stanley chuckling and said to the widow, "Pardon?"

The widow looked wide-eyed at the boy, suddenly realizing he'd learned more Polish in his time with her than she'd imagined. "A blessing for those around me," she lied.

"Quack, quack," Stanley mumbled under his breath, and laughed.

Electrified bulbs burned overhead as an usher guided the widow and Stanley down one of many aisles covered in cinders, sawdust, and pine shavings.

"Smells like Mr. Harris's barn," Stanley said. "I wish Sophie could be here to see this."

The widow chortled as she slid halfway down the length of a makeshift pew. "Now wouldn't that be a story. The Catholics who brought their mule to meet Mr. Sunday." She grinned and tussled Stanley's hair. "Myrtle Evans would have a field day with that one." This got them both laughing so hard, the people in front of them turned and glared.

Stanley stared right back and said, "*Zeby cie kaczka kopnęła*," with a perfect Polish accent.

Shock flashed across the widow's face, but wouldn't settle in. Some other expression worked its way forward. "Quack, quack," she managed just before a fit of giggles took hold of the pair again.

The widow knew they needed to compose themselves, so she and Stanley stopped looking at each other, and focused on the tabernacle. And they did eventually settle, with no more than an occasional hiccup or two of laughter.

White muslin stretched across an empty stage, twenty feet wide and ten feet tall, with Preachers' Row on the right and dignitaries on the left. Mayor Jermyn sat in the front, waiting to be introduced. Jury-rigged telephone lines and telegraph instruments surrounded the platform, guaranteeing quick reporting and extra editions of local newspapers. Behind the pulpit, choir members from all over Scranton sang hymns of invitation in preparation for Billy Sunday's appearance.

"We'd like to sit up close," Mildred Evans told the usher who was guiding her down the sawdust-covered aisle toward the same pew where the widow and Stanley sat.

"I'm sorry, ma'am, the front seats are reserved."

"Well, then move over," Mildred said, tapping Stanley on the shoulder. "There's nothing wrong with your legs, now is there?"

The widow pursed her lips as she slid down to the end of the row with the boy in hand.

At his mother's urging, Evan Two-Times slid in next to Stanley.

The widow bristled. If Evan thought he was going to sit there and make unkind remarks to Stanley, he had another think coming. She eyed the troublemaker and waited.

Evan stared at Stanley's handless forearm for a couple of minutes. "Can I see?"

Stanley smiled, unpinned the cover, and pulled back a corner, before the widow could react. "Look!" he said proudly. Red ropes of thickened flesh twisted across the surface. "Gets itchy sometimes," he explained, scratching the stump.

"Stanley!" the widow yelled. "Just what do you think you're doing?"

He quickly pulled the cover over, and Evan pinned it in place. Both boys giggled and nudged each other playfully.

When everyone had settled into their seats, Homer Rodeheaver stepped onto the platform, turned to the choir, and applauded. "As Mr. Sunday's music director, I must say, it's been a blessing to work with so many trained voices. Beautiful." He started to clap again, and the audience joined in. "Just beautiful," he repeated at the end of the applause. "Now, before Billy Sunday takes the pulpit, I'd like to read the roll call of organizations which have come to attend this meeting in a body." He peered out into the reserved sections. "We are supposed to have with us today the Boy Scouts of Green Ridge. Are you here? Rise up and let us have a look at you."

About thirty boys between the ages of ten and eighteen stood at their seats.

"My, how good you look. What a nice healthy lot of young people you are and how well the uniforms fit you. Now tell me your favorite song, and we'll sing it for you."

"'Blessed Assurance'!" the smallest boy yelled.

Mr. Rodeheaver turned to Mr. Ackley at the piano and said, "You heard the man," and everyone at the revival stood up to sing.

After the song ended, the music director called out, "Where are the iron workers from the Scranton labor unions?" Six rows of people stood. "I see you have brought your wives along with you too, eh? That is wise. Never let the boys go out alone. Not even to the tabernacle. Now, what is your favorite song?"

"'The Old Rugged Cross'!" one of the men shouted, and Mr. Ackley began playing again.

The roll call continued in this fashion for about an hour, ending with the Masons from the Moon Lodge in Providence. "A fine Christian organization," Rodeheaver said. "Brothers in Christ. And who is your Worshipful Master?"

Warren Maxsom raised his hand.

"We'll be pleased to sing a song for you. Tell me your favorite."

"With all due respect," Warren said, "the Boy Scouts got to it first."

"'Blessed Assurance,'" Rodeheaver said to Ackley. "A finer song we'll never hear." Ackley nodded in agreement and began to play the tune a second time.

At the end of the song, the crowd of about two thousand noticed for the first time that Billy Sunday had somehow slipped in, and now stood waiting on the platform behind a simple wooden pulpit. Women smoothed their skirts and men buttoned their jackets. Even the children knew to straighten up on the hard wooden benches, thanks in equal parts to instinct and stern parental warnings received earlier that morning.

"I have a message that burns its way into your soul and into my heart!" Billy Sunday shouted. "My words may be strong, but they are bloodred with conviction!" He pounded his fist against the pulpit and leaped out to the front of the platform. "I must cry out!"

Several of the dignitaries appeared to be confused by Sunday's rapid-fire style of speaking, but women in the congregation waved white handkerchiefs and cried out, "Amen!"

"*Be not deceived*, Paul tells us in Galatians, *God is not mocked: for whatsoever a man soweth, that shall he also reap*." Sunday pulled out his handkerchief and patted his damp face. "I know of no more suitable text in all the Bible for the subject that I have in hand for this morning's service." He paused as if mustering fortitude for a distasteful chore. "For-bid-den a-muse-ments." He stretched each crude syllable to its limit, before spitting into his hanky. "I'm speaking of theatre, cards, and dance." Several heads bobbed along Preachers' Row.

"You know that the theatre had its beginning in the church and was intended to be the handmaid of religion." Sunday pranced back and forth across the length of the platform, daring every fixed eye to keep up with him. "It produced so much fuss and trouble that they were compelled to drop it. Unless the theatre is redeemed, it will fall by its own stinking rottenness." He pulled a wooden bow back chair forward, swung his foot upon the seat, and pointed at the people in front of him. "If you want obscenity, you will find it in the theatre. Nowadays, your show has to be tainted in order to gather the coin."

Spontaneous "Amens" erupted from the crowd.

"The capacity for amusing people along decent lines seems to have gone by. Instead, you will find divorce smeared all over the stage, and adultery even lurking in the flies. Why, there are shows where they have beds right in the middle of the stage, and carryings-on which, if they happened in your own homes, would result in a visit from the police!"

About ten rows back, Miss Reese, the third grade teacher, swooned and dropped onto the sawdust-covered aisle. Those nearby fanned her until two men from the temporary first-aid station arrived and carried her out.

Billy Sunday kept on preaching to a mesmerized crowd: "I suppose some of you may wince at the plainness with which I speak, but remember, it costs me severe pangs of regret to be compelled to do it." He grabbed hold of the chair, pointed it backward, and straddled the seat. "You don't thrash the devil with highfalutin words."

Stanley and Evan sat in the pew with their mouths hanging open. Neither one had ever seen the likes of Billy Sunday. Occasionally, the widow would glance at the boys, making sure Stanley in particular hadn't had an attack of nerves with all the excitement. At one point he pulled on the widow's sleeve and whispered, "This is even better than the minstrel show."

"*Boże. Boże*," was all she could manage as she looked at the boy in wonder.

"A-muse-ments." Sunday stretched the word, but in a more reasoned tone this time. He leaned forward in his chair, striking a relaxed pose. "People say to me, *Billy, what harm can come from a game of cards*?" He smiled at his audience like a bulldog before it attacks. "Ever since the day that cards were invented," Sunday shouted, "they have been the tools of the gambler!" He stood up and climbed onto the chair. "I say, if you have any cards in your home, you had better throw them in the fire or else throw your Bibles in the furnace! The two won't mix!"

Many in the audience averted their eyes in shame.

"Oh, you need not gasp! I am handing it to you straight!" He took off his brown suit jacket, twirled it overhead, and threw it to the back of the platform. "There is no use having Bibles around your house if you are going to make a joke of His Word by playing Bridge. Every pack of cards is but another stepping stone to hell!" He jumped off the chair, walked to the edge of the stage, crouched down, and leaned over. Cupping his hands around his mouth, he directed his next words toward hell. "There's a square-shooter in Scranton by the name of Billy Sunday, and he's gunning for you, Devil."

The crowd applauded, wept, and praised the Lord. Sunday mopped up his sweat and wrung out his handkerchief. He picked up an imaginary bat and hit an imaginary ball. Cheers rose from the benches. The evangelist smiled, and everyone clapped once more.

Stanley poked at the widow's arms. "An out-of-the-park home run!" he yelled, and clapped his hand against his thigh.

The widow's eyes darted to Myrtle and Mildred with their arms flung straight up in the air. She glanced about the tabernacle and noticed a similar spectacle repeating itself throughout the crowd. She'd never seen such behavior in a house of God.

"A-muse-ments!" he shouted for the third and final time. "The dance." He grabbed his jacket before stepping behind the pulpit once more. "It's a hugging match set to music." He put the jacket on slowly, smoothed the lapels, and pounded his fist into the podium. "The dance is a sexual love feast!"

Startled by such vulgarity, the widow shifted uneasily, and noticed that many in the audience were doing the same.

"The church is honeycombed with the rottenness of society. Somebody has to come out and run the risk of incurring your displeasure." He waited for everyone to settle, and continued, undeterred: "The lowest-down rascal in any community is a dancing Methodist!"

At that, Myrtle Evans stood up and hollered, "Hallelujah!" She grabbed her husband by the collar and yanked him up. "Nothing worse than a Methodist!" she shouted.

"Do you know," Billy Sunday went on, "that three-fourths of all the girls who are ruined owe their downfall to dance? People say to me, *Billy, but didn't they dance in the Bible?* Yes, they danced in the Bible." He took a beat. "And they committed adultery too!" He pounded his fist again, headed to the front of the platform, and raised his hands to his mouth as a megaphone. "And they got punished!"

"That's telling them, Billy!" Mayor Jermyn shouted. Then, remembering his position, he sat back in his seat.

"When you sow the theatre, you reap adulterers!"

Row after row stood and applauded.

"If you sow card games, you reap a bunch of gamblers. When you sow the dance, you reap a crop of brothels."

Applause thundered throughout the tabernacle.

Billy Sunday waited a full minute for the audience to calm down. "And if you sow saloons, you reap a lot of puking drunkards." He paused and smiled. "But that's another sermon for another service." He returned to the pulpit and closed his eyes. "Let us pray . . . Lord," he yelled up to the rafters, "it's me, Billy!"

Heads dipped in prayer, but most eyes stayed open to

see what the evangelist had in store.

Sunday glanced across the audience. "I want to thank you for this throng before me." He looked up with a beatific smile, as if he could see God Himself. "Help them this morning. Let them know that if they accept Jesus as their Lord and Savior, they will be saved. Go over to Providence and Bull's Head. Go to Green Ridge, Hyde Park, and every square foot of this valley. Don't miss anybody, Jesus. Go downtown to the hotels and respectable businesses, but don't forget to stop by the theatres and brothels. Save them all, Jesus. The policemen, the firemen, the fellows who deliver the mail. And the lawyers. Oh, Jesus, there's a bunch that needs lots of help." He grinned, and at least half the audience smiled back at him. Sunday pointed toward a dozen men sitting at the telegraph machines and telephone lines. "And the newspapers. Aren't you proud of them, Lord?" He turned around. "And bless the singers sitting behind me." He looked over at his musical director sitting by the piano. "How many churches, Rody?"

"Fifty-three," Mr. Rodeheaver said.

"That's right. Bless all fifty-three churches serving in this choir." Sunday turned back around. "And the miners, Lord, especially the miners. They labor underground to supply our great nation with the anthracite that sustains us. Help all these fine people to know that there's nobody but Jesus Christ who can save them. Inspire them to hit the sawdust trail this very day. Amen."

The audience returned a rousing, "Amen!"

Mr. Ackley pulled his stool closer to the piano and began to play "Onward Christian Soldiers," one of several hymns Sunday liked to use when he invited folks to come down front to be saved. People streamed out of their seats and into the aisles. The sawdust muffled the sound of their footsteps as they moved forward. The evangelist personally greeted each "trail hitter" with a welcoming smile and a glad handshake before directing him or her toward representatives from local churches. As Billy Sunday often said, "You can't no more go to heaven without joining the church than you can go to England without crossing the ocean."

Janet Paul, one of Sunday's many assistants, sat next to him, counting in an even voice for the benefit of the pressmen. "Eighty-one souls saved, eighty-two, eighty-three, eighty-four souls saved . . ."

Stanley tugged on the widow's sleeve. "I want to hit the trail!"

She looked around at the frenzied crowd pushing out of the pews. "I'm afraid you'll get trampled," she said.

"But I'm being called forward!"

She looked at him skeptically at first. "If you think so." She smiled. "*Mój drogi*, I suppose it is all right. We all pray to the same God." She stood up. "I'm going with you, though."

"We're already saved," Myrtle said, as the two passed by. "No need for us to go up front."

"At least I'll be able to say I met Billy Sunday," Stanley countered as he stepped into the aisle.

The widow puffed up as she glanced at Myrtle, who seemed to be considering his point.

"It's not every day a fellow gets to meet a famous ballplayer," the boy added.

The widow turned back to see if Myrtle had caught this last remark, before pushing Stanley forward in silence.

When Janet Paul called out her last count, "Two hundred and ninety-seven souls saved!" Sunday declared it to be a "goodly number." Homer Rodeheaver picked up his trombone and played "Stand Up for Jesus," signaling the ushers to take up the collection.

At the conclusion of the service, Billy Sunday said, "I expect everyone back at two o'clock." He smiled. "And don't forget to bring a friend."

CHAPTER THIRTY-ONE

OWEN TREKKED DOWNTOWN IN SEARCH of a gin mill. He had wanted to do right by Grace, but Myrtle had a point. Seeing him, "today of all days," would be too difficult, especially with the baby a month or so out. Better to stay away from her. Yet whenever he thought about Grace buying that tin of lye, he couldn't help feeling she needed him. On one hand, Grace ought to know better than to put down lye this time of year. Then again, why should she know better? Wasn't that a husband's job? Shouldn't he be there to spread lye, lift sacks of flour, and tend ashes? His place was with her. But she'd never take him back as long as he was drinking, and God as his witness, he needed to drink. This battle continued inside his head until he stopped in front of a speakeasy, a few blocks shy of the tabernacle.

As was the custom at such places, he headed around back and checked in all directions before knocking. A man on the other side of the door eyed Owen through a peephole and hollered out, "We're not open on Sundays. It's the law in this town!" Owen shoved his hands into his pockets, feeling the cold for the first time that day, and turned to leave. He glanced up at the graying sky, and took note of the snowflakes starting to fall around him.

"Look where you're going!" a man shouted.

"Sorry," Owen replied, stepping out of the way. "Didn't

see you coming." He continued walking, then turned around. "I don't suppose you're going inside."

"'Course not," said the man, though he didn't make an effort to leave. "It's Sunday." He pulled up the collar on his oversized coat, leaned against a post near the door, and started to roll a cigarette.

"Hey," Owen said, looking at the man for the first time, a short guy, down on his luck if his disheveled appearance was any indication, with the ring finger missing on his left hand. "Don't I know you?"

"Not likely." He struck a match.

"Carl, from the cockfights, about twelve—no—more like fourteen years ago."

Carl tipped his head up. "The fellow who wanted my piano for his girl," he said. "Do you still have her?"

"The piano or the girl?"

"Either one."

"I'll tell you over a drink, if you really want to know."

Carl continued leaning.

"First beer's on me," Owen added.

"You should've said so." Carl crushed his cigarette with the toe of his boot and knocked on the back door. "I'm here about a horse," he said to the man who opened the peephole.

"And him?"

"He's with me. Tell Ferri I'll vouch for him." With that, the man inside slid the bolt and opened the door. Carl looked back at Owen. "I never would've made you out as a drinker. Just goes to show, you should never bet on the character of a man."

"Why's that?" Owen asked as they walked up to the barkeep.

"He'll lose you money every time."

* * *

Ushers put down new sawdust before the start of the two o'clock service; caretakers fed coal to each of the fifteen potbellied stoves. The women who'd sung in the choir that morning seated themselves in the congregation. Mr. Ackley intended to feature the men's voices at the afternoon meeting, and the women's later that evening. Betty Leas suggested that the ladies from the Providence Christian Church sit together in the pews she'd asked Pearl Williams to save for them. Most abided—though, understandably, a few chose to sit elsewhere with their families.

The crowd at the tabernacle quadrupled to eight thousand by the time Rodeheaver stepped out to introduce a couple dozen new groups, including the members of local Eastern Star chapters and the Salvation Army. As with the first service, Rodeheaver worked up the crowd, but this time they knew to watch for Billy Sunday's entrance during the singing.

And the evangelist did not disappoint. He strutted out onstage during the last verse of "I'm Bound for the Promised Land," carrying a signed baseball bat, a gift from the Scranton Miners ball club. He took a couple of swings and jumped right into his sermon: "They tell me a revival is only temporary." He swung a few more times, stood the bat upright, and leaned into it. "So is a bath," he finally said, "but it does you good." He laughed easily, and everyone in the audience applauded.

Sunday's second sermon of the day focused on backsliders. He spoke of careless Christians and serious ones who, in the end, weren't serious enough. He told stories of heathen women, adulterous men, and somehow managed to work around to a king named Cyrus who tried to bribe a beautiful woman named Panathea to join his harem. When she refused to dishonor her husband, the king sent him into battle. According to Sunday, whose tone turned sentimental,

Panathea knew what this meant. He shook his head, indicating no good could come. "She waited while the battle raged, and when the field was cleared she screamed her husband's name and finally found him wounded and dying. She kneeled," Sunday dropped to the floor, "and clasped him in her arms." He hugged his own body, rocking back and forth. "And as they kissed," he looked up with tear-filled eyes, "his lamp of life went out forever."

Moans rippled throughout the tabernacle.

Sunday stood up and dusted himself off before finishing the story. "King Cyrus heard of the man's death and went to the field. Panathea saw him coming, careening on his camel like a ship in a storm. She called, *Oh, husband! He comes.*" Sunday glanced at the floor as if addressing a body at his feet. "*He shall not have me. I was true to you in life, and will be true to you in death.* And she drew her dead husband's poniard from its sheath," he grabbed the baseball bat from the pulpit and held it like a knife, "drove it into her own breast, and fell dead across the body. King Cyrus came up and dismounted. He removed his turban, kneeled by the dead husband and wife, and thanked God that he had found in his kingdom one true and virtuous woman that his money could not buy nor his power intimidate."

Some in the audience wept. Everyone leaned forward, waiting for the message in this emotional illustration.

Sunday concluded, "The problem of this century is the problem of the first century. We must win the world for God." He pounded the bat against the pulpit. "And we will win just as soon as we have men and women who will be faithful to God and not sell out to the devil."

Applause broke out in the congregation, compelling people to hit the trail, some for the second time that day. Toward the end, Midge Howells, a well-known motorman on the Green Ridge line who'd attended the first service, entered the tabernacle. He'd stopped his streetcar filled with passengers out on North Washington Avenue, long enough to come inside and walk down front.

"My only regret," he said to Billy Sunday, who extended the glad hand of faith, "is that I didn't come forward this morning."

After a late lunch, Grace lumbered over to the couch with both hands pressed into her lower back. "Just let me rest my eyes for a few minutes," she said to Violet, who followed her into the parlor from the kitchen. Grace brought one hand around and rubbed her belly. "Carrying this sort of a load wears on a person." She smiled as she stretched out on the cushions and closed her eyes.

"What are you waiting for?" Grief asked, balancing on the arm of the sofa.

"All in good time," Grace murmured.

Violet watched from a chair, but said nothing. She pulled her knees up to her chest and wrapped her arms around them.

"What is it you have in mind? Surely, you can tell me now." Grief reached for her thigh but tumbled forward, catching himself on the gate-leg table. He stood, smoothed his soiled shirt, and limped over to the doorway. "Hand me the lye. I'll stop this foolishness," he said, glaring at Violet, "once and for all!"

"Not another word out of you," Grace shot back, her eyes still closed.

"Pardon?" Violet leaned forward.

"I'll tell you what you can do for me."

Violet jumped up. "Anything."

"*Anything*," Grief mimicked from across the room.

"Play Mother a song on the piano."

Panic flooded Violet's face as she dropped back into the

chair. Her hands gripped its wooden arms, fingernails digging into the varnish. Her breath stuck like a stone in her throat. She hadn't touched the keys since she'd played for the three days Daisy lay dying.

"Make it something joyful," Grace said, either unaware or in spite of her daughter's torment. "Today is a special day."

Grief stepped in front of Violet and looked into her eyes. "A last hurrah, perhaps?" he cackled as he turned toward Grace.

"Not another word," she said. "I mean it."

Violet shuddered.

"Did I ever teach you the sparrow song?" Grace started humming.

Violet remained bolted to her chair, too frightened to move.

Grace sang the chorus in a quiet voice.

I sing because I'm happy
I sing because I'm free
His eye is on the sparrow
And I know He watches me . . .

Grief slapped his palms together. "Lovely," he said, "just lovely." He stood over Grace, breathing heavily as she sang the first verse.

Why should I be discouraged
And why should the shadows fall . . .

She held the last note, and opened her eyes to look at Violet. "I should have taught you that one," she said. "It's one of your father's favorites." She held up her hand and fingered the keys of an imaginary piano. "A light touch. A pianist should never overpower her singers. Remember that."

Grief stroked Grace's brow, laughing to himself. "She won't have to remember for very long."

Grace ignored him and continued singing.

Why should my heart be lonely
And long for heaven and home—

Grief interrupted, "I have a song she might like to try." He strutted to Violet, stood directly in front of her, and bellowed out of key:

Daisy, Daisy, give me your answer do
I'm half crazy, all for the love of you—

"Stop it!" Grace yelled from the couch. She took a breath, peered at Violet who was shaking in her seat.

"How about getting Mother a glass of milk," she suggested, trying to sweeten her voice. "And maybe a piece of sugar bread to settle my stomach."

Violet let go of the chair and stumbled into the kitchen, legs trembling, tears running down her face.

Grief followed the child as far as the doorway. His eyes remained fixed, as if seeing her for the first time.

Grace lay on the couch, concentrating on her breathing.

"Just one spoonful is all it takes," Grief called back to Grace as he stole another look at her daughter.

"I don't like it when you're peevish," Grace whispered.

"I don't know what you're waiting for," he said, taking out his sterling silver buttonhook and pointing it at Violet's throat. "It's time to make the girl pay for what she did," he tiptoed back to Grace, "to your beautiful Daisy." He danced to the end of the couch and caressed her bare feet with his free hand.

"It was an accident." Grace struggled to keep her voice low. "A terrible accident."

"You don't believe that any more than I do," he said. "Why else would you indulge me these many months?"

"As if I had a choice!" she shouted. Remembering herself, she started again in a whisper, "She's my child."

"I think you're afraid of her." He poked Grace's foot with the hook, and seemed both surprised and delighted when he drew blood. He watched for a moment as the red drops bubbled to the surface, before running down toward the cushions.

Grace lay still.

He pushed on: "Here's a thought. Ask her what happened that day. Find out once and for all, and we'll see if confession really is good for the soul." He lifted Grace's foot to his mouth and sucked up the blood. "Unless," he dropped the leg and looked into her eyes, "it's *your* soul that needs saving."

Grace squeezed her eyes shut and held her breath.

"So, it's true," he said, shaking his head. "Poor Gracie. The lye is for you." He circled the couch. "Then the confession should be yours as well." He leaned down close to her face and whispered, "Say it. You know she killed Daisy, just say it." He yanked Grace up from the couch and shook her. "Say it!" he shrieked. "Say it! Say it! Say it!"

"You killed Daisy!" Grace screamed, just as Violet walked back into the room.

CHAPTER THIRTY-TWO

OWEN AND CARL STUMBLED OUT of the speakeasy around six thirty that evening and stepped into half a foot of fresh snow.

"Well, I'll be damned." Carl lit a cigarette and looked up at the sky. "Don't seem to be stopping."

"Can't be that bad. The streetcars are still running," Owen said, as one pushed past with a plow attached in front. He took another swig from the nearly full bottle of whiskey Carl had won with a pair of loaded dice, and handed it back to his new friend. "Anyway, you said we should find Grace."

"Hell yeah," Carl nodded. "That woman is all you can talk about."

Arm in arm, the two men staggered down North Washington Avenue through sheets of falling snow. Carl slipped on a patch of ice, pulling both of them into a snowdrift. "Stop horsing around!" Owen yelled. He stood up unsteadily and brushed himself off.

"Sorry." Carl extended his hand to Owen, who yanked him upright. "Wasn't looking where I was going." He searched the pile of snow, found his whiskey bottle intact, and smiled.

The pair pushed on, bowing their heads against the weather. Occasionally, they veered into the street before finding the slippery sidewalk again.

"Where you going?" a voice called out.

Owen lifted his head and tumbled backward into Carl. Before them, the tabernacle seemed to rise up like an enormous chariot bathed in light. A man in a fur-trimmed coat and an oddly shaped fedora stood alone, crowned in electric sunlight.

"I say," the man tried again, "where you headed?"

Owen fixed his eyes on the voice. "I'm looking for Grace," he slurred.

"Well, you've come to the right place, brother." He guided the men toward the tabernacle's main entrance. "Go ahead and take a seat. You'll find grace waiting for you inside." He reached his hand out to Carl. "Billy Sunday," he said, keeping his arm outstretched and his fingers open.

Carl took a long swig of whiskey, wiped off his mouth with an icy hand, and began reciting,

Here's to the glass we so love to sip,
It dries many a pensive tear;
'Tis not so sweet as a woman's lip,
But a damn sight more sincere.

At the conclusion of his toast, Carl handed the half-empty bottle to Sunday, and followed Owen into the tabernacle.

"Are you still out here, Billy?" Rodeheaver yelled, as he pushed open one of the side doors.

"Just taking in some fresh air," Sunday called back.

Rodeheaver glanced around at the blanket of snow. "Do you think we ought to cancel tonight's service?" He pulled his coat tight.

"Not on your life," Sunday said, holding up the bottle of whiskey. "There's at least two men inside who are in need of the Lord's Word. Found them myself not five minutes ago." He came around and opened a door at the back of the building. "Just remember, Rody," he held up the bottle a second time, "the Lord always provides." The two men chuckled as they stepped inside.

"Myrtle said Grace should be here." Owen's eyes roved drunkenly over the crowd. He stumbled partway up the main aisle before noticing his first familiar face. Davyd Leas sat in a pew next to his three boys. "Have you seen my wife?" Owen leaned against a pole to keep from falling down.

Davyd looked up. "I don't believe she's here, on account of her condition," he said, "but Betty could say for sure." He pointed at the singers seated behind the platform. "She knows more about women's matters than I do."

Owen wandered up the aisle toward the choir, when Carl pulled him by the arm.

"I need to sit down for a spell," he said, dropping into the first pew in front of the pulpit and resting his head against a pillar.

Owen staggered over to Preachers' Row, where Reverend Halloway sat talking to the minister from Bethania Presbyterian. "Where is she?" he asked.

Reverend Halloway turned around and shook his head. "She's home. Best place for her, if you ask me." He watched as Owen swayed back and forth. "Let's get you a seat." He stood up and took Owen by the arm.

"I have to find her." He pulled away with such force that he lost his balance and landed on his back in the sawdust.

Reverend Halloway motioned to Davyd Leas, who quickly ran down front to help. The two men lifted Owen, brushed him off, and placed him at the end of a second-row pew behind Carl.

"Let him sleep it off," Davyd said. "Maybe he'll wake up a new man."

Reverend Halloway nodded. "God willing."

By the time Rodeheaver and Ackley finished preparing the crowd for Billy Sunday's entrance, at least a foot of snow had fallen, covering the skylights that dotted the tabernacle's turtle-back roof. Inside, fifteen coal stoves and four thousand bodies provided enough warmth to convince those in attendance to stay put and wait out the storm.

"I am the sworn, eternal, uncompromising enemy of the liquor traffic!" Billy Sunday bellowed as he ran out on stage. "Seventy-five percent of our idiots come from intemperate parents. Eighty percent of our criminals are whiskey-made!" He began pacing back and forth across the stage. "I find men behind prison bars and ask, *What put you here?*" Sunday stopped dead in his tracks and shouted the answer. "Drink!" He started moving again. "I stand by the scaffold and ask, *What made you a murderer?*" He cupped his ear toward the audience.

"Drink! Drink! Drink!" the crowd screamed, some so enthusiastically that they fell faint and had to be tended to by the ushers.

Carl sat up in his seat and yelled, "Drink!" with a fist in the air and his eyes still closed. Then he settled his head against the pillar and went back to sleep.

Sunday threw off his jacket and loosened his tie. He leaned forward as if speaking confidentially. "The saloon is the sum of all villainies. It is the crime of crimes. It is the mother of sins."

Resounding "Amens" punctuated each sentence.

"The devil and the saloon keeper are always pulling the same rope."

"Save us!" someone shouted from a back row.

"Now you're talking." Sunday smiled. "If you believe in a greater Scranton, if you believe in men going to heaven instead of hell," he hollered as he lifted a chair and threw it across the platform, "then down with the saloon!"

"Amen!" the crowd shouted. "Amen!"

Myrtle's eyes rolled back and she fainted into her husband's shoulder. Mildred swooned alongside her.

The widow looked sympathetically at Mr. Evans, squashed up against a pole by the weight of both women.

"One never likes to be outdone by the other," he called over.

Myrtle gave him a good pinch, sat back up, and pushed Mildred off her.

"The wrath of an outraged public will never be quenched until the putrid corpse of the saloon is hanging from the gibbet of shame!" Sunday strode over to the pulpit, reached inside, grabbed a half-empty bottle, and waved it in the air. He jumped down off the platform and stormed toward the first row, where Carl slept off the last of his drunken stupor. "Not one hour ago, I wrestled this poison out of the hands of this whiskey-soaked man!" He pulled Carl up by the shirt for all to see, before dropping him back on his bench. Carl stirred, shaking off the grogginess that weighed on him like a coat of lead.

Sunday smashed the bottle against the wooden post, soaking the audience in the first three rows and sending glass across the sawdust-covered aisle. Startled, Owen sobered on the spot.

"The saloon is a rat hole for a wage earner to dump his pay!"

At the words *rat hole*, Owen wriggled in his seat like an insect pinned to a wall.

"The only interest it pays is red eyes and foul breath." Sunday pointed a finger at Carl. "You go in with character and you come out ruined!"

Owen held his head, trying to collect his thoughts.

Sunday turned his ear toward the door. "Listen up, folks." He waited for everyone to settle. "There's a storm raging outside these walls, but I tell you, it's nothing compared to the blizzard of misery that befalls not only the drunkard, but those he loves."

A vision of Grace and Violet flashed in Owen's mind and stung his eyes. He hid behind his calloused hands, but his quaking shoulders betrayed him.

Sunday turned back toward his congregation. "It impoverishes your children, and it brings insanity and suicide!"

Suicide. The word taunted Owen like a dare. He kneaded his temples to stop the pain coursing through his head.

Sunday rushed back on stage and yanked Ackley up from the piano as a prop. "It will take the shirt off your back!" He made a pretense of ripping off the pianist's clothing and pushed the man to his knees. "And yank the last crust of bread out of the hand of the starving child." Ackley looked up and feigned begging. "It will take the last cent out of your pocket, and will send you home staggering to your family." Sunday pulled the man to his feet and sent him back to the piano. "It will steal the milk from the breast of the mother and take the virtue from your daughter."

"God save us all!" someone shouted from the rear.

"He's our only hope," Sunday shot back, "because the saloon is the dirtiest, most low-down, damnable business that ever crawled out of the pit of hell!" The preacher pulled his handkerchief out of his pocket and mopped up the sweat on his forehead and neck. He paused for a moment, retrieved his toppled chair, and straddled it.

Everyone leaned forward, waiting for him to continue.

Sunday stood up slowly. "The saloon is a liar!" He sent the chair flying a second time. "It sends the boy home with a lie on his lips to his mother; and the husband home with a lie on his lips to his wife."

A lie on his lips to his wife. These words tumbled like dice inside Owen's head, knocking into and over and around each other. *A lie. To his wife. On his lips.* He struggled to make sense, to hear truth, but the pain inside screamed louder.

"It's a murderer!" Sunday stepped behind the podium and pounded his fist.

The howling wind slammed back as if to register its displeasure, with Sunday or the devil, no one could say for sure.

The evangelist stopped and listened as the snow beat against the windows. "Oh God," he closed his eyes and prayed, "get out there and grab that blizzard by the snout and shake the daylights out of it so that this crowd may get home tonight."

Sunday opened his eyes and leaned over the pulpit glaring down at Carl. "God's wrath be upon you if you do not change your wicked ways." Sunday peered across the crowd and concluded quietly but resolutely, "Repent or go to hell."

The applause began hesitantly, as if unsure of the appropriateness of this last statement, but swelled soon enough into thunderclaps. Sunday motioned the crowd forward, like a coach at third waving a runner home. In spite of the storm raging outside, hundreds hit the sawdust trail. Ackley started playing "Amazing Grace," that evening's hymn of invitation. Most of those in line caught up by the second verse.

'Twas grace that taught my heart to fear,
And grace my fears relieved;
How precious did that grace appear
The hour I first believed.

Grace. Words swelled in Owen's mind, squeezing into

crevices usually filled with whiskey. Daisy, he thought. And rat holes. His head started spinning. Grace. She ought to know better. Violet, sweet Violet. A lie on his lips to his wife. A lie. And then he remembered. She did know better. The words stood at attention.

Lye on the lips of his wife!

Owen jumped up from the pew and turned his back on Billy Sunday's promise of salvation. He pushed and squeezed his way up the aisle, in the opposite direction of those rushing forward.

"You can't go out in this!" Carl hollered from the front of the line, his eyes aglow with newfound fervor.

Owen bent down, scooped some sawdust into his pockets to keep his hands warm in the frigid air, turned up his collar, and opened the door.

"It's suicide!" Carl warned.

"Exactly!" Owen yelled back as he ran into the grievous night.

At the end of that evening's revival, about fifteen hundred people, who lived close by, set out for home.

Just before ten o'clock, Sunday called out to the twenty-five hundred marooned inside the tabernacle, "*God will provide as God hath plenty.*"

Everyone hushed so the evangelist could be heard.

"I've been talking to these fine pressmen." He pointed around the platform. "Seems all of the telegraph wires are down, but a few of the phone lines still work, praise the Lord."

Cheers rose up from the crowd.

"Now, I hate to send the dishpans around a second time," he said, nodding to the collection plates, "but we're running out of coal to feed the fires, and we'll need to feed our bodies as well." Sunday pulled a ten-dollar bill out of his wallet and handed it to one of the ushers. "I'll be the first to contribute. And we'd be much obliged to anyone else who can give. Remember the story of the widow's mite when you're reaching into those pockets."

C.E. Shelp and two of the men in his employ braved forty-five-mile-an-hour winds and two feet of snow to deliver coal to the tabernacle by ten thirty. "Took twenty minutes to urge the horses through some of them drifts," Shelp said. Several of the men in attendance at the revival volunteered to carry the coal inside.

Just before midnight, patrol wagons arrived with enough sandwiches and ground coffee to feed everyone twice over. "Compliments of the *Truth*," one policemen explained.

"And the *Times*," a reporter called out.

"And the *Republican*," a third man chimed in.

The women in the choir took charge of setting out the food and boiling coffee in the collection plates on top of the potbellied stoves.

"Women and children first," Myrtle said, pushing past a group of men from the Odd Fellows. "Just like the *Titanic*," she added, to dispel any doubts about her right to be fed ahead of them.

CHAPTER THIRTY-THREE

You killed Daisy!

The accusation had exploded from Grace's lips like a forgotten shell in the barrel of a shotgun. "God, forgive me!" she wailed. "Forgive me! Forgive me!" She dropped to the couch and covered her eyes.

"Don't buckle now." Grief smiled, sweeping loose strands of hair behind Grace's ears. "I'm bursting with pride." He lifted her chin, pointed her face toward the kitchen, and licked his lips. "Behold what you have wrought." He took a step back, giving her an unimpeded view.

Violet stood in the doorway, stunned, wounded, ravaged, milk in one hand, sugar bread in the other. The late-afternoon sun broke from the gray sky and burned through the window behind her.

Forced to shield her eyes, Grace turned away from her daughter. "Look what you did!" she hissed at Grief, now standing on the opposite side of the room. "Jealous, that's what you are."

Jealous? Violet wanted to rush over to her mother and tell her that she was not a jealous girl. That she was sorry, so very sorry for what had happened that horrible day. That she loved her sister at least as much as she loved her mother and father. And that no one had to blame her for what happened. She blamed herself enough to fill the bottomless hole that Daisy had left behind.

And she wanted to say all of it from the comfort of her mother's arms, but Violet's impudent feet and tongue would not abide. She stood as still as the stone Mary in the widow's front yard.

"Fascinating," Grief said as he stepped over to the girl. He slid the buttonhook out of his pocket and dragged it lightly across her cheek.

Violet twitched.

Awareness bubbled up and soured in Grace's stomach. "Stay away," she warned, "or . . ."

"Or what?" Grief slinked back to his corner.

Violet set the milk and sugar bread down on the closed lid of the piano, took her coat from the hook on the wall, and walked out the door.

"It's long past supper." Grace's brow furrowed at the realization. "I thought she'd be back by now."

"Give her a little more time," Grief said to Grace, who sat across from him at the kitchen table. "She'll come back when she's finished sulking. Anyway," he patted her arm and glanced at the empty kettle waiting at the sink, "we have other priorities tonight."

Grace stared absently at their reflections in the window, Grief's withered appearance, her wasted one. She looked down at the swollen mound stretching the folds of her skirt to their limit, and wondered at a baby's ability to thrive under such woeful circumstances.

"Perhaps a cup of tea," he suggested in an even tone. "It always seems to soothe you."

She stretched a hand toward his lips. He nibbled a little—a finger here, and knuckle there—seemingly indifferent to such paltry scraps.

"I know!" Grief jumped up excited. "I'll start the kettle."

"Why the hurry?" Grace stood, went to the sink, and pumped water. "When did this become your idea?"

"I'm devastated, truly," he said, patting his pinched chest with a bony hand. "But I need to be supportive of my Gracie." He reached toward her and rubbed the small of her back. "Who is it that said, *What touches us ourselves shall be last served?*"

"Where could she have gotten to this time of night?" Grace stoked the fire and placed the kettle on the stove. She spooned spearmint leaves into the hinged tea ball and placed it on the table next to the empty tea pot.

"Shakespeare, I suppose. Though don't ask me where." Grief walked to the shelf, grabbed the tin of lye, and set it in the middle of the table. "I never much cared for his plays." The two sat back down and waited. "Though I have to admit, some of his sonnets intrigue me." He started reciting.

When in disgrace with fortune and men's eyes,
I all alone beweep my outcast state . . .

"She's so young," Grace said.

And trouble deaf heaven with my bootless cries,
And look upon myself, and curse my fate . . .

"How will she manage alone?"

Grief broke from his reverie to reassure her: "She's not alone." He counted off, starting with his left thumb. "She has Hattie, the widow, Stanley, and that husband of yours." Only his pinky remained folded. The boiling kettle rattled on the stove, so he reached around with his right hand and pulled it off the flame. He poured the water into the pot and dropped the tea ball inside to brew. "And she has me," he added, lifting the last finger, before stroking Grace's cheek with his open palm.

"You!" Grace pushed the hand away. "I'll not stand for it!" She slammed her fist on the table.

"Come now," he said, tapping the lye into the teapot and swirling it gently. "After all, she's about the age you were when I first came calling. Probably even a shade older." He closed his eyes a moment. "So tender, so ripe." He opened his eyes and grabbed hold of the teapot. His hand quivered a bit as he poured and pushed the cup in front of Grace. "What's good for the goose," he laughed, "is good for the gosling. Isn't that what they say?" He lifted the cup to Grace's lips. "As if you could stop me."

She pushed him away with such force, he tumbled backward in his chair, toppling the teapot, cup, and lye as he fell. "I'll not let her near the likes of you!"

Grief lay unconscious at her feet.

Grace snatched her coat, threw it around her shoulders, and opened the front door. Horrified, she stared out at the night, noticing the storm for the first time. Snow fell from the sky, only to be tossed about by the merciless wind. A white shroud rendered yards, sidewalks, and streets indistinguishable from one another. Who could survive such a night? Certainly not a child, Grace realized as she stepped onto the porch.

When Violet had walked out the door, she'd found Sophie chewing on an empty burlap sack in the backyard. "How'd you get here?" Violet looked over at the Harris's barn and noticed the open door. "Stanley wouldn't want you wandering the neighborhood."

She tugged on what could best be described as a leash. The widow had fashioned it out of her late husband's belt the day Stanley had announced that Sophie would no longer need a bridle. "No sense wearing the thing if no one's going to ride her," he'd said. "And no one's going to ride her. She's worked her share already."

It had taken Violet over an hour to coax the mule back into the barn. Sophie would take a step or two, and stop to nuzzle Violet, licking away her tears. By the time she finally got the mule settled in her stall, watered, and fed, the snow had begun in earnest.

Hours later, Violet lay huddled beneath the hay in the Harris's barn, sidled up against Sophie's warm belly. How could I think that Mother would forgive me, she thought, that anyone could forgive me for what I did?

She shivered, even as Sophie pressed her body closer. The tears, which hadn't stopped flowing in the hours since she'd left the house, froze to thin lines of straw around her. "I'll run away," she said aloud. Sophie whinnied, but Violet ignored her objection. She looked up at the ceiling. "Sorry, Stanley," she said, before turning her attention back to the mule. "I'll need your help. This night's not fit for walking." She stood up to see if the worst of the storm had passed. A foot and a half of snow wrapped its way around the barn. The wind had dropped at least another foot alongside the door, and still had not let up. Violet burrowed back under the hay and waited.

Grace clung to the porch banister, dizzy from squinting through the wind-swirled snow. She's out there somewhere, Grace thought, as she tried to make out a child's shape in the blizzard. And it's all my fault. Though virtually snow-blind, Grace knew the widow's house to be a straight shot across, so she bowed her head and set out, hoping to find Violet there, warming herself at the stove. Grace tried to push through the snow, but her legs tired quickly, and she had to resort to raising and dropping them like a soldier on parade. A few minutes later, she arrived on the other side of the street and, clinging to the banister, pulled herself up the front steps. After shoveling a good amount of snow away from the door with a coal bucket and bare hands, Grace squeezed her way inside and yelled, "Violet!" Only the howling wind moaned in reply. Grace shook the ice out of her skirt, as the flame inside the stove flickered and died. She grabbed an afghan from the widow's couch and headed back into the night.

In spite of Sophie's best efforts, Violet trembled underneath the hay. She drew her hands up into her coat sleeves, but that didn't stop the numbness from spreading down her fingers.

"We're in trouble," she whispered toward the mule's ear, shutting her swollen eyes for just a minute.

"Wake up!" Daisy cried. "It's time for school."

Violet resisted the urge to stir. She wanted to savor the warmth of her bed.

Daisy shook her by the shoulder. "I'm not going to let you make me late on my birthday."

When Violet finally opened her eyes, she found Daisy standing at the door of their bedroom. She wore her beautiful white store-bought dress, and a matching bow bloomed from her head like a peony in early summer.

"I have a surprise for you," Daisy teased. "It's a dandy."

Violet slipped out of bed, feeling the chill of the day through her muslin nightgown.

"Last one out's a rotten egg," Daisy called back as she ran down the hall and out their front door.

Violet scurried after her into the yard.

"Get on," Daisy said from atop Sophie's back. She fingered the mule's white mane and waited.

Violet hesitated.

Daisy started clapping. "Come on. It's my birthday!"

Sophie nudged Violet's head, and leaned down low so she could swing her leg up and over.

"Hold tight!" Daisy yelled from in front. "And keep an eye out for Myrtle Evans. Nothing she likes more than to catch us up to no good."

Grace pushed against the wind and snow, back across the street, this time to Louise's house. When she finally managed to let herself in, Grace found the place as empty as the widow's. The last bit of heat from the banked stove leaked through the rag-stuffed window frames, like the final traces of warmth on a fresh corpse. Grace shivered, as she lumbered to the back door and headed for the Evanses' house, not even stopping to wipe the ice from her frozen eyes.

The wind slapped pellets of snow against her cheeks and neck. Grace pulled the afghan up around her face and inched forward. Next, she arrived on Myrtle's back porch, only to find the door bolted against her. Another time, Grace would have found it odd that Myrtle had locked her door, but she didn't have the energy to think about such matters now. Instead, she dropped to her knees, out of exhaustion as much as a need to pray. "Please, Lord!" she yelled. The wind absorbed her voice, but Grace kept on, hoping God might hear her plea even if she could not. "I'll make it right, somehow. Just don't take her away from me!"

She thought to say more, but when no words came, she opened her eyes and stood. The wind changed course, and for a moment Grace saw Violet floating on a pillow of snow. She tried to make sense of the vision while she pushed past the drifts. There it is again, she thought, as the gusts momentarily calmed enough to let her see in the storm. Grace pressed on, weaving and stumbling toward her house. Just before reaching the door, she fell into what seemed to be a mountain of snow. When she stood up, she discovered what the vision was—an unconscious Violet, draped across Sophie's back.

Grace threw the afghan over her daughter, pulled at Sophie's leash, and led the mule and child up the porch steps. In spite of her increasing back pain, she lifted Violet off the animal's back and carried her into the house. She sat with her on her lap in front of the hissing stove, alternately rubbing Violet's hands and feet between her palms.

Sophie squeezed her way into the kitchen uninvited. The wind slammed the door shut behind her, causing Grace to swing around.

Grief opened one eye, but snapped it shut when Grace threw a look down at him. She glanced up at Sophie standing by the cupboard. Savior or not, a mule did not belong in the house.

Sophie dipped her head as if she understood, took a few steps backward, and folded herself onto the floor, quite inconspicuously for a mule. Grief moaned under the weight of the beast, but Sophie didn't seem to notice. She licked at Violet's ankles dangling in front of her.

"Daisy," Violet muttered, as if waking from a deep sleep.

"Mother's here," Grace said, turning back toward the fire. "Thank you, Lord, for answered prayer," she added, wrapping her body around her daughter.

Just at that moment, the pains of childbirth began.

CHAPTER THIRTY-FOUR

OWEN STARTED THE TWO-AND-A-HALF-MILE TREK from the tabernacle downtown to Spring Street in Providence, with one thought on his mind. Grace. How could he have been so wrong? Of course she knew when to put down lye. Hadn't she seen him do it plenty of times? And he'd even left the empty tin on the kitchen shelf this past October, so she'd know he'd taken care of the rats before the first good frost. *Lye on the lips of his wife.* He shivered as he pushed through the howling gusts that pounded him with snow.

Violet stirred in Grace's arms. "Daisy," she said, again.

"Mother's here," Grace cooed in her ear, soothing the waking child. She kept one arm around Violet and grabbed hold of the chair's seat with the other, squeezing as hard as she could, waiting for the pain to pass.

Sophie stretched her neck and gently nuzzled the two of them.

With her eyes shut tight, Violet inhaled her mother's scents: spearmint, perspiration, Welsh cakes, lilacs, and vanilla. She nestled a minute longer, feeling like she belonged on this lap. Outside, the whistling wind beat against the weathered boards.

When the pain let up, Grace wrapped both arms around

her child, hugged her once more, and shook her gently. "You have to wake up now," she whispered.

Violet jumped down from her mother with a start and hopped to the other side of Sophie. "You don't want me here." She tugged at the mule's leash, but Sophie wouldn't budge. Violet ran over to the hook on the wall and grabbed a woolen scarf.

Grace's face twisted at the start of another contraction. "I need you." She glanced from her stomach to Violet. "My time's come early." The pain exploded. Now she squeezed the chair with both hands. "Besides," she closed her eyes and measured each syllable through her clenched jaw, "I won't let you go out into this night again. You'll die out there."

Violet burst into tears. "It's what I deserve!" she sobbed.

"No!" Grace stood and started walking around the table, away from Sophie and Grief, toward Violet. "I love you!" She reached for her daughter, who scrambled away.

"How can you love me?" Violet looked around for her coat. When she couldn't find it, she picked up the afghan lying alongside Sophie and headed for the door. "I'm the one who killed her!"

Violet put her hand on the knob, and her mother dropped to the floor, unconscious.

Owen's breath turned to ice against his buttoned collar, his fingers numb inside his sawdust-lined pockets. Although he bent his head to the wind, he still had to blink to keep his eyelids from freezing shut. He watched the blizzard circle round his legs. "Knee high!" Owen yelled, as if someone had called out to him from a window or porch for a check on the snow. "Knee high," he repeated, though he couldn't say why. A compulsion gripped him, forced him to say those two words over and over. "Knee high. Knee high." They seemed to be the start of something, or the end of it. "Knee high," he said again, searching, but for what? Some saying? Some truth?

Owen turned onto Green Ridge Street, halfway home. First he'd have to make it down the steep hill where all the moneyed people lived, then up, past the mine and the river. He started his descent, and the words rattled inside his head. *Knee high. Knee high.* His shins seemed to catch fire as he pushed through the piling snow, so he lifted and lowered his legs, trying for a bit of relief, but found none.

At the bottom of the hill, with his eyes almost frozen shut, Owen tripped on a buried railroad tie and fell headfirst into a six-foot snowdrift. He struggled to stand, but couldn't get his footing on the ice-slicked plank. Each time he tried, his muscles resisted, as if they believed they had finally found rest. The snow stung his face and filled his nostrils. So this is it, Owen thought. I'm going to die here. He didn't mind so much for himself. After all, he hadn't shown an interest in living for the better part of a year. But he worried now about Grace and Violet. They deserved better than this. Than him. Was anyone out there who could intervene? Owen ached to believe in a God who shepherded lost souls, who scoured the woods for His lost children, even those who had run away. Owen's God hadn't bothered with him for some time. Then again, the same could be said of Owen.

Snow burned his shins. He realized he was on his knees—the second time in as many days. A sign? He pulled his hands out of his pockets to cover his face, inhaling the scent of freshly cut wood. His fingers twitched against his raw skin. When did I become so lost?

The words circled again in response. *Knee high*, familiar, yet incomplete. "Knee high . . ." He held the last syllable expectantly, as if to coax whatever followed. In a moment, the truth sliced through the silence of his tomb—an adage used by local farmers when describing the progress of corn. "Knee high," he mouthed, "by the Fourth of July." And he wept.

The Fourth of July. Grace hadn't wanted him to buy those sparklers. And he'd been the one to scold the children and send them away. "Outside, both of you, while you still can." He moaned into his cracked palms.

Grace's face flashed before him, the face he'd followed out of the mine on Christmas Eve. He tried again to find his footing, this time positioning his feet between the icy railroad ties. With a good deal of effort, he pushed himself up and out of the snowdrift and continued toward home.

Violet ran back to her mother and tugged on her arm. "Wake up!" she cried. She draped the afghan around her, sat down on the floor, and cradled her mother's head. "Not you too!" She held her mother against her chest and rocked her.

Grace's eyes fluttered open. She stared into her daughter's face, reached up, and traced the creases in her brow. "Don't cry," she said, pulling her daughter toward her.

Violet's head settled at her mother's bosom, a place she'd known in another life. One where Father left for work each morning and returned at night. Where Mother made hair ribbons to match their dresses and kneeled with them to say their prayers. "*Now I lay me down to sleep.*" A time of pianos and pies. "It'll get better before you get married." Of laughter and kisses. "Ready or not, here I come."

A life with Daisy. Violet burst into shuddering, gasping sobs.

Grace tightened her grip around the child. The pain swelled up inside her once more. "*In sorrow thou shalt bring forth children*," she whispered, recounting God's punishment to Eve. She closed her eyes and gritted her teeth. "*The wages of sin.*"

Violet shot up in horror. "Why should you suffer for my sin?"

Grace managed one word in the midst of her labor: "Forgiveness."

"How?" The crying stopped, but Violet still trembled. "I killed her. You said so yourself."

"Forgive me." Grace's breathing evened out. She pulled Violet into her. "I'm so ashamed," she whispered.

"Ashamed?" Violet shook her head in disbelief.

"I blamed you. What kind of mother does that?"

"But I killed her," Violet repeated.

"It was an accident." Grace hugged her child. "I was out of my head with grief."

The pain reared up again. Grace clutched her stomach, and in an instant, they found themselves sitting in a puddle of warm liquid.

Grace spoke slowly, erasing most of the anxiety from her voice. "Take the oil cloth off the table, spread it across my bed, and come back for me."

Violet jumped up. She pressed a rag against the front of her damp dress and grabbed the cloth.

"I love you," Grace said, clenching her jaw with the pain. "Now hurry. The baby's coming."

Grace lay on the covered mattress, while Violet removed her mother's felt slippers and rubbed the soles of her stockinged feet. "Such a good girl," Grace said, once the pain subsided. Runnels of sweat ran off her face, soaking the blue and white ticked pillow. "I wish I could spare you this." Shivers of goose flesh dotted her arms. "I'll need a clean sheet," she said, pointing to the closet.

Violet tugged at the linens folded on the shelf above the clothes bar. They all fell on her head, and landed in a heap on the floor. Panic shot through her as she waited to be scolded for making a mess.

"Just set them on the rocker," Grace said breathlessly.

She turned her head toward the window and stared out at the storm. "We'll probably need all of them before this night's over."

Violet returned to the foot of the bed and snapped a sheet open. It billowed softly as it landed across her mother's legs.

Grace drew the sheet up to cover her body, rolled down her stockings, and took off her clothes. "No sense getting an eyeful of something you're not ready for," she said, pushing the garments to the floor. "Now bring me my nightgown."

Violet's hands trembled when she pulled the gown off the hook and passed it under the sheet to her mother.

"Maybe you can just feel your way through," Grace suggested, though she sounded doubtful. The flame from an oil lamp flickered in the otherwise dark room. "And turn down the wick some."

Violet stood rigid at the bottom of the bed, transfixed by fear. At that moment, she could no more tend the wick than birth a baby. "I don't know how . . ."

"You're all I have," Grace replied, before the contractions started again.

Several minutes passed before Grace could speak. "Lord, help me," was all she could manage, and then the pain exploded. She clenched two handfuls of sheet and gritted her teeth.

Violet searched her mind for any bit of knowledge about babies. They had to be "delivered," but she had no idea what that meant. *A woman's time. A blue baby. Born without breath*. Janie Miller once told her, "Doc Rodham brings babies in that black bag of his," but Violet knew there would be no doctor tonight.

Grace shrieked, as she slid down the length of the mattress, opened her knees, and pressed each foot against a bedpost. "Get out!" she snarled toward the rocker, her teeth clenched, her eyes on fire. "You'll not go near my children!"

Violet turned with a start, but saw no one. "It's me, Mother. Violet."

"He's gone," Grace said, "for now." She drifted into the fog of pain.

Violet's hands disappeared under the sheet, but her eyes remained locked on her mother's. "Tell me what to do," she begged.

Her mother rolled fitfully in and out of consciousness.

Violet stretched her arms in further, until they landed on a slippery mound. Instinctively, she cupped her hands around what she knew to be a head. "Wake up!" she screamed, knowing somehow that her mother had to "deliver" the baby whole.

Grace's eyes remained closed, but she pushed her feet against the bedposts and howled.

Violet felt a shoulder pass through and waited for the other.

Grace bore down again and moaned, as if competing with the wind outside.

The baby remained frozen in place.

Grace pushed down once more, but with less force. She opened her eyes and looked pleadingly at Violet. "Don't be afraid," she whispered at the end of the breath.

Violet slid her fingers inside, felt for the shoulder, and loosened it from its hold. The baby gushed into her hands fully formed, but still attached, somehow, to her mother. She pulled it out from under the sheet and, even with the dim light, saw the blood. So much blood. It seemed to have come from her mother. The bedding was soaked with it. The baby painted in thick, curdled coats of it. And now Violet's arms were covered in it as she cradled the slippery infant in her arms.

Grace lay silently in the bed, her eyes open.

The baby rested in Violet's hands, silent as well. In a panic, Violet placed the infant on the bed, wiped some of the blood away with a towel, and grabbed the oil lamp. She tipped the light toward the bed. A girl, she noted, before spotting the dark cast to her skin. *A blue baby. Born without breath*. She set the lamp back on the table, catching the chain of her birthday locket on the metal knob. The necklace tore from her neck and fell to the floor, but Violet didn't dare look down. She lifted the baby and slapped her back, like Father had done to her one time when she choked on a piece of hard candy. The infant slumped in her hands like a ragdoll. Violet slapped her again, praying she would make some sound.

In the distance, the manic winds tolled the bells at Providence Christian Church. From Violet's arms, her sister suddenly added her cry to the cacophony.

CHAPTER THIRTY-FIVE

I'VE DONE SOMETHING GOOD, Violet thought, as she looked at the baby in her arms. Maybe the others would see that before remembering the rest. Maybe they wouldn't be so quick to give her the looks they'd been giving her since that day. She glanced at her mother who had somehow roused herself long enough to instruct Violet on how to cut the cord. She'd fallen asleep soon after, but her color was better and her breathing was even. That was something anyway.

Violet's efforts at swaddling hadn't been so successful, though. The blanket was too loose to contain her squirming sister. Her sister. I have a sister. Again.

The baby's eyelids flickered, then opened, revealing two orbs, bluer than the bluest summer sky. Daisy's eyes. Violet scoured them but could find no trace of judgment. Yet almost everyone blamed her. Not that they ever asked her what happened. At first, they were too busy tending to Daisy. Later, too busy grieving her. They discussed it, of course, but they talked around Violet, not to her. Most folks took Myrtle's version of the incident as gospel, adding their own suppositions with each telling. And like everyone else, the more Violet heard the different accounts, the more she believed them.

After all, she was jealous of her sister, and she did throw that sparkler.

All of it true.

But not the truth.

When the pastor had washed away Daisy's sins, he'd washed away her common sense as well. Violet could find no other explanation for her sister's transformation that Fourth of July.

"If a body is old enough to choose Jesus as her Lord and Savior," Daisy had explained for the third time in the hour since her baptism, "she's ready to *put aside childish things*. First Corinthians, Chapter 13, verse 11."

Violet had dropped the jacks and ball onto their bed, next to the jumping rope and the china doll. Daisy sashayed out the door, still wearing the white cotton dress with the pleated skirt. The matching bow bloomed from her head like a peony. Not fair, Violet thought, catching her own reflection in the window. She pulled at the hem of her yellow hand-me-down and fingered her recently shorn hair. Violet hated her sister for being first, for being nine.

She had dropped backward, arms outstretched into the swell of a hand-knotted bed quilt. Indignation cozied up alongside her. Eleven months separated the girls, but to Violet's thinking, it may as well have been eleven years. Daisy got the store-bought dress since she was old enough to be taken to church. Daisy needed quiet because her advanced studies required concentration. Daisy hadn't been forced to cut her hair short. Not a single louse in all those curls. And such beautiful blue eyes. And that voice, like an angel. Will she be singing in the *gymanfa ganu*? All the old Welsh hymns will be sung. Even the photographer, hired to commemorate the baptism, declared her features to be "perfectly suited for the camera." Their father called her *little lady*. Their mother called her *pet*.

Just thinking about it had made Violet's blood boil, and she gave her sister a good shove in the kitchen when she saw her chance. She hadn't intended to send Daisy into Mother, especially with a pie in hand.

Once their father had sent them out to the yard, Daisy drilled her heel hard into the toe of Violet's boot.

"Ow!"

"Jealous."

"Ungrateful." Violet gave her sister a quick push, then ran back to the safety of the porch steps. Neither girl was fool enough to start up so close to their parents. She sat down on the porch, unlaced her boot, and inspected her foot. If a bruise formed up, and she hoped one would, she'd show it to Mother.

Daisy sat on a rock at the end of their yard, folded her head into her arms, and began to cry. Violet hadn't expected this particular response, and it made her feel uncomfortable. She removed her other boot and wondered if someone else's tears could wash away her own anger. Unwilling to apologize—after all, Daisy had pushed her first, a fact their mother could attest to—but anxious to put the matter behind them, Violet considered the situation. She flung her boots onto the porch, and like manna from heaven, the answer appeared. At least two dozen sparklers tumbled out from behind the copper wash tin. Their father must have hidden them there as a Fourth of July surprise for the girls. She grabbed the fireworks and a nearby box of matches, and walked barefooted to the end of the yard. With her hands hidden behind her back, Violet said, "I brought you a surprise."

Daisy kept her head on her lap.

"It's a dandy. Promise."

Daisy lifted her face and glared.

Violet swallowed. "I'm real sorry—about spoiling your dress, I mean."

"What surprise?"

Violet flung her arms around front and revealed her find.

Daisy stood up, snatched the matchbox, and said, "You oughtn't to be playing with fire."

Stung by Daisy's rebuff, Violet's eyes filled with tears.

"I'm sorry too—about your foot, I mean." Daisy carefully pulled a sparkler out of the bunch as if drawing straws. "Hold this. Real tight."

Violet dropped the others, and gripped her sparkler with both hands.

Daisy grabbed a match and dropped the box on the ground. "I'll light yours, then one for me. We'll put the rest back so Father won't find out and switch both our hides." She looked across the yard. "And keep watch for Myrtle Evans. Nothing she likes more than to catch us up to no good."

Daisy struck the match and tipped it toward the firework in Violet's hand. Nothing. She ran the flame back and forth overtop, and leaned in close to inspect the situation, trying to decide whether or not she had selected what the boys in the neighborhood called a "lemon."

Sparks exploded in a flash. Both girls jumped and laughed, frightened and embarrassed at once. The orange flare sizzled down the rod throwing off pinpricks of fire, then sputtered and died before it had a right to.

"Not fair," Violet said, scraping at the unused portion with her thumbnail. "I didn't get a full turn."

Daisy bent down, grabbed another sparkler, and handed it to her sister. "This one's it."

Violet pressed both sticks together, glancing quickly toward their house, and then the Evanses's. Before Daisy could light another match, the first sparkler resurrected itself half an inch from Violet's fingers. Daisy started to warn her sister, but the words caught in her throat. She tried again but only squeaked a split second before the red-hot ember reached Violet's left thumb. Myrtle stepped out onto her porch just in time to see both sparklers ignite, raining onto Violet's startled hands. Her fingers opened and the sparklers scattered like shooed pigeons. Unfettered, the fireworks tumbled to the ground, catching Daisy's hem on their descent.

"Violet!" Daisy's warning landed as accusation.

Time hesitated as the twin sparklers crackled at Violet's feet. A glowing strand of light quivered on Daisy's charred skirt before bursting into a patch of blue flame. Violet's heart pounded painfully against her chest. *Help her!* Violet willed her arms forward, but they would not obey. *Scream! Run!* She stood frozen in place. A soft breeze stirred, nudging time along. The girls locked eyes in horror as the dress erupted into flames.

Their parents ran out into the yard, Mother first, who smothered the fire. Father gathered Daisy in his arms and carried her toward the house. As they passed by, Violet searched her sister's eyes for the condemnation, loathing, or, at the very least, the recrimination she deserved. Instead, she found an expression so unexpected, it turned the familiar into something jarring, like that first sip of milk when you think it's lemonade, or the opening note of any song, other than the one you were waiting for. No matter how good, for that instant, the milk tastes sour and the key sounds flat.

In that same way, Violet misread her sister's expression. It didn't fit her expectation, so Violet decided it was far worse than she'd imagined.

But now, as Violet gazed at the baby who looked at her with Daisy's eyes, all she saw was love.

CHAPTER THIRTY-SIX

SOME TIME AFTER ONE O'CLOCK in the morning, Owen pulled himself up onto the porch, much the same way he'd crawled out of the snowdrift an hour earlier. He shoved legfuls of snow away from the threshold. Desperation surged through him, giving him the strength to shake the door loose of its icy frame. He spilled into the kitchen and found himself staring at the rear end of a curled-up mule. He shook his head several times, trying to jar the hallucination from his head. Sophie turned her neck to look at him. Owen stepped closer, righted the overturned chair, and stretched his hand toward the animal, hesitantly, certain he'd finally lost his mind. Sophie swatted his cheek with her tail, before settling back to sleep. Dumbfounded, Owen looked around, trying to make sense of his surroundings. The cupboard was his. The sink and the motto above it. And he certainly knew the rag rug at his feet. He glanced at Sophie again. The tea kettle, cup, and open tin of lye lay next to her back legs. He opened his mouth, but not a sound emerged. The frigid air had stolen his voice.

Owen ran toward the bedroom, certain he'd find Grace lifeless on their bed. He took a breath, turned the knob, and froze at the sight before him. An oil lamp flickered from a table in the corner. Shadows danced across blood-soaked sheets on an empty bed.

Owen fought to make sense of the scene, to shape it into something he understood. He grabbed the lamp and tipped it closer to the mattress. What in God's name had happened here tonight? Somewhere, behind the throbbing pain at his temples, a whisper of truth floated by, and landed just short of Owen's reach. Outside, the wind whipped up and rattled the old house to its bones. Owen spun around and faced the noise. When he turned back, he saw the locket, caught in the light of the lamp. "Violet," he whispered, and rushed across the hall to his daughter's bedroom.

He pushed through the door and lifted the lamp with a trembling hand. Grace and Violet slept under the hand-knotted bed quilt, their bodies curled toward each other and the baby cooing between them. The flickering light skipped across their sleeping faces like smooth rocks over a still pond. Afraid of waking them, Owen turned down the wick and closed his eyes. For a long time, he stood in the darkened room and listened to the rise and fall of their measured breathing.

Dawn squeezed its light around each side of the gossamer curtain in Violet's bedroom, alerting Owen to morning. He peered down at the Bible, opened on his lap for the last few hours. Each page announced its intention in gilded letters—*Births* on the left-hand side, *Deaths* on the right. He set the book on the night table next to the photograph of Daisy, stepped over to the window, and pulled back the curtain. Drifts of snow, some three-feet high, settled in the yard like tufts of cotton. He closed his eyes and offered up a silent prayer of thanks before turning back.

Violet lay in her bed, staring up at him. "When did you—"

He stopped her with a finger to his lips, and leaned down to kiss her forehead. "Good morning, doll baby," he whispered.

Grace stirred on Daisy's side of the bed, and slowly opened her eyes.

"I didn't want to wake you," Owen said, his voice still hoarse. He picked up the Bible and sat back down in the chair.

Grace looked at him without saying a word.

"I know I have no right to ask," he started, staring down at the floor, "but, if you'll have me . . ."

Grace watched him in silence, but didn't move.

"There's no excuse," he started again. "I won't ask for forgiveness." He fumbled with the pages on his lap. "Can't even give that to myself." He closed his eyes and dropped his head. "I'm broken. Don't know if I can change that." He opened his eyes and pulled his chair up to Grace. "But if you give me a chance," he took her hand in his and stroked it gently, "I'll have every reason to try."

He waited.

Grace shifted away from him, and leaned into the middle of the bed. When she turned back, she held the swaddled baby in her arms. "Lily," she said, facing the infant toward Owen.

He lightly brushed a scabbed finger across the baby's silky cheek. "She has Daisy's eyes."

"And her birthday." Grace paused to put the baby to her breast. "Near as I can tell. I've this one to thank." She bent down and kissed the top of Violet's head. "We wouldn't be here without her."

Owen lifted the Bible and patted his knee. Violet scurried out of bed and onto his lap. He wrapped both arms around her, book and all. "What would I do without you?" He tucked his head into her neck as tears fell from his eyes.

Violet pressed her nose against him, taking in his tobacco smell.

"Thank you," Owen whispered in her ear, and set the

Bible across both their laps. "It ought to be you who writes it," he said, reaching for the pen and ink.

Violet's hand trembled slightly, as she dipped the pen and started writing on the page entitled, *Births*.

Lily Morgan.

Violet glanced at her own record of birth, to get the next line right.

Born in the year of our Lord.

She knew the rest of the information by heart.

March 1, 1914.

She smiled at her mother and finished writing.

Just before midnight.

Violet fanned the words.

Owen turned to the page entitled, *Family Temperance Pledge*, and took the pen out of his daughter's hand. He looked at Violet with one thought: *And a child shall lead us.*

Owen read aloud.

We the undersigned solemnly promise
By the help of God
To abstain from the use of all
Intoxicating drinks as a beverage.

He silently noted the pair of signatures under the pledge, his father's and his own. This time, he thought as he dipped the pen into the inkwell and tapped it on the side of the jar, will be the last. He spoke each word.

I here now take the pledge and sign it in the name of the Lord.

—Owen Morgan, March 2, 1914

He set the pen back on the table and took Grace's hand. Lily slept soundly at her breast.

Violet leaned down and blew lightly on the page, encouraging the ink to dry.

PLANTING SMALL SEEDS

In planting very delicate flower seeds, fill eggshells with fine dirt, and when nearly full put in the seeds; cover lightly with a little more dirt, keep moist, and when the plants are large enough to transplant, it can be done without disturbing the little delicate roots, as the shell can be broken away instead of digging out the plants.

—*Mrs. Joe's Housekeeping Guide*, 1909

The "Billy Sunday Snowstorm." Won't soon forget it. Worst blizzard in these parts since '88. According to the *Truth*, four souls perished during the night. No one from Providence Christian, thank God, but tragic, nonetheless. Of course, it could have been far worse. At least they had the chance to meet their Maker with pure hearts, assuming they attended the revival beforehand. Not everyone in this world is so fortunate.

Over two thousand souls saved by sunup, or so they claimed. We're not surprised. Snowed in with such a marvelous evangelist, who wouldn't be saved? The real question is, will they be attending church six months down the road? The proof of the pudding is in the eating, as we always say.

A shame to see them tearing down the tabernacle. Always intended to be temporary, though. No sense wasting good wood. There's talk of a new ICS building going up on that corner. We could think of worse things in the name of progress.

In any event, the Good Lord spared man and beast that night. We still can't believe that harebrained mule made it without a scratch. Took two people to get her out of the Morgans' kitchen, Stanley pulling in front, Owen pushing at the rear. A wonder neither one of them got kicked in the head. Made quite a mess of that house while she was there. That's what you get when you go and make a pet out of an animal God intended for work.

Still, that Polish boy had to have been delighted after all he's suffered. Nice to see him getting on so well these days. Lucky to have the widow looking after him. Now there's a woman who believes in an education. Swears she'll see Stanley clear through law school. And we're pleased to hear her say it, even if we can't imagine anyone fool enough to hire a one-handed lawyer. Then again, we don't have much use for the two-handed kind, either. We're simple folks. Read our Bible. Follow God's Word. Keep to ourselves. Never go looking for trouble.

Quite the opposite, in fact. Why, just the other day we were remarking on how good it is to see Owen Morgan finally past his difficulties, and home where he belongs. Even if he didn't hit the sawdust trail, we're pleased to welcome him back into the fold. We always had faith in him. Grace too. Just took her a little longer to come around, but who can blame her? Certainly not us. She had her hands fuller than most. And Violet. Never did think that child could harm her own blood, no matter the gossip. Just goes to show, some people will say anything to hear themselves talk.

Hard to keep quiet about Pearl Williams, though. Seems to be making a fool out of herself over that horse trainer from the track. Carl something. A little fellow with a finger missing on one hand. Don't much like the looks of him. A handsome woman like Pearl could do better. Just the same, thinking about that husband who left her makes us realize, she could do worse. And Carl did start attending services pretty regular after Billy Sunday. Let's hope he keeps it up for her sake. Hate to see a woman like Pearl disappointed. Seems to be having herself a grand time if we do say so ourselves.

And we're happy for her. Shows courage to take up with a man at that age.

THE END

REFERENCES

Chapple, Joe Mitchell. *Mrs. Joe's Housekeeping Guide*. Cleveland, Ohio: The Chapple Publishing Company, Ltd., 1909.

Much of the dialogue attributed to A.P. Gill, Homer Rodeheaver, and Billy Sunday was found in three sources:

Bruno, Guido. "Billy Sunday, Who Makes Religion Pay." *Pearson's Magazine*. April 1917: 323–332.

The Scranton Times. Various articles on Billy Sunday's visit to Scranton. January–March 1914.

The Tribune-Republican. Various articles on Billy Sunday's visit to Scranton. January–March 1914.

Most of the sermon material attributed to Billy Sunday was found in the sermons "Theatre, Cards and Dance," "Backsliding," and "Get on the Water Wagon," all written by William Ashley Sunday.

For further reading on Billy Sunday:

Betts, Reverend Frederick W., D.D. *Billy Sunday: The Man and Method*. Boston, Massachusetts: The Murray Press, 1916.

Ellis, William T., L.L.D. *Billy Sunday: The Man and His Message*. Philadelphia, Pennsylvania: The John C. Winston Co., 1914.

Rodeheaver, Homer. *20 Years with Billy Sunday*. St. John, Indiana: Christian Book Gallery, 1957.

For further reading on Scranton and coal mining:

Bowen, George W. *Diamonds of the Mines*. Scranton, Pennsylvania: International Textbook Company, 1928.
Greene, Homer. *Coal and the Coal Mines*. Boston, Massachusetts: Houghton, Mifflin and Company, 1889.
Hitchcock, Frederick L. and John P. Downs. *History of Scranton and Its People, Vol. I*. New York, New York: Lewis Historical Publishing Company, 1914.
International Correspondence Schools. *The Coal Miner's Handbook*. Scranton, Pennsylvania: International Textbook Company, 1913.

ACKNOWLEDGMENTS

I'm Scranton born and raised. We shovel our neighbor's sidewalks when it snows, and send meals to folks when a loved one passes. Generosity is the rule, not the exception. I began this journey called *Sing in the Morning, Cry at Night* with nothing more than a few details about a family tragedy and a legendary blizzard. Several years later, I'm humbled by the giving spirit I encountered along the way.

I am a writer and a teacher, not a historian, so I need to recognize the efforts of numerous people who shared their expertise with me. Many thanks to Harold Bowers and the miners at the Lackawanna County Coal Mine; Richard Stanislaus and the workers at the Anthracite Heritage Museum; Cheryl Kashuba, Alan Sweeny, Bob Booth, and the staff at the Lackawanna Historical Society; Bob Shuster from the Billy Graham Center Archives; the librarians at the Albright Memorial Library; Greg Williams, corporate sales manager at the Radisson Lackawanna Station Hotel; Kathy Gavin, owner of Stirna's Restaurant; and Bill Ferri, owner of Ferri's Pizza.

And since I only speak English, thank you to Jessica Dziadas and her grandmother, Tatiana Szerniewicz, for assisting me with the Polish in the book, and my "cousins" Eddie and Jennifer Thomas for the Welsh translations.

Years ago, James and Jane Widenor organized all of the First Christian Church's historical documents and created a "Memorabilia Room." Because of their efforts, I was able to research my church's history and create the fictional Providence Christian Church.

And thanks to Jane Widenor for allowing me to interview her. Her stories, and those of Laura Davis, Marion Thomas, and Violet Williams, three church members who've long since "gone home," enriched my writing. Thank you also to Gayle Williams for sharing her grandmother's life story.

To my "reading weekend" buddies and dear friends—Jane Baugess, Carol Kochis, Ann Lehman, Kim Mancini, and Judy Nudi—thank you for your encouragement, and to Carol, in particular, for giving me the widow Lankowski. Thanks to Kim and Mark Nied for answering my questions, and to my students at Pocono Mountain, past and present, for inspiring me to dream.

Thank you to Cary Holladay, my fiction professor at Memphis University, for telling me to "find an MFA program when you get back to Scranton." A week later I enrolled in Wilkes University's creative writing master's program. Thanks to all of my classmates for cheering me on, even with the extra semester! And special thanks to Dawn Leas, Ronda Bogart, Rick Priebe, and Tom Borthwick for seeing me through to the end.

I'm also grateful for the faculty at Wilkes, especially Bonnie Culver, Jean Klein, J. Michael Lennon, Nancy McKinley, Jan Quackenbush, and Chris Tomasino. Their lessons forever changed my writing and my life.

And thanks to my "workshoppers" who committed to reading the whole manuscript: Laurie Loewenstein, Nina Solomon, Theasa Tuohy, Deirdre Sinnott, Liz Dalton, Monique Lewis, Heather Bryant, Suzanna Filip, and Mary Horgan.

Special thanks to my mentor and publisher, Kaylie Jones, who somehow saw the promise in my story, even when I struggled to see it myself. My book is what it is because of her. She gave me strength and confidence, and she gave me her piano. For that, I'll always be grateful.

And thank you to Johnny Temple of Akashic Books, for taking a chance on a teacher from Scranton, Pennsylvania.

I'm thankful for my family, those related by blood and by heart. To Jeff Aukscunas, for all those hours at the microfilm machine and, more importantly, for all the years of friendship. When I first told you about my idea, you said, "Now that's a book I'd like to read." You made me believe I was onto something. Thanks for all the love and laughs.

And to Michael Bonser for more love, more laughs, and an undeniable faith in my talent.

Thank you to my great-aunt, Louise Lynch, for allowing me to ask so many questions. And to my mother, Pearl Taylor, and my grandmother, Alice Howells, for sharing your love and stories through the years. I only wish you were all still here so I could listen better.

And to the McGraws, Alice, Jimmy Jr., Jimmy III, and Megan. I am in awe as I watch how you support each other through seemingly insurmountable odds. Your faith and courage inspire me. And to my sister, Alice, thank you for your unconditional love.

Finally, my heartfelt thanks to my father, Carl Taylor, my companion on this journey. You never said no to mine tours, museums, or pizzerias. And you answered my questions about everything from birdcalls to cockfights. I love you for always daring me to dream, while standing close enough to catch me.

Taylor 1281460